D0734277

Margaret Peterson Haddix

GREYSTONE SECRETS

THE STRANGERS

GREYSTONE SECRETS

THE STRANGERS

MARGARET
PETERSON HADDIX

ART BY ANNE LAMBELET

KATHERINE TEGEN BOOKS
An Imprint of HarperCollins Publishers

Katherine Tegen Books is an imprint of HarperCollins Publishers.

Greystone Secrets #1: The Strangers
Text copyright © 2019 by Margaret Peterson Haddix
Illustrations copyright © 2019 by Anne Lambelet

Library of Congress Cataloging-in-Publication Data

Names: Haddix, Margaret Peterson.
Title: The strangers / Margaret Peterson Haddix.
Description: First edition. | New York, NY : Katherine Tegen Books, an
    imprint of HarperCollinsPublishers, [2019] | Series: The Greystone secrets
    ; #1 | Summary: Told from separate viewpoints, Chess, Emma, and Finn
    Greystone, ages twelve, ten, and eight, investigate why their mother went
    missing and uncover their ties to an alternate world.
Identifiers: LCCN 2018013963 | ISBN 9780062838377 (hardback) | ISBN
    9780062892034 (signed edition)
Subjects: | CYAC: Missing persons—Fiction. | Brothers and sisters—Fiction. |
    Family life—Fiction. | Secrets—Fiction. | Supernatural—Fiction.
Classification: LCC PZ7.H1164 Str 2019 | DDC [Fic]—dc23 LC record
    available at https://lccn.loc.gov/2018013963

Typography by Aurora Parlagreco
19 20 21 22 23 PC/LSCH 10 9 8 7 6 5 4 3 2 1

❖

First Edition

For Meg

ONE

FINN

The three Greystone kids always raced each other home when they got off the school bus, and Finn always won.

It wasn't because he was the fastest.

Even he knew that his older brother and sister, Chess and Emma, let him win so he could make a grand entrance.

Today he burst into the house calling out, "Mom! We're home! It's time to come and adore us!"

"Adore" had been on his second-grade spelling list two weeks ago, and it had been a great discovery for him. So *that* was what it was called, the way he had felt his entire life.

Emma, who was in fourth grade, dropped her backpack

on the rug beside him and kicked off her red sneakers. They flipped up and landed on top of the backpack—someday, Finn vowed, he would get Emma to teach him that trick.

"Twenty-three," Emma said. There was no telling what she might have been counting. Finn hoped it was a prediction of how many chocolate chips would be in every cookie Mom was probably baking for them right now, for their after-school snack.

Finn sniffed. The house did not smell like cookies.

Oh well. Mom worked from home, designing websites, and sometimes she lost track of time. If today was more of a Goldfish-crackers-and-apple-slices kind of day, that was okay with Finn. He liked those, too.

"Mom!" he called again. "Your afternoon-break entertainment has arrived!"

"She's in the kitchen," Chess said, hanging his own backpack on the hook where it belonged. "Can't you hear?"

"That would mean Finn had to listen for once, instead of talking," Emma said, rubbing Finn's head fondly and making his messy brown hair even messier. Finn knew she didn't mean it as an insult. He was pretty sure Emma liked talking as much as he did.

Chess was the one everyone called "the quiet Greystone." He was in sixth grade and had grown four inches in the past year. Now Finn had to tilt his head way back just to see his brother's face. He also cupped his hand over his ear and pretended to be listening really, really hard. There was a low mumble coming from the kitchen—maybe a man's voice?

"Is Mom watching TV?" Chess asked. "She never does that during the day."

The kids all knew their mother's routine. She never listened to anything but classical music while she worked, because she said songs with words were too distracting. And when she really didn't want to be disturbed, she worked in a windowless room in the basement. The computer down there didn't even connect to the internet.

The three Greystone kids called that "the Boring Room."

Now Finn laughed at his older brother.

"Are you going to stand around asking stupid questions when you could get your answer just by walking into the kitchen?" Finn asked. "Let's go eat!"

He dashed toward the kitchen, dodging both Emma's backpack and the family's cat, Rocket, lying in the middle of the floor. He yelled, "Mom, can I cut up apples? It's my turn, isn't it?"

Mom was standing at the kitchen counter with her back to Finn, but she didn't turn around. She had both hands clenched onto the edge of the counter, as if she needed to hold on. Her cell phone lay facedown on the floor by her feet. Her laptop sat on the counter in front of her, but it was tilted up, so Finn couldn't see what was on the screen.

"Mom?" Finn tried again.

She still didn't turn around. It was like she didn't even hear him, like she was in a soundproof bubble.

This was not like Mom. She had never acted like this before.

Then she began to moan: "No, no, no, no, no. . . ."

TWO

EMMA

Emma had had a substitute teacher that day. The sub had dressed all in gray and had gray hair and a gray face and even a gray voice—somehow, Emma decided, that was possible. And the sub made the entire day so dreary and dull that Emma had started looking for and counting weird things about the day just to keep herself awake.

The thing was, if you started looking for weirdness, suddenly everything seemed that way. Wasn't it weird that the pattern of coats hanging up on the classroom hooks went blue-green-red, blue-green-red twice in a row? Wasn't it weird that the sub could have a gray voice? (Or was that just normal for her?)

By the time Emma got off the school bus and began racing toward the house, she'd counted twenty-one things she considered indisputably weird. To her way of thinking, that actually made the day pretty interesting, and she was excited to tell Mom about the new trick she'd discovered for surviving school.

Then she noticed that the porch light was still on, even though Mom usually turned it off when Emma and her brothers left for school.

And then, stepping into the house, Emma noticed that the living room curtains were still drawn tight across the windows, and so were the blinds on the bay window at the back of the house. This turned the living room's cheery yellow walls dim and shadowy; it made the whole house feel like a cave or a hideout.

Twenty-three weird things in one day. What if that was a normal amount, and Emma had just never noticed before?

She'd have to count again some other day—or, really, lots of other days—to know for sure.

Finn and Chess started yammering on about Mom and the kitchen and TV. Emma joined in and then rubbed Finn's head, because it felt good to do something normal again. Mussing Finn's hair was like petting a dog—you had to do it. Finn had thick, unruly hair with odd cowlicks that sprang up no matter how much Mom smoothed them down. Finn being Finn, he claimed this meant his hair had superpowers.

And . . . now Finn was racing off to the kitchen, shouting about apples.

Emma looked up at Chess, and they both shrugged and grinned and followed Finn.

But when they got to the kitchen, Mom wasn't hugging Finn and reaching out to hug Emma and Chess, too. Finn stood in the middle of the kitchen, staring at Mom. Mom stood at the counter with her back to the kids, all her attention focused on her laptop.

And the voice coming out of the laptop was saying, "The kidnapped children are in second and fourth and sixth grade."

THREE

CHESS

"Mom?" Chess said quietly.

His mother's shoulders shook. And then, as if she was fighting for control, her whole body went still.

Just like before, Chess thought.

Of the three Greystone kids, only Chess remembered the awful day their father died. Chess had been four; Emma, two; and Finn, only a baby. But even Chess's memories of that day were more like puzzle pieces he kept in a box in his mind, rather than one continuous video: Chess remembered the two sad-faced police officers at the door; he remembered the red Matchbox car he'd been holding in his hand when the door opened; he remembered the way Mom's shoulders shook before her back went ramrod straight, and she turned around to face Chess and Emma and Finn.

Now Mom was reaching for the top part of her laptop, as if she planned to shut it and hide whatever it said. Something made Chess stride quickly across the kitchen and grab her hand to stop her.

"Someone was kidnapped," he said. He caught a glimpse of a few words at the bottom of the computer screen. "Three kids in Arizona. Was it anyone you know?"

"No . . . ," Mom whispered.

Her dark eyes were wide and dazed. The color had drained from her face.

Shock, Chess thought. The school nurse had come in and taught a first-aid unit to the sixth graders earlier that year, and Chess was proud of himself for remembering the symptoms.

It was just a shame he couldn't remember any treatment.

Maybe he was feeling a little shocked himself. It was scary that anyone would kidnap anyone. But Arizona was a thousand miles away. And it wasn't like there would be some crime ring going around kidnapping kids from any family who had a second grader, a fourth grader, and a sixth grader.

"Mom, maybe you should sit down," Emma said.

Hmm. Maybe that was one of the treatments for shock.

Chess shot his sister a grateful look and took his mother's arm, ready to help ease her toward the kitchen table.

"Rocky, Emma, and Finn Gustano were last seen leaving their school, Los Perales Elementary, in Mesa," the voice coming out of the laptop speakers said.

Finn started cracking up.

"Isn't that funny?" he cried. "Two of those kids have the same first names as me and Emma! That's the third Finn I've ever known. Well, not that I actually know this one, but . . ." He slugged Chess in the arm. "Don't you feel bad that *you* don't have the same name as some kid who's famous now? And I bet when they find these kids, they'll get all the ice cream they want, and all the toys they want, and their parents probably won't make them do homework ever again!"

But what if nobody ever finds these kids? Chess thought.

He wasn't about to say that to Finn.

"Yeah, I've never met another kid named Rochester." Chess forced himself to fake a smile at Finn. "Or with the nickname 'Chess.' Oh well."

"Maybe you should *sue* Mom for giving you such a different name," Finn suggested.

"Or maybe I should sue for getting such a boring, ordinary name," Emma countered. "Did you know there are three other Emmas in fourth grade? And eight others in the rest of the school!"

But Chess tuned out his brother and sister. Because Mom lifted one hand and pointed toward the laptop screen. The way she held her hand was like a nightmare, like a Halloween ghost, like someone under a witch's spell in a fairy tale. It was like she could only point, not speak.

"We're repeating the information we have about the Gustano children," the voice coming from the laptop said. A photo of a friendly-looking, dark-haired boy appeared on the screen. "The oldest of the three kidnapped siblings, Rochester Charles Gustano, who goes by Rocky, just turned twelve last Tuesday. . . ."

Chess's hearing blanked out temporarily. His middle name was Charles, too. And his twelfth birthday had been last Tuesday.

How could there be another Rochester Charles, born the exact same day as him?

And how could that other kid have been kidnapped?

FOUR

FINN

Everybody was acting too serious. They'd all stopped talking. Even Emma. She'd taken the last two steps to join Mom and Chess at the counter, to stare silently at the laptop screen.

"Hello?" Finn said. "It's snack time—remember?"

Nobody answered.

"Remember how you're always telling me I have to quit right away when I'm playing computer games and you think it's time for me to do something else?" Finn tried again.

He walked over and reached his hand for the power button on the laptop. He wasn't *really* planning to switch it off—he'd heard too many lectures from Mom about not messing with her work. He just wanted to tease Mom a little, until she acted normal again.

Emma surprised him by grabbing his hand. At first it seemed like she was just trying to stop him from doing something dumb. Then it started feeling like she *needed* to hold his hand.

Finn stood on tiptoes and peered at the screen. He saw three pictures in a row, each with names and ages beneath. The kids in the pictures all had brown hair, just like Finn and Chess and Emma did, and they stared out at Finn with stiff school-picture-day smiles on their faces, as if they'd gotten the same warning Finn always got: "Remember, this is your official photo for the entire year, so no goofing off!" The youngest boy, the one Finn was already thinking of as Other-Finn, was perfectly snaggletoothed, with one adult front tooth partly grown in and one front tooth missing entirely.

Finn felt a little jealous. He'd lost both his front teeth two weeks after picture day last fall, and for some reason Mom wouldn't agree to let him have his picture retaken just because of that.

"But Mom, this is what I look like in second grade," he'd argued, sticking his tongue into the hole where his teeth used to be just for the sheer joy of it. "Don't you want to remember me this way forever?"

"Don't worry," Mom had said, laughing and pretending to try to catch his tongue before he yanked it back. "I'm not going to forget, regardless."

Finn dropped his gaze to see if Other-Finn was just a smidge older, and if that was the reason he'd been lucky enough to lose both his front teeth right before school picture day.

Finn Michael Gustano, it said below the picture. *Born 3/4/11.*

"He has the same middle name as me?" Finn said, stunned. "And wait—does three-four mean March fourth?"

"He has the same name as you," Chess said, sounding dazed. "And the same birthday."

"And that Emma is Emma Grace, just like me," Emma added. She kept her gaze aimed at the screen, as if she was too surprised to look away. "And her birthday is April fourteenth, too."

"That's crazy," Finn said. "Weird, weird, weird. Did they just steal our names and birthdays? Or—I know." He yanked his hand away from Emma, put his fists on his hips, and tried to look stern. "Mom, did you let that other family clone us?"

He wanted everybody to laugh. He *needed* everybody to laugh. And then Mom would shut the laptop and forget those other kids; she would bring out snacks and ask Finn and Emma and Chess about school. Just like usual.

But Mom did none of those things. Even when Finn went over and snuggled against her, she didn't move.

She just kept staring at the kids who'd been kidnapped.

FIVE

EMMA

"Finn, you're being silly," Emma said. "Clones would *look* like us, not have the same names and birthdays."

The girl on the computer screen had straight light brown hair while Emma's was darker and wavy. It was hard to tell from a tiny picture, but the other girl may have even had bluish-purple eyes, while Emma's were dark brown, almost black. Also: The other girl's chin was rounder, her cheeks were fuller, her gaze was a little too . . . peaceful. In every picture anyone had ever taken of Emma, she looked like she was trying to solve complicated math problems in her head.

Sometimes she was. Having your picture taken was *boring*.

Seeing the picture of someone with your exact same birthday and almost your exact same name who'd been kidnapped wasn't boring. It was the weirdest thing that had happened all day. But like all the other weirdness she'd catalogued that day, was it really all that stunning?

Emma was glad Finn's question had awakened her brain again.

"Statistics," Emma said. "Probability. There are billions of kids in the world. Probably millions of girls named Emma who have two brothers. Maybe thousands who have one brother named Finn, hundreds—or, well, at least *dozens*—who have a brother named Rochester. There's probably some formula you could do to figure out the chances that parents who like the name 'Emma' would like the other two names, too. And for the birthdays—there are only three hundred and sixty-five *possible* birthdays anybody could have. Three hundred and sixty-six, if you count leap day. So you just need three hundred and sixty-seven people in a room together to be sure that at least one pair has the same birthday."

"How many do you need to have *three* pairs of birthdays all the same?" Chess asked.

Emma was pretty sure there was a way to figure that out,

but her mind was attacking the harder problem: How would you calculate the chances that two sets of siblings would have the same names, in the same order? You'd have to know the number of all possible names, wouldn't you? Since people could just make up any name they wanted for their kids, was that even possible to put a number on?

Emma didn't like it when math failed her.

"The . . . kidnapping," Mom whispered. "The odds that anyone's children would be kidnapped are . . . are . . ."

"Tiny," Emma finished for her. "But this is like the chances of winning the lottery. There are overwhelming odds against anyone winning the lottery, so it's stupid to buy a ticket. But *somebody* is going to win. *Somebody* gets to be the one in a million. Or else it'd be zero-in-a-million chances. But it's *only* one person who has that good luck."

"Being kidnapped sounds like *bad* luck to me," Finn said, giggling. Then he furrowed his brow and pointed at the laptop screen. "Or are you saying those kids used up all the bad luck, so *we* never have to worry about being kidnapped? Thank you, Other-Finn and Other-Emma and Other-Rochester! Hope you get found soon!"

Mom seemed to shake herself and looked down at Finn as if she was seeing him—*really* seeing him—for the first time since he'd walked into the kitchen. Then she lifted her head, and her gaze darted first to Emma, then to Chess. She reached out and hugged all three kids, pulling them together so tightly that Emma could barely breathe.

"You *don't* have to worry about being kidnapped," she said in her usual firm voice. "I promise. I'll do everything I can to prevent that."

It would have been really reassuring, except that Mom's voice quivered at the very end.

And why would Mom think she'd need to prevent anything?

SIX

CHESS

Chess woke up in the middle of the night with aches in his legs. *Growing pains,* he thought. Mom had explained them to him a year ago, and then she'd helped him look them up online. Finn had asked, "What? It hurts to grow as tall as Chess? Maybe I'll just stay short!"

Finn was still so little he thought you could control things like that. Chess couldn't remember his own brain ever working that way, thinking he got to choose whatever he wanted. For as long as Chess could remember, he'd had to be the responsible oldest kid, the one who had to help Mom with Emma and Finn. The mini grown-up.

Was it just because Dad had died when all three of them were so young? Or did the other Rochester, the one who'd been kidnapped, feel that way, too?

Chess could picture the other Rochester—Rocky—crouched beside his younger brother and sister in some locked, windowless back of a van somewhere, or some locked, windowless basement. The younger kids would be crying. But Rocky would be telling them, *Everything's going to be all right. I'll take care of you.* Even if he was really thinking, *There's no way out! What are we going to do?*

Chess could picture it too well.

Those kids have probably already been rescued, he told himself. *They probably got balloons and welcome-home banners and toys and ice cream—just like Finn said—hours ago.*

But Chess had seen how Mom kept checking her phone under the table all through dinner, and even afterward, while everyone was doing homework. She also kept her laptop balanced on her knees when, as a special treat before bedtime, she let them watch the first half of *The Lego Batman Movie.* She *said* she was just typing up invoices to send out for her business, the kind of mindless work she could do while keeping one eye on animated Legos. But Chess was pretty sure she'd been checking news websites, too.

Mom would have told them if there'd been any news about the kids in Arizona being rescued.

Chess stretched his legs, then he slipped out of bed. Sometimes it helped to stand up. Sometimes it helped to walk.

He decided to go get a drink of water, but just as he put his hand on his doorknob, he heard another door open down the hall. Chess peeked out. The nightlight in the hallway cast eerie shadows, but he could tell that Mom's door was open, down at the opposite end of the hall. A moment later, he heard the creak of the third step down on the stairway.

So Mom's going downstairs, Chess thought.

Sometimes when she couldn't sleep, she got up and worked in the middle of the night. She always said, "That's the great thing about working for myself! I can work all night and sleep all day if I want to! I don't have a boss telling me what to do!" But Chess wondered if that happened more often when she was worried or upset.

Did she ever wake up in the middle of the night and try to remember everything she could about Dad, the way Chess did sometimes?

And was that maybe the reason she decided to get up and work instead?

Chess decided to follow her. He tiptoed down the hall and went down the stairs by twos—it was only the third and the ninth ones that squeaked, so his descent was totally silent. He didn't want to wake Emma or Finn. Sometimes when the younger kids weren't around, Mom would tell Chess things she wouldn't tell them.

But when Chess got down to the first floor, Mom was nowhere in sight. With all the curtains and blinds drawn, Chess had to navigate by the thin slats of moonlight that trickled in along the edges. Once he got to the kitchen, he also had the red glow of the digital clock on the stove.

It was 3:15 a.m. exactly when Chess noticed that the door to the basement was slightly ajar.

Seriously? Chess thought. *It's the middle of the night, and Mom still has to go down to the Boring Room to keep from being distracted?*

He started down the basement stairs but froze when he heard Mom talking.

"I thought you'd never call!" she was saying.

Who would call Mom in the middle of the night? Who would she *want* to talk to then?

Chess strained his ears, trying to listen for even the barest hum of a reply, but there was nothing. Maybe the person on the other end of the phone call was whispering.

"Do *not* tell me to calm down!" Mom said. "This is exactly what I was afraid of!"

The pause was shorter this time, then Mom exploded again.

"Oh, right, it's not my kids," she said. "Not *yet*. But it's *somebody's* kids. It's kids I can imagine really well, because I know exactly what an eight- and a ten- and a twelve-year-old are like. And I'll tell you, they're completely innocent. They're—"

The person on the other end of the phone call must have interrupted her. But maybe she interrupted him—or her—right back, because she didn't pause long enough to take a breath.

"It's not a coincidence, Joe," she said. She didn't even sound like Mom now. She sounded cold and mean and cutting. "You have to fix this. Or so help me, I will."

SEVEN

FINN

Finn could smell the French toast as soon as he woke up.

"Special breakfast?" he shouted. "It's a special break-fast day? Is school canceled? Is it a snow day? Or a holiday nobody told me about?"

He jumped out of bed and raced out into the hall. Emma was standing sleepily in her own doorway, sniffing the air.

"It's sixty-eight degrees out," she said. Finn was pretty sure she knew that because of a weather app, not from the smell of the air. But there was no telling with Emma.

"Okay, it's not a snow day," Finn admitted.

"Not a holiday, either," Emma said sadly. She leaned in

close and whispered, "It might be a bad-news special break-fast."

Finn remembered that the last time Mom had made French toast, it was because she'd gotten overwhelmed with her job and had to work an entire Saturday. That French toast was like an apology for not taking the kids to the park.

"There shouldn't be any such thing as bad-news special breakfast," Finn said. "It's going to make me stop liking maple syrup."

"You will *never* stop liking maple syrup," Emma said.

That was probably true. Finn was pretty sure he'd be able to drink it by the gallon, if Mom ever let him.

"*I* think it's going to be about good news," he said. "Maybe they found those kids in Arizona, and Mom's celebrating."

Finn expected Emma's face to light up at that idea, but she stayed serious.

"Finn, don't worry about those other kids," she said. "They—"

"Chess! Emma! Finn!" Mom called from downstairs. "Are you all up and moving?"

"I'll wake up Chess!" Finn shouted back. He realized Emma had yelled the same thing. They both took off running for Chess's room. Normally Chess was the first one up, so this was a treat, too.

As soon as he shoved past Chess's door, Finn launched himself toward the bed.

"Time! For! Breakfast!" he shouted as he landed. He bounced up and down with each word.

Beside him, Emma yelled, "Get up! Get up! Get up!"

Her bounces coordinated perfectly, too.

"We should be in the Olympics," Finn said, giggling. "Mom should sign us up for gymnastics. We'd win all sorts of medals."

He braced himself for Chess to push him and Emma off the bed. Maybe Chess would growl like a bear and pretend to be angry, and then they could have a mock wrestling match before breakfast.

But Chess just lay there. He blinked once, then twice. He had dark circles under his eyes, like he hadn't gotten enough sleep. But he'd had the whole night for sleeping.

"Chess?" Finn said, tugging on his brother's arm. "Talk to me, dude. Let me know you're in there!"

Finn saw Chess's face change, as if someone had flipped a switch. One moment, he looked groggy and sad—and just *wrong*, with those circles under his eyes. Finn might have even said Chess looked old, which was crazy.

The next moment, Chess had a goofy grin plastered on his face, but even that felt wrong.

"Arr, matey, who dares to disturb the pirate captain's

slumber?" Chess growled, which was from a book Finn had loved when he was little. Normally this would have been just as much fun as the bear growl and the wrestling match. But something was wrong with Chess this morning. He wasn't just pretending or acting; it was more like he was pretending to pretend and acting like he was acting. He had layers. Lots of them.

What if that had always been true about Chess, and Finn had just never noticed before? What if noticing was a sign that *Finn* was growing up?

Finn kind of wanted to tell Chess and Emma this. Maybe both of them would sling their arms around his shoulders and say, "Ah, grasshopper, let us initiate you into this stage of growing up. We're so proud of you! Neither of us figured out anything like that until we were nine!"

But Finn kind of didn't even want to think about it.

Mom poked her head into Chess's room just then. She put a stack of laundry on Chess's dresser.

"Come on, kiddos—get a move on!" she said. "As soon as you're all dressed, I have a special breakfast ready for you. . . ."

"It's because you have bad news, isn't it?" Finn blurted out. "We're having bad-news French toast. Like that day we couldn't go to the park."

For a moment it seemed like Mom had been wearing a

mask, and the mask slipped. It was almost like how Chess's face had changed, except in reverse. For just that one moment, it looked like Mom might start crying the way really little kids did, with a trembling lip and huge puddles of tears in each eye. But then Mom smiled and came over and ruffled his hair.

"You're onto me, huh?" she said. "I guess I'll have to save the French toast for good-news days from now on. Anyhow, it's not really bad news, just . . ."

"Spit it out," Emma demanded.

On a normal day, Mom probably would have scolded Emma for how sassy and disrespectful that sounded. But today Mom just gulped and smiled harder.

"I found out this morning that I have to go away for a few days," she said. "For work. I'm sorry."

"Oh, that's not *so* bad," Finn said. And maybe he was acting and wearing a mask a little bit, too. Mom didn't travel for her job very often, but when she did, Finn always felt strange the whole time. Even when he was at school and wouldn't have seen her, anyhow. "Tell you what, you *could* make French toast every day between now and then, to make it up to us."

Mom laughed, but it sounded especially fake. And sad.

"Finn, this is really last-minute," she said. "I have to leave today. How about if we have bad-news French toast today, and then a celebration special breakfast when I get back?"

"When will that be, Mom?" Chess asked.

Chess wasn't one of those kids who yelled at adults—neither were Finn or Emma. And Chess had actually spoken more quietly than usual, not louder. But Finn got a picture in his mind of Chess slashing a sword through the air and driving its point into the ground, like someone issuing a dare.

Finn glanced quickly back and forth between Mom and Chess. They both looked perfectly normal for a Tuesday morning. Chess's hair was mashed on one side and sticking out on the other. He was wearing his Lakeside Elementary Safety Patrol shirt over his pajama bottoms. Mom had on an old Ohio State University sweatshirt that had once belonged to their dad, along with old jeans with a rip in the knee that had happened because she'd worn them a lot, not because she bought them that way. Her hair, which was just as dark and curly as Emma's, was pulled back into a messy ponytail.

Still, Finn felt a little bit like he was watching strangers.

Mom started acting like she really needed to straighten one of the pictures on Chess's wall, above his bed.

"I'm not quite sure when I'll be back," she said as she reached for the frame. She kept her head turned away from the kids. "Things are a little up in the air. I . . . I may not even be able to call home every day."

Mom *had* turned into a stranger. She didn't leave things

up in the air. Whenever she went away, she left behind a list of what she was doing every day, and exactly where she would be, and how the kids or their babysitter could reach her every single minute, even if her cell phone broke.

Finn stopped feeling like he'd reached a new stage of growing up. No matter how much he tried to hold it back, his bottom lip started to tremble.

EIGHT

EMMA

Hello? Mom? Don't you see you're going to make Finn cry? Emma wanted to shout. *You do not do that to a second grader right before school!*

"So you'll have Mrs. Rabinsky stay with us while you're away?" Emma asked quickly. Mrs. Rabinsky was an old, grandmotherly type who made no secret of the fact that Finn was her favorite of the three kids. The idea of even just one afternoon and evening of Mrs. Rabinsky asking constantly, "What would you like for dinner, Finn?" and "Finn, could you tell us more about your day at school?" and "Do you want me to read you a bedtime story, Finn?" kind of turned

Emma's stomach. But she wasn't going to complain if it would cheer Finn up now.

"Actually, no," Mom said. She had her face turned to the side, but Emma could see that Mom was biting her lip. "I'm, um, still working out those arrangements, too. Like I said, this just came up. You know I'll cancel the trip if I can't be sure the three of you are all right."

"So why don't you just cancel the trip already?" Finn asked eagerly. "If it's not that important. If it's cancel-er-able."

Mom didn't laugh and tell him that "cancel-er-able" was not a word.

"Finn . . . ," she began.

"Two things can be important at the same time," Chess said tonelessly. "Mom's job and spending time with us, both."

Emma glanced over her shoulder at her older brother. Chess was just quoting an explanation Mom gave all the time. But did he actually think that was going to help, when he sounded so much like he was reading from a script?

Emma waggled her eyebrows warningly at Chess and mouthed at him, *Sound normal!*

The truth was, sometimes she, Chess, and Mom all acted like Mrs. Rabinsky. As if taking care of Finn and keeping him happy was the most important thing.

"*I* think Mom's going to have some big adventure,"

Emma announced. "And she'll bring back great stories. And presents."

This time, Mom did laugh. But it was an odd laugh, one that trailed off awkwardly.

"Emma, I'm just meeting with a client in Chicago who needs a lot of hand-holding," she said. "I don't think it will be much of an adventure. But I will bring presents. Okay?" She looked down at the clock on Chess's bedside table. "Now, seriously, everyone—move!"

They all scattered for a frenzy of clothes changing, face washing, and teeth brushing. Emma skipped combing her hair, because she wanted to be the first one down to the kitchen. She had a secret, and she hadn't quite decided yet if she wanted to tell Mom.

Last night after everyone had gone to bed, Emma had crept back out of her room and gone downstairs and slipped Mom's cell phone out of her purse. Disappointingly, Mom was one of those parents who thought kids should wait until middle school before getting phones of their own; she also didn't think looking at a screen right before bedtime was a good idea. So Emma had had to be sneaky. She'd typed in the password, which Mom probably didn't know Emma knew. And then, sitting alone in the dark, Emma had looked up everything she could about those kids in Arizona.

They'd actually been kidnapped on Friday. So three whole days had passed while three kids named Rochester, Emma, and Finn in Ohio had no idea that three other kids named Rochester, Emma, and Finn had been kidnapped in Arizona.

That was weird. It seemed like Chess, Emma, and Finn should have known instantly about everything that happened to their Arizona doubles. Like Emma should have felt a twinge in her side when she was sitting in social studies class and realized, *Oh no! The other Emma Grace is in danger!*

It felt like Chess, Emma, and Finn should have known all along that those other kids existed.

Emma found a site dedicated to missing children, and she tested herself looking at the page about the Emma from Arizona. *Why does this make me feel so weird? Would I feel this way if Emma Chang, Emma Pulaski, or Emma Jones from school were kidnapped?*

She would feel sad about *any* kidnapped kid. But she would feel even more sad if it was someone from her school, regardless of the kid's name. Just being from her school was enough of a link.

Emma had had the name Emma her entire life. She was used to sharing it with other girls.

She wasn't used to sharing it with another Emma who

also had an older brother named Rochester and a younger brother named Finn. Not when they also all had matching birthdays.

She tried to make herself feel better staring at all the details about Arizona Emma that were different: *Look! Arizona Emma is only four foot five, not four foot seven like me! And she weighs five pounds less, too!* When Emma clicked over to the other kids' information, she saw that the kidnapped boys' heights and weights were different from Chess's and Finn's, too. That made sense: Chess was taller than practically every other boy his age; Finn was one of the shortest kids in his class.

Emma zoomed in on the pictures of the two kidnapped brothers, which she hadn't looked at closely before. The younger boy's ears tilted slightly, making him look a little elfin, just like Finn. Other-Finn had the same mischievous gleam in his eye, too. Rocky Gustano held one eyebrow higher than the other, as if he hadn't expected the picture to be taken just then—Chess always looked surprised in pictures, too.

Both boys—and Other-Emma, too—had skin a shade or two darker than any of the Greystone kids'. But that could just be from living in Arizona, where there was more sunshine.

Or it could just be the way the pictures showed up on the

phone screen. If the Gustano and Greystone kids were standing side by side, maybe their skin tones would look identical. Maybe their hair and eye colors would, too.

None of those details are things I can count, Emma told herself. *But with things that are numbers, like height and weight, I could throw those into the equation if I wanted to calculate the odds of those kids having so much in common with us, and . . .*

It really bothered Emma that she couldn't calculate the odds, because of not knowing all the possible names in the world.

Because without that, she kept thinking, *This isn't random. There are too many similarities. We* are *connected to those Arizona kids. Somehow.*

That was what she wanted to tell Mom. Even if she had to confess that she'd used Mom's phone without permission.

But when Emma reached the kitchen, she found Finn already sitting at the table, digging French toast slices out of the dish where Mom had been keeping them warm. And Chess arrived right on her heels.

"Emma, your hair," Mom said. She pressed her hands against her own head and moved them outward, pantomiming an explosion.

That probably *was* what Emma's hair looked like. She hadn't actually checked the mirror.

"It's the humidity, isn't it?" Mom said sympathetically.

"Chess, you go ahead and start eating. Emma and I will go back upstairs and work on her hair together."

Perfect! Emma thought. She'd have Mom to herself.

But just then, Mom's phone pinged. Mom yanked it out of her purse and gave a relieved sigh.

"You don't have to go to Chicago after all?" Finn said hopefully. Syrup dripped from his forkful of French toast and rolled toward the dimple in his right cheek.

"No, sorry, I do," Mom said. She quickly typed something into her phone. "It's just, now I know who's taking care of you three while I'm away. She said yes. The perfect person."

"Who?" Chess said.

Emma saw Mom hesitate before she looked up from her phone. Mom glanced at the clock on the stove, then she put down the phone and pulled the ponytail rubber band out of her own hair. She scooped Emma's hair back and wrapped the rubber band around it.

"Sorry, Emma, I think we've got to go with the quick fix today," Mom said. She reached over and turned the water on in the sink, cupped her hand under the faucet, then slid that hand over Emma's hair, smoothing down all the stray locks. "There. Now go eat."

"*Who's* staying with us?" Emma repeated Chess's question

as she sat down and began filling her plate alongside him.

"Do you remember Ms. Morales, who was PTO president at Lakeside the year before last?" Mom said.

"Why would we?" Chess asked.

"You're making us stay with a *stranger*?" Finn wailed.

Mom looked back at her phone, but not before Emma caught a glimpse of Mom's face.

Is Mom . . . panicking? Emma wondered.

Emma felt like she was trying to solve some huge math problem that didn't involve numbers but people and events: The kidnapped kids in Arizona. Mom's unexpected business trip. And now this, the unknown babysitter. And Mom's panic.

None of it felt random.

Mom's trip is connected to the Arizona kids somehow, Emma thought. *And even though she doesn't want to, she's leaving us with some woman we don't even know because, because . . .*

Emma didn't know the answer to that part.

What if this was like the kind of huge math problems that Emma hadn't gotten around to studying yet?

The ones that didn't actually have any solutions?

NINE

CHESS

Chess should never have gone back to bed last night. He should have continued down the basement stairs and turned on the lights and said, *Mom, I heard you on the phone. What did you mean when you said, "This is exactly what I was afraid of"? And "Not yet"? Do you think Emma and Finn and I are in danger of being kidnapped, too? What's going on?*

He'd *almost* done that. He'd even touched his toes to the next step down.

But then he'd heard Mom sniffle. And it was definitely an "I'm about to cry" sniffle. And that made Chess freeze.

What if this has something to do with Dad?

That was the only reason Mom ever cried. After that day when the police officers came to the door, Chess remembered lots and lots of nights when he woke up and heard Mom crying. As a four-year-old, he'd go curl up beside her and try to wipe away her tears. And then one night she'd said, "Chess, this helps me, but I'm not sure it's good for you. Whenever you're sad, please come and tell me. You can cry on my shoulder anytime you want. But you really shouldn't have to comfort me all the time. You're only four!"

After that, Chess had started pretending he didn't hear her crying. He made himself stay in bed whenever he heard weeping. Not because he wanted to. But because he knew it made Mom sadder if he was sad, too.

All of that had happened eight years ago, but still, just that one sniffle last night had made Chess move his foot back from the stair below. It had made him decide, *I'll ask Mom about everything tomorrow. When she's not crying. First thing in the morning, when I get up before Emma and Finn.*

And then he'd accidentally slept later than Emma and Finn. And now Mom was leaving. And just as his job last night had been to keep from making Mom sadder, he knew that now she was counting on him to keep Emma and Finn from freaking out about having to stay with a stranger.

"Ms. Morales is the woman Finn always called Perfume Lady," Mom said, sounding desperate. "Remember? Because he said she smelled good?"

"Oh, right," Chess said, even though he didn't remember. Finn and Emma had puzzled looks on their faces, too.

"So she'll make our house smell like perfume?" Finn asked doubtfully.

"No, the three of you are going to stay at her house," Mom said. They had never done that before with a babysitter. "You know, she has a daughter, too, and it wouldn't be fair to make them uproot their lives when they're doing a favor for us."

So there's some strange kid we have to get used to, too? Chess wanted to wail. It'd be fine for Emma and Finn. Finn got along with everybody, and Emma didn't care whether people liked her or not. But being around people he didn't know always made Chess feel like he had to be on his best behavior.

It wasn't like his *worst* behavior was ever that bad. But being on good behavior wasn't relaxing.

"Ms. Morales will pick you up after school," Mom said. "You know what that means, don't you?"

"We get to wear the same clothes and never brush our teeth the whole time you're away?" Finn asked, a gleam in his eye. "Because we're going to her house after that, not ours, and staying there until you get back?"

Finn's actually going to be okay with this, Chess thought in amazement. *He's acting like it'll be an adventure.*

Of course, Finn hadn't heard Mom in the basement last night saying, "This is exactly what I was afraid of."

"No, you don't get to re-wear clothes and have dirty teeth," Mom said briskly. "I'll pack suitcases for each of you and give them to Susanna." She glanced at the kitchen clock for probably the fifth time since Chess had stepped into the room.

"So what does it mean that Ms. Morales is picking us up after school?" Emma asked. Chess knew it was wrong, but he was glad that she sounded sulky. Maybe Emma and Chess together could get Mom to explain what was going on. They just needed to get Finn out of the kitchen so they could ask.

"It means you get to use the code word," Mom said. "Remember the code word?"

"Succotash!" Finn shouted. "I get to tell Ms. Morales I like succotash!"

"No, silly," Emma said. "Get it straight. *She* has to say succotash first. It wouldn't be much of a code if you told her what it was."

Mom had gone to some special parents' meeting a year or two ago about keeping kids safe, and she'd come home determined that the kids all know a code word any adult could say to them to prove that they were trustworthy.

43

Together, the three kids—mostly Emma and Finn—had decided that "succotash" was the best word to use.

"Because," Emma had explained, "nobody who's going to kidnap you would promise, 'Hey, little kid, would you like some succotash?' No kid's going to get kidnapped because they loved corn and lima beans too much!"

The family had turned it into a big joke that night. Finn had decided that succotash was the funniest word in the universe. And Emma and Finn had started taking turns pretending to be kidnappers. They'd even written fake ransom notes asking for millions of dollars and then, just to be silly, millions of dollars' worth of succotash.

"A kidnapper would have to be crazy to think we were rich enough to pay a ransom!" Emma had laughed.

It was true: The Greystones weren't rich.

But last night in the basement, Mom said, "Not yet," like she thought we were in danger of being kidnapped, Chess thought. *More danger because of those other kids with our names being kidnapped . . .*

His stomach roiled, and he put his forkful of French toast back on his plate.

Two years ago, even as Finn and Emma laughed and laughed and laughed, Mom had tried to explain that she wasn't *really* worried about kidnappers.

"It's just a precaution," she said. "Because what if my car breaks down sometime when I'm supposed to pick you up, and somebody else has to do it for me? I just want you to know who's trustworthy and who isn't. That's all."

Because Mom is really all we have, Chess thought. *Other kids have two parents, and sometimes even three or four. And they have grandparents and aunts and uncles and cousins, or even brothers or sisters who are already grown up.*

Except for Mom, the only relatives the Greystone kids had were each other.

The only ones who were still alive, anyway.

Now Chess really wasn't hungry. He pushed back from the table.

"Okay," Mom began. "So I've told you about Ms. Morales, and your suitcases, and the code word, and—"

"Are we taking Rocket with us?" Finn asked.

The family cat had just come strolling into the kitchen. He flicked his tail twice, as if to say, *What? Were you going to forget about me?*

"Oh, um, Susanna is allergic to cats," Mom said. She squinted her eyes and twisted her mouth, as if she was just now trying to figure out what to do about Rocket. "I guess I'll leave him with lots of food, and I'll tell Susanna to bring one of you over here every other day to clean his litter box."

Emma scooped Rocket into her arms, even though that meant that his tail got dangerously close to the pool of syrup on her plate.

"What if Rocket's lonely?" she moaned. "We should come *every* day, just to keep him company!"

"No," Mom said sharply. "That's asking too much of Susanna. She's already doing us a big favor—we don't want to inconvenience her any more than we have to."

Emma had her face buried in Rocket's gray fur, and Finn was watching syrup drip from his fork. So Chess was the only one who saw the way Mom's face quivered.

Then she caught Chess watching her, and her expression softened.

"I just want you to be considerate," she said. "I know you'll pick up after yourselves, and offer to help anytime you can, and . . ."

"Sounds like this is going to in'venience *us*," Finn said.

Mom turned her back on all three kids. Chess watched carefully to see if her shoulders started quaking. But she just stood still for a minute, and then she turned the water on in the sink.

"Oh—five minutes until the bus arrives," she called out over the sound of the rushing water. "Let's clean off the table and get a move on!"

Normally Mom would have helped. Normally she would

have noticed that Chess had barely eaten two bites and that Finn had licked all the syrup off his second piece of French toast but not actually bitten into it. Normally she would have noticed that a few unruly locks of Emma's hair were already slipping out of her ponytail rubber band and Emma had started absent-mindedly twirling one of them around her finger. In a few minutes, Emma's hair would probably look as messy as Albert Einstein's again—even as her brain was trying to solve quantum physics or the mysteries of time travel or some other mathematical or scientific conundrum.

Mom—look at us! Chess wanted to yell.

But he didn't, and she didn't turn around.

In no time at all, the three kids had cleared the table, loaded the dishwasher, and hurried to the front door to grab their backpacks.

At least Mom followed them to the door. She lifted the backpack strap over Finn's shoulder and then hugged each of them in turn.

"Have a good day at school," she said, her arms around first Finn, then Emma. "Be good for your teachers and Ms. Morales."

She could be any mother anywhere in the world, saying goodbye to her kids headed to school any day of the week.

But then she got to Chess. She wrapped her arms around his shoulders, engulfing him and his overstuffed backpack.

With her mouth near his right ear, she whispered, "And don't forget anything."

Chess pulled back.

"Wait—what?" he said confusedly. He peered into his mother's face. "Did you just say—"

But Mom was already turning his shoulders, aiming him toward the front door. Finn had opened it and was already leaping off the front porch, skipping all the steps; Emma was holding the door open for Chess.

Mom gave Chess a gentle shove.

"Go on," she said. "Don't . . . don't worry."

"Mom—" Emma began.

But Mom shook her head and reached for the door. To shut it.

"The three of you will be fine," Mom said. It sounded like she was trying to convince herself. "Absolutely fine. You have each other. Oh, look! There's the bus! Hurry!"

Chess looked down at his sister, and it felt like they were coming to understand the same thing at the same time: *Mom doesn't want us asking questions. Mom doesn't want to explain anything.*

Chess stumbled down the porch steps and blindly aimed his feet toward the driveway down to the bus. He kept his head down, as if he didn't trust his legs to move without him watching. Or maybe it was that he didn't trust his head not to swivel back toward Mom and the rest of his body to follow.

Once he reached the bus, he went to the very back seat—
and only then did he turn around to look back toward the
house and Mom.

Mom still stood in the doorway, her face frozen in an
attempt at a smile. And she kept waving and waving and
waving, as though she believed she'd never see Finn and
Emma and Chess again.

TEN

FINN

Finn sat in a sea of empty desks. His class had already said the Pledge of Allegiance and listened to the morning announcements. (The most important one: Lunch was going to be pizza.) And still his friends Tyrell and Lucy hadn't shown up. Now he was supposed to be reading quietly while Mr. Habazz helped some other kids with math. Normally Finn loved any Commander Toad book (though he couldn't read them quietly, because he always laughed). But today he kept looking up from *Commander Toad and the Big Black Hole* to stare at the empty desks.

It made him think about Mom leaving, too. Was she still

at home, or had she driven to the airport already?

Why hadn't Finn asked what time she was leaving?

What if Finn suddenly got a stomachache? How would he know whether he was supposed to go home or to that strange woman's house?

Maybe Finn should get a stomachache, just so he could go home and spend every moment possible with Mom, until she had to leave.

If she hadn't left already.

His stomach did feel kind of funny.

"Finn, don't worry, I'm sure your friends will be here soon," Mr. Habazz said from across the room. "I got a message from the office that there's a late bus."

Just then, the speaker at the front of the room crackled, and Finn heard the school secretary say, "Pardon the interruption—bus thirty-two has just arrived. Teachers, please admit the late students to class."

Lucy, Tyrell, and three other kids came dashing into the classroom.

Tyrell raced to the front of the class and cried out, "Someone crashed into our bus!"

Lucy dropped her backpack and put her hands on her hips.

"Tyrell, you know it was just a bump, not a crash!" she said. "'Crash' sounds like somebody got hurt."

"But the police had to come!" another of Finn's friends, Spencer, added.

Mr. Habazz sighed.

"Okay, take five minutes," he said. "Tell the story. Then we'll get back to work, and you can save the rest of the conversation for recess, okay?"

"This green car came out of nowhere and hit us!" Tyrell said. "It was like the driver didn't even *see* us and, you know, that bus is as big as a house! And—bright yellow!"

"Who has a question for the bus thirty-two kids?" Mr. Habazz asked the rest of the class.

Mr. Habazz kept alternating between having the kids from the bus talk and letting the other kids ask questions. It made Finn a little sad that every answer made the crash sound less and less interesting. Even Tyrell had to admit, "No, I don't think there was a dent. But they wouldn't let us get off the bus to look. And we had to sit and wait *forever*."

At least five minutes passed without Finn thinking about his mom being away.

Finally, Mr. Habazz said, "Okay, bus thirty-two kids, time to sit down. Back to our normally scheduled programming. Silent reading or page ninety in the math book."

His heart wasn't quite in it, but Finn whispered to Tyrell, "At least *you* got to have an adventure this morning. I wish *my* bus had been in a crash. I mean, as long as nobody got hurt."

"Finn, we were saving the big news for you!" Tyrell said as he slid into his seat. "Lucy said maybe we shouldn't tell, but . . ."

"But what?" Finn asked.

"Tyrell, you know Finn's mother was not robbing that bank!" Lucy said, dropping a book onto her desk.

"Robbing . . . what?" Finn asked. "*My* mom? No way!"

"When that car hit us, we were right beside the bank," Tyrell said, talking fast the way he always did when he got excited. Which was pretty much . . . always. "You know, the one with the red sign? Anyhow, your mom came running out of the bank carrying a big bag, big enough that it was like she might have told the bank lady inside, 'Give me all your cash.' And then she got in her car and pulled out of the parking lot, and Finn, she even squealed her tires! Like she was making a quick getaway!"

Finn's mother did not ever squeal her tires. Much to his disappointment.

"You must have just seen someone who *looked* like my mom," Finn said.

"Nuh-uh, it was her," Tyrell said. "And that was your car, because it had the scratches on the side where you and Emma crashed your bikes into it. . . ."

Tyrell saw Finn's mom all the time. He knew Finn's mom's car, too. In fact, some of the scratches on it were probably from Tyrell's bike, not just Emma's and Finn's. Tyrell hung out at Finn's house so much that a neighbor had asked once if they were twins—even though Tyrell was black and Finn was white.

So Tyrell should have known that Finn's mom would never rob a bank.

"Nobody from the bank chased out after Finn's mom," Lucy said. "*Someone* would chase a bank robber. Probably she was just in a hurry."

"She—" Finn started to tell about how Mom was going on a business trip to Chicago. How she had been in a big hurry this morning.

But suddenly Tyrell grabbed Lucy's arm.

"Lucy!" he cried. "What if the *green car* was chasing Finn's mom? And that's why he didn't see the bus? Because she turned in front of us, and then . . . boom! We were in the way! Our bus stopped the green car from catching up with Finn's mom! What's it called when someone helps someone else with a crime? We're—"

"Accomplices?" Lucy asked.

"Oh, my beloved chatty kids! Finn, Tyrell, and Lucy!" Mr. Habazz called from across the room. "*Silent* reading, remember? Do you need to move to different seats so you're not so tempted to talk?"

"No, Mr. Habazz," the three of them chorused together.

Finn, Tyrell, and Lucy all bent their heads over their desks. Finn tried very hard to look like he was reading about Commander Toad standing at the edge of the black hole. But the words swam before his eyes.

"Don't listen to Tyrell's crazy stories," Lucy whispered. She had special skills when it came to not getting caught talking: She kept her eyes down and made it look like she was just moving her lips as she read. "*I* know your mom wouldn't rob a bank. Tyrell knows that, too. He's just having fun."

It's not fun today, Finn wanted to say. *Not when my mom's going away. And when kids with the same name as Chess and Emma and me got kidnapped. And . . .*

He didn't let himself think about anything else that might not be fun. But he still couldn't make himself read.

He just sat there staring at pictures of black holes.

ELEVEN

EMMA

When Ms. Morales came to pick up the three Greystone kids at the end of the school day, she was wearing a lot of makeup and hairspray. She also had on high heels, dramatically flared black pants, and a frilly blouse with swoopy sleeves. Emma thought that if it were wintertime, Ms. Morales could lie down on the ground in that outfit and make snow angels without even moving her arms.

"—and your mother tells me that your favorite food is succotash?" Ms. Morales was saying.

"Yes, ma'am," Chess said. Then his face turned bright

red. Emma wasn't sure if it was because he'd had to claim in public that he liked lima beans, or if he was afraid someone else in the school office would overhear their secret code word.

Or maybe it was just because he was twelve. Mom had explained once that sometimes when kids got into sixth or seventh grade, they started getting embarrassed easily. She'd explained that to Emma and Finn when Chess was away at a friend's house. Emma and Finn had thought this news was hilarious, and they'd both told Mom, "That is *never* going to happen to us."

Emma wasn't embarrassed, but it felt really weird to walk out the school door with Ms. Morales. Ms. Morales's clothes might as well have been shouting, "Hey! Everybody! Look at me!" Emma was more used to being around people whose clothes talked in a normal voice and didn't saying anything but, "Enh, look at me, don't look at me, who cares?"

Though Emma herself did have a Math Olympiad T-shirt she really loved. Was it also like shouting to walk around with the words "Math kids get pi" on your clothes?

"My SUV's over there," Ms. Morales said, pointing out into the parking lot. "There's been a tiny change of plans, because your mom ran out of time to drop your suitcases off at my house this morning. So we're going to swing by your house to get them. You can check on your cat while we're there and attend to the kitty litter, so we won't have to go back until the day after tomorrow."

"But Mom will be back by then, right?" Finn asked, stepping off the curb.

"Sorry, honey," Ms. Morales said, ruffling Finn's hair. "She still doesn't know when she gets to come home."

Finn stuck his lip out like he was sulking, which wasn't like him. But Emma liked Ms. Morales a little better, that she'd known to mess up Finn's hair.

"I can do the kitty litter," Chess said.

"That's nice of you to offer, but your mom said it was Emma's turn," Ms. Morales said.

Emma felt a little like her own mother had tattled on her.

But I didn't say I wouldn't *do the kitty litter!* she wanted to protest. *I was just . . . thinking about more interesting things!*

"Susanna!" one of the teachers on bus duty called over to Ms. Morales. "Great to see you back! We miss you at PTO!"

"Oh, believe me, I miss Natalie's elementary school days, too!" Ms. Morales called back. "Life was so much simpler then. . . ."

What did that mean?

Other teachers and parents kept calling out to Ms. Morales, but she kept shepherding the kids toward the parking lot, even as she stayed a few steps back from them. It almost felt to Emma as though Ms. Morales didn't want everybody to know the Greystone kids were with her.

Because we're *not wearing makeup and hairspray and swoopy clothes?* Emma wondered. Then she giggled, imagining what the three of them would look like with makeup and hairspray and swoopy clothes.

"It's the white SUV at the far end of the lot," Ms. Morales said under her breath, like a spy. Or a gangster. "Go around and get in on the passenger side. *Not* the side that faces the school."

Okay, that was weird, Emma thought.

She looked toward Finn and Chess. Her eyes met Chess's; Chess instantly started patting Finn's back.

"Hey, Finn," Emma said. "Look how big that SUV is. And it's white. What do you bet the Morales family named it Moby Dick, like the whale? Moby for short? Won't it be fun to drive around in Moby?"

Finn turned back toward Ms. Morales.

"*Is* your car named Moby Dick?" he asked.

"Er—no," Ms. Morales said. She was looking around and barely even glanced at Finn. "I guess I never thought of naming it."

They reached the SUV then, and Emma huddled close to Finn as they circled around it.

"Don't worry," she whispered. "You still have Chess and

me with you. It's not like you'll be totally stuck with people who don't even name their cars."

Emma started to reach up for the handle of the front passenger door, but Chess shook his head.

"Someone's already sitting there," he whispered. "The daughter—Natalie?"

He opened the side door, and first Finn, then Emma, then Chess climbed in. As Emma settled into the middle seat, she peeked toward the front. All she could see of the girl sitting there was a waterfall of brown hair and the edge of a cell phone the girl was hunched over.

The girl didn't turn around or say hello.

Ms. Morales climbed into the driver's seat.

"Everybody, this is Natalie," Ms. Morales said. "Natalie, this is Chess, Emma, and Finn."

"Hi!" Finn shouted. "Nice to meet you!"

"Yeah," Emma said.

"Er, um," Chess said. His face turned red again.

Natalie *might* have made the kind of grunting noise prehistoric cave people made to one another before anyone invented language. But it was kind of hard to tell because Finn had been so loud.

Natalie's posture didn't change in the least. She didn't turn her head. Her fingers kept flying over the surface of the cell phone.

Ms. Morales sighed as she put her seat belt on.

"Natalie, wasn't it nice to see the elementary school again?" Ms. Morales said in one of those fake-cheerful voices grown-ups used all the time. "Where you have so many happy memories?"

Natalie might have grunted again, and this time the sound could have gotten lost in the noise of the engine starting up.

Something dinged.

"Oh, Natalie, could you check that text message?" Ms. Morales said as she turned the steering wheel far to the right, to back out of the parking space.

Emma found herself deeply curious about what Natalie would do next. Would she:

a) Grunt again, and maybe even make it audible this time?

b) Keep typing on her own cell phone and totally ignore her mom?

c) Actually reach into her mother's bright red purse and pull out Ms. Morales's phone and read the text message aloud? In a normal voice even?

Emma would have said there was no chance the answer was c. If she'd had a million dollars to bet on the odds of each answer, she would have put it all on a or b.

But after Natalie let out a loud sigh of her own—the

kind of sigh that said someone was in the greatest agony ever—she reached into the red purse on the floor between her and her mother. She slid her mother's cell phone through her curtain-like waterfall of hair, studied it silently, and then announced in a bored voice, "It's from those kids' mom."

Then she dropped the phone back into her mother's purse.

Emma was so busy deciding whether to count Natalie's bored tone as normal that she let it fall to Finn to cry, "What did Mom say? Is she going to call us? Is she coming home tonight?"

Ms. Morales switched the SUV from Reverse to Park and scooped up the phone. She glanced at the screen, then turned to face Finn and Emma and Chess.

"I'm so sorry," she said. "Your mom was texting to say that her meetings are going really, really late, and she's not even going to be able to call you this afternoon or evening. What would you like me to say back to her?"

Emma took a deep breath and grabbed Finn's hand. She squeezed it hard.

Don't let Finn cry, she thought. *Don't let Finn cry. Not in front of this awful girl Natalie.*

Was it possible that if Emma hadn't had Finn to think about, she might have needed to tell herself, *Don't let me cry. Don't let me cry. Not in front of Natalie?*

"Can we just type the answer ourselves?" Chess asked. Probably Ms. Morales and Natalie wouldn't be able to tell that his voice wobbled a little. Probably only Emma noticed, because she knew him so well.

Ms. Morales handed the phone back, and Emma peeked over Chess's shoulder.

Chess here, he wrote. **We're fine. We all had a good day at school and are with Ms. Morales now. Can you talk to us tomorrow morning? Do you know when you're coming home?**

"Tell her we love her!" Finn yelled, and Chess added that.

Emma stared at the phone screen. Three little bouncing dots appeared, which meant Mom was writing back.

Emma waited. In the driver's seat, Ms. Morales waited, too.

Natalie kept typing away on her own phone, as if nothing else mattered.

I hate not getting to talk directly! popped up on the screen. **Susanna, please pass this along to the kids: I promise, I will make it all up to you when I get home. Just think about all the fun we'll have then! I am trying to finish up as fast as I can, so I can come home as soon as possible. So I need to stop texting and get back to work. I love you all so, so much!**

63

Mom must have thought Chess gave the phone back to Ms. Morales right away, since she was writing to Susanna, not him. That was weird. Mom hadn't even answered Chess's questions.

This was not like Mom at all.

Chess started to hand the phone over to Ms. Morales, but Emma said, "Wait a minute." She took the phone from Chess's hand and tilted it to make it look like she was adding a message of her own. But really she was scrolling back through the text conversation, to see what Mom had told Ms. Morales earlier in the day.

Maybe Mom had actually told Ms. Morales how long she was going to be gone, and it was just such a horrifyingly long time that no one wanted to break the news to the kids.

Well, Emma would rather know.

But Emma reached the top of the text conversation between Mom and Ms. Morales, and the *only* texts from Mom were the ones she'd just sent this afternoon, about how she didn't have time to call.

What did that mean?

Maybe Ms. Morales is just one of those people who deletes text messages right after she reads them, Emma told herself. *Or maybe she has a work phone and a personal cell phone, and all the other messages were on that other phone.*

Or maybe there was something really weird going on.

We aren't being kidnapped! Emma told herself. *Not like the kids in Arizona! Ms. Morales knew the code word! Mom* arranged *for her to pick us up! She told us so!*

But none of those thoughts were comforting.

After Emma gave the phone back and Ms. Morales turned back around to drive, Emma slipped her other hand into Chess's. Now she was clinging to Finn on her left and Chess on her right.

Whatever was going to happen, at least they could deal with it together.

TWELVE

CHESS

Ms. Morales's daughter, Natalie, was a Lip Gloss Girl.

Chess hadn't recognized her until he heard her voice. He still hadn't seen her face, and he hadn't figured out until she spoke that she didn't have the same last name as her mom, and her *real* name was Natalie Mayhew.

Natalie Mayhew and the other Lip Gloss Girls had kind of run the whole school last year, before they moved on to middle school.

There'd been a moment last spring when Chess was out at recess, pretending to be part of a baseball game—but not pretending very hard, because nobody was actually going to hit the ball that far into the outfield. And Natalie and three other Lip Gloss Girls had walked over to him, and one of them had said, "You know, you're kind of cute."

And then Natalie had added in a scornful voice, "For a fifth grader, anyway."

What was Chess supposed to say to that?

Chess didn't say anything, and the four girls had walked away, all of them with hair rippling down their backs like they were princesses in some Disney movie.

For weeks after that, Chess had tried to figure out what he should have said. Would "Thanks!" have sounded conceited? Would "You're really pretty, too" have sounded like he was a jerk? If he'd tried to say anything, could he have gotten the words out without snorting or belching or stammering or doing something else that made him seem like a total dork?

It was probably a good thing that he'd just stayed silent.

But Chess had wondered if that moment was something he could have talked about with his dad, if his dad had still been alive. Dad probably would have been able to give him all sorts of advice about how to talk to girls.

Of course, Chess could have just asked his mom. But . . . it wasn't the same.

Now Chess was sitting in the SUV with Natalie Mayhew, and his little sister was holding his hand. And, over on the other side of Emma, Finn was holding *her* hand, so the three of them probably looked like really, really little kids going off to preschool or something like that.

Chess felt his face go hot again. He was not going to let go of Emma's hand just because Natalie Mayhew was sitting in the front seat and could turn around at any minute and see him.

She probably wasn't going to turn around, anyhow.

She probably didn't even remember talking to him last spring.

She was a *middle school* girl now, and she'd probably forgotten about everything that happened in elementary school.

Before Chess knew it, Ms. Morales was pulling up in front of the Greystones' house.

"You can park in the driveway," Finn volunteered. "Mom won't mind. And Rocket stays in the house, so it's not like he'd come out and make you sick. Because of your allergy."

"That's okay," Ms. Morales said. "I'm already parked. I'll just stay here and take care of some work email. Natalie can go in with you and help you carry out your suitcases."

Natalie Mayhew is going to come into my house? Chess wanted to scream.

"Ooo—let's see if she obeys this time," Emma whispered

in his ear. "Can Natalie put down her phone that long? What's your prediction?"

Chess watched Natalie. She seemed to be texting one-handed as she shoved her door open. She slid out the door in one smooth move and began walking up the driveway. As far as Chess could tell, she didn't take her eyes off the phone screen once. She also didn't stop texting.

"Never mind," Emma whispered to Chess.

Chess followed Natalie, Finn, and Emma toward the house. He was a little afraid Finn would suggest, *Hey! Let's race like we always do!* And then probably Natalie would laugh at the way Chess ran. But even Finn seemed weighted down, his steps sluggish.

Even the cowlicks in Finn's hair seemed to droop.

When they got to the door, Chess pulled out the key and turned it in the lock. The house already had a closed-up feeling to it, as if it had been empty for days, not just a matter of hours. Three suitcases sat by the door: Chess's was an ordinary blue, Finn's had a giant Pokémon logo, and Emma's was bright red and covered in stickers.

"Really, I can carry my own suitcase," Finn said, and his voice echoed a little. "Natalie doesn't have to help."

"Mom would have made me come in here anyway," Natalie muttered without looking up from her phone. She leaned back against the wall by the door.

"Why?" Emma asked, as if this was something that deeply fascinated her.

"Don't worry about it," Natalie said. "Just take care of your cat. Or dog. Whatever it is."

"Weren't you *listening*?" Finn said. He sounded offended. "Rocket's a cat!"

"Yeah, yeah," Natalie said. She kept her head bent over the phone. But Chess could have sworn he saw her eyes dart right to left, her gaze shooting past the phone.

Maybe she really was looking around their house. She just didn't want them to know she was looking around the house.

Chess wanted to share this observation with Emma, but he couldn't do that with Natalie standing right there.

"I'll help you with the kitty litter," he offered to Emma. "Finn, why don't you go pet Rocket and keep him company for a few minutes?"

"I'll have to find him first!" Finn said. He bent down and looked under the couch.

"He's probably on the window seat in Mom's room," Emma said. "That's where he goes when no one's home."

Chess was a little worried that Finn would say, *How do you know where Rocket goes when no one's home? If nobody's home, nobody's here to see him!* And then Emma and Finn could get into one of those "If a tree falls in a forest, and nobody hears it, does it still make a sound?" discussions. And Natalie Mayhew would just stand there rolling her eyes.

But Finn said, "Okay," and raced toward the stairs.

Oddly, Natalie followed him.

Chess wanted to call out to her, *Hey, who said you were allowed to go upstairs? Who even invited you into our house?* But that would have been rude. It would have made it seem like he didn't trust Natalie.

Was there any reason not to trust Natalie?

Mom trusts Ms. Morales. Mom knew Ms. Morales had a daughter. So . . .

"Are you going to help me or not?" Emma asked, backward-walking toward the kitchen and the door down to the basement.

"Oh, er—yes," Chess said.

He and Emma were partway down the basement stairs—past the step where he'd stood in darkness the night before, listening to his mother's phone call—before he figured out what he wanted to say to his sister.

"Do you remember Natalie from last year, when she went to our school?" he asked.

"No," Emma said.

Chess guessed there was a big difference between him being just one year younger than Natalie and Emma being three years younger.

"Natalie was part of this group of girls . . . they all wore lip gloss," he began.

"Really?" Emma said, as if he'd just said something like *Cheetahs can run up to seventy-five miles per hour* or *Bats are the only mammals that can fly.* "Girls wear makeup in sixth grade? Do girls in your class do that this year?"

"Um . . . some do," Chess said. "I guess. But it's not the same as . . ."

Why was he having so much trouble explaining this to Emma?

Emma got ahead of him again, jumping past the last three steps. Now she was almost where Mom had stood the night before.

Maybe Chess should tell Emma what he'd heard Mom say on the phone, instead of trying to explain about Natalie.

But what if that just scares her?

It was scary that Mom had said, "You have to fix this. Or so help me, I will" to some strange person—Joe?—at three a.m. And then just four hours later she was announcing an unexpected business trip.

It was scary that her last words to Chess had been "Don't forget anything."

But telling Emma about all that wouldn't make it any less scary.

Mom's the one I need to talk to, Chess decided. *She'll call tomorrow morning, I bet. I'll just have to take the phone somewhere private, away from Emma and Finn. And away from Ms. Morales and Natalie. And then I'll get Mom to explain.*

Chess needed to hear Mom say, "Everything's under control. Don't worry." Maybe he even needed to hear her say, "The police have found those kids in Arizona and they're perfectly safe. They're back with their parents, and the kidnappers will be in prison for the rest of their lives. And, really, it was just a false alarm, me thinking those kids had anything to do with us."

"Can you hold the bag for me?" Emma asked.

She crouched down beside the litter pan, the scoop in one hand, a plastic grocery store bag in the other. Chess walked over and took the bag from her.

"Natalie's a teenager," Emma said as she dug the scoop into the litter. "Mom told Finn and me that sometimes kids start acting weird about the time they turn thirteen. Or even just twelve. Like you."

She dropped the clumps of litter into the bag and jokingly flicked the empty scoop at him.

"*I* don't act weird," Chess said.

"Oh yeah?" Emma challenged, taking the bag from him

and tying the handles together so it wouldn't leak. "Then why are you just standing there all moony, talking about Natalie? Why is it different if *she* wears lip gloss than if girls in your class wear lip gloss?"

"I'm not—" Chess began.

But just then he heard Finn shout from upstairs:

"Chess! Emma! Get up here now!"

THIRTEEN

FINN

Finn had really wanted to pet Rocket. It could have made everything at least a little better.

Finn hadn't even had a chance to tell Chess or Emma about Tyrell saying Mom was a bank robber. Mom would never do that, and even if she had, wouldn't the police have already caught her? Wouldn't they have come for Chess, Emma, and Finn, too? Finn was pretty sure that was how things worked.

Still, Finn wouldn't have minded snuggling with Rocket and whispering into his furry ear, *Tyrell says Mom robbed a bank, and Mom went to Chicago, and Chess and Emma and I have to stay with some lady we don't know, and, oh yeah, some kids with our names were kidnapped, so . . . purr, Rocket, purr! I need to hear you purr!*

Finn looked in his and Emma's and Chess's rooms, but Rocket was nowhere in sight. He saved Mom's room for last, because he thought looking there would make him miss her even more. But Emma was right—Rocket *loved* sleeping on Mom's cushioned window seat, especially on sunny afternoons.

Finn walked into Mom's room, and the blinds were drawn, so there wasn't any sunny spot on the blue cushion by the window. The whole room was dim.

Someone flicked on the light behind him. It was that girl, Natalie. He hadn't even heard her come upstairs.

"You go walking around in the dark, you'll run into something and get hurt," she said. "Then my mom will get mad at me for not protecting you."

"I can walk around my own house without getting hurt," Finn said. He waited, because he was pretty sure she was going to say, *Oh yeah?* And then he'd have to say, *Yeah, what's it to you?* Something about Natalie made Finn want to argue with her. And Finn didn't even like to argue.

But Natalie just gave a half snort and tilted back against the wall. She kept her head down, looking at her phone, and her long brown hair slid forward, hiding her face.

Good, Finn thought. *I don't want her watching me pet Rocket.*

He didn't want her in Mom's room, either, but he decided to ignore that and focus on finding Rocket.

Rocket wasn't under Mom's bed.

Rocket wasn't curled up in the chair where Mom piled clothes sometimes when even she was too lazy to put things away.

Rocket wasn't perched on the top of Mom's dresser, where sometimes he acted like he was a lion or a tiger out in the jungle waiting to pounce on his prey.

"Is that your cat's tail under the dresser?" Natalie asked in a bored voice.

"Huh?" Finn said, looking down. "Oh. Yeah."

Rocket's striped gray-and-black tail curled out from behind the dresser. Finn bent down and saw that Rocket was lying upside down, his paw swiping up toward a cord plugged into the wall behind the dresser.

"Rocket! Don't play with electrical cords," Finn said, reaching for the cat.

But Rocket seemed to think Finn was playing, too, and batted his paw at Finn instead. The cord caught on Rocket's claw and whipped toward Finn.

"Is that—? Oh no!" Finn said. "Mom forgot her phone charger! How's she going to call and text us when her phone dies?"

"I bet she has a backup charger," Natalie said, sounding more bored than ever. "Or she can buy one."

"No, she—" Finn was not going to explain to Natalie that this was Mom's special charger, with a sticker on it from each kid: Finn's was a grinning cat; Emma's, a pink robot; and Chess's, a tiny zigzag like a Harry Potter scar. "We have to mail it to her! Overnight!"

Finn unplugged the charger and tugged on the other end of the cord, which went under the back of the dresser.

The cord did not come snaking out. It seemed to be caught inside the dresser.

Finn switched to yanking on the bottom drawer. If he could move that out of the way, he could see where the cord went.

The drawer slipped out and sagged toward the floor. This drawer held Mom's sweaters, neatly folded and stacked. Finn tilted sideways, his eyes even with the top of the drawer, so he could see the cord winding down from the back of the drawer and into the middle pile of sweaters. He shoved the top sweater away—and there, hidden beneath it, still attached to the cord, was something that almost made Finn's heart stop.

It was Mom's phone. She'd left it behind, too.

FOURTEEN

EMMA

Emma took the stairs three at a time, right alongside Chess.

"We're coming, Finn!" she yelled. "What's wrong?"

Emma and Chess were only at the top of the basement stairs; all she could hear from Finn was, "Because Mom . . . Mom . . ."

Emma raced through the kitchen and then sprinted through the living room to the next flight of stairs. Rocket came galloping toward them from the opposite direction, streaking down the stairs and then around the corner toward the basement.

"That's not good," Emma muttered.

"Cats spook easy," Chess said. "And Rocket—"

Emma stopped listening and lunged for the stairs. She saw Finn and Natalie in the doorway to Mom's room. They appeared to be playing tug-of-war with Natalie's phone—had Finn tried to take it away from her?

That didn't seem like Finn.

Then Finn turned the phone to the side and Emma caught a glimpse of the case: hard plastic with a crookedly drawn heart and the words "We love you, Mommy."

The phone they were fighting over wasn't Natalie's.

"You've got Mom's phone?" Emma said, screeching to a halt when she reached the landing. "So Mom's home?"

"*No*," Finn said. "She left her phone in her *drawer*. Where she *never* leaves it. So who put it there? And who just texted us pretending to be her?"

"I tried to tell him," Natalie said breathlessly. "She's probably texting from her laptop or an iPad or something like that. Some other device. *You* tell him. Maybe he'll believe you. He tried to bite me."

"That wasn't my teeth, that was the cat's claw," Finn said with great dignity. "You shouldn't have tried to grab the phone away from Rocket and me. Emma? Chess? What's going on?"

Natalie made a sweeping gesture with her arm, the kind

that clearly said, *Be my guest. You talk sense into him.*

"I . . . I guess Mom could text from her laptop," Emma said, trying to remember if she'd ever seen Mom do that. It *seemed* possible. "But—"

"Mom would never leave her phone behind on purpose," Chess said firmly from behind Emma. "She wouldn't forget it, either."

Emma wanted to cheer, *Go, Chess!* He might have been acting kind of moony and weird about Natalie down in the basement, but now it was almost like he'd sprung in front of Finn, put out his arms protectively, and shouted, *Don't you make fun of my brother! He knows what he's talking about!*

And Chess wasn't just talking about Mom's phone. He was talking about the crooked heart and the "We love you, Mommy" on the case, too.

Mom wouldn't forget that, either.

"Something's wrong," Emma said. She reached out and grabbed Finn by the shoulders, pulling him closer. She kept both arms around him, with her face nestled against his messy hair. So now it was all the Greystone kids together facing off against Natalie. Three against one.

Natalie held up her hands in an "I surrender" pose. But, oddly, she didn't lean back against the wall or mutter "Never mind" or let her hair hide her face while she did nothing but text. She peered directly at the three Greystone kids, with a look in her brown eyes that might have even been kindness. Or . . .

Pity? Emma thought.

"Look," Natalie said softly, her hands still up in the air. "Usually when my mom tells some friend—or acquaintance—that she'll babysit her kids for a few days, no questions asked, it's because . . . well, you know. Sometimes parents fight. And sometimes a woman needs to go away, while things cool down. So she can work things out. And . . . cell phones have GPS, and sometimes even when you think you've disabled it, well . . . Haven't you heard your parents fighting? Don't you see—"

"Our dad is dead," Chess said flatly.

"It happened *eight* years ago," Emma said.

"Oh, sorry," Natalie said, and Emma liked that she didn't make it all fake and dramatic, *I feel so bad for you! What a terrible thing!* It was more like Natalie was sorry, but she was distracted from that by trying to figure everything out with this new information.

That was how Emma liked to deal with information, too.

"Then I guess in your mom's case," Natalie went on, "it'd be a boyfriend who—"

"Mom doesn't have a boyfriend," Emma said.

"Are you sure?" Natalie asked, and it was almost like she was taunting Emma and apologizing, all at once. "Maybe she just hasn't wanted to introduce you to him yet. Maybe she goes out at night after you're asleep, and—"

"Mom doesn't go anywhere at night but the Boring Room!" Finn roared.

"The what?" Natalie asked.

"Her office," Chess said tonelessly. "In the basement."

Natalie took a step back.

"Okay, look," she said. "Do any of you know your mom's code, to unlock the phone? I think maybe there's a way to see what other devices the texting is linked to, and then at least the little guy will see that she really did send those texts, and there's nothing wrong. Or . . ." Natalie winced and finished in a hurried mumble, "At least, there's nothing wrong that she isn't trying to fix."

"I don't know any code," Finn said.

Emma looked back to find Chess shaking his head silently.

"Emma?" Natalie said.

Emma didn't say anything.

Finn whimpered.

"All right! All right! I know the code!" Emma admitted.

She glared at Natalie. "But you do *not* get to watch me type it in. And you don't type anything on Mom's phone we can't see. I don't want you changing anything. And you *just* look at the texting."

"Sure," Natalie said.

Finn slipped the phone into Emma's hand. Emma could have sworn she felt the crooked heart against her palm, even though it was just a Sharpie drawing on plastic and perfectly flat.

Mom loves us, Emma told herself. *Mom would never go off without us—or her phone, to link to us—without a good reason. Either Natalie's right, or something weird happened and* Mom's *in danger, or . . .*

Emma couldn't think about the rest of that sentence. She kept one hand on Finn's shoulder and used the other to tilt the phone out of everyone else's sight and type in Mom's passcode: 111360. The reason Emma remembered it so well was because she knew where it came from. One time she and Mom had been talking about numbers, and Mom had said that they were symbolic. Three ones in a row, she said, always reminded her of Chess and Emma and Finn, not just the number 111.

"But the three of you together add up to a way bigger number," she'd said.

"Like three hundred sixty?" Emma had answered. "That's two squared times three squared times ten. And there are three hundred sixty degrees in a circle. And the line that makes a circle goes on and on and on, without any end."

Emma had been in kindergarten or first grade then, and Mom had laughed.

"Oh, Emma," she'd said. "What all are you going to do in this world, my little mathematician?"

The way she'd said it had made Emma feel proud. And a little possessive. Later, when she noticed that Mom had started using 111360 as her cell phone passcode, Emma wanted to keep the information to herself. She was the middle child, stuck between adorable Finn and responsible Chess—sometimes she just needed something to be all hers.

The keypad vanished from the screen, revealing the menu page. Emma held the phone out so Natalie could see the screen. Natalie squinted at the texting symbol at the top.

"Your mom uses an encrypted texting service?" Natalie said. "*That's* interesting. What did you say she does?"

"*We* didn't tell you," Emma said.

"But she's a graphic designer," Chess added, just as Finn said, "She makes websites."

Emma tried to decide if she should glare at her two brothers. But she was too busy watching Natalie's fingers fly across the screen.

"Huh," Natalie said. She bent closer and started to lift the phone higher. Emma pulled it back down.

"You don't see anything we don't see," Emma reminded her.

"Are you sure you want to . . . ? Oh!" Natalie jerked back, knocking the phone to the side.

Chess's hand shot out, steadying it again.

"Mom sent another text?" he asked. "Or—lots of them?"

Now it was Chess lifting the phone higher. Emma had to stand on tiptoes to see the screen, which was suddenly full of one green bubble of words after another. Emma read only, **Tell the kids I can't believe this! My schedule today is just as crazy today as yesterday but** . . . before Natalie was scrolling farther down, through bubble after bubble after bubble.

"Technically, she hasn't sent these yet," Natalie said. She sounded apologetic again. "It's like she's got some auto-service set up, so these are set to go out at certain times. Tomorrow morning, tomorrow afternoon, then . . ."

Emma caught only bits and pieces of each text: . . . **so, so sorry . . . Believe me, this is not what I want . . . don't want to interrupt at school . . . wish so much I could be home with . . . really do wish I could call** . . .

Then the words on the screen stopped moving, and Natalie slapped her hand over the last bubble of text. Emma could see only the date above that bubble: It was for Tuesday, May 12. Exactly one week away.

"Let. Us. See," Finn said.

Natalie started shaking her head, her long hair whipping out like snakes.

"No," she said, and now her voice turned pleading. "You don't want to read this. Maybe you'll never have to. It's actually to my mom. And it's the kind of thing that—"

Emma and Chess and Finn together ripped the phone out of Natalie's grasp.

And then Emma saw the last words on the screen:

Please tell the kids this was the last thing I wanted to happen. But I have to stay away for good, to protect them. That's the only way to keep them safe. Tell them, you'll always have each other. But also tell them never to look for me. I'm mailing you a letter to give to them today. It will explain everything—when they're ready.

FIFTEEN

CHESS

"Mom would never do that to us," Chess said.

"Unless she had to," Emma said. "Mom always says she would do anything to protect us."

Chess hated how Emma could be so brutally logical, even at a time like this.

Even if she sounded like she was about to cry.

Chess put his arm around Emma's shoulder, so now all three Greystones were linked: Chess holding on to Emma, Emma holding on to Finn.

But it's not the same without Mom, Chess thought.

How could she possibly be gone for good? How could anybody not cry, if that was true?

Chess felt too frozen to do anything. But Finn sniffed. Then he whirled around and buried his face in the hollow between Chess's shirt and Emma's sleeve. He *was* crying.

Natalie reached out like she wanted to pat Finn on the back, but Emma glared and clutched Finn closer. It was possible that Chess's face had shaped itself into a glare, too. He seemed to have lost control of his expression.

Natalie drew her hand back.

"Parents are so awful!" she snarled. "I hate my mom, too. And my dad. But even they never—"

"*Our* mom isn't awful," Finn mumbled into Chess's shirt and Emma's sleeve. "She loves us."

"Finn's right," Emma said fiercely. "Mom probably needs *our* help. We need to see that letter. Now, not next week."

"We can't get it out of the mail," Chess said. "We don't even know where and when she's putting it *in* the mail. But if she typed it on her computer . . ."

Natalie raised an eyebrow at Chess, like he was supposed to understand something the younger kids wouldn't. Maybe she was trying to say, *What if you really* don't *want to see that letter? What if it's too awful to read?*

Chess shook his head at Natalie. If he hadn't minded

Finn and Emma overhearing, he would have said out loud, *My father* died *when I was four. You think I'm scared of a* letter?

No, he probably wouldn't actually say that. But he could think it.

Whether it was true or not.

"If she left her phone here, maybe she left one of her computers, too," Emma said. "The one she doesn't use for work. And maybe the letter's on that. Or we can use that computer to get to the cloud, where she might have saved it."

"*I'm* going to go find it," Finn announced, and Chess knew without looking that Finn would have his lip stuck out and his face set, a vision of obstinacy.

But then Chess did glance down at his brother, thinking it would help his own resolve. And Finn had tear tracks down his cheeks, along with a bubble of snot threatening to balloon out of one of his nostrils. His whole face trembled.

Finn looked like he *wanted* to act stubborn, but he'd gotten stuck on forlorn.

"Finn, why don't you look around up here," Chess suggested. "I'll check on the first floor, and Emma can try the basement. She needs to go back down there to throw away the kitty litter she scooped, anyway."

It felt good to be making plans—taking charge—even though his voice shook. And Emma shot him a glance that Chess knew meant, *Why do you have to be so bossy?* Still, Emma started down the stairs, and Chess quickly followed her.

Because if he hadn't, he would have had to meet Natalie's gaze again. And she might have even asked the question Chess was trying very hard not to think about. Chess hoped it *never* occurred to Finn or Emma.

Natalie's mom had agreed to take care of the Greystone kids for a night or two. Or maybe three. But if Mom wasn't coming back—or even if she only got delayed—what would happen to the Greystone kids then? Where would they go? Who would take care of them?

This is crazy, Chess told himself. *A misunderstanding. A mistake. Of course Mom's coming back. That will happen regardless. Whether we find her spare computer or not. Whether we do anything or not.*

Still, as soon as he got down to the living room, Chess began looking under pillows, pulling out drawers.

Because there had to be something he could do.

He had to prove that none of this was true.

SIXTEEN

FINN

"You can go help Chess or Emma," Finn told Natalie as he opened Mom's closet. "I've got this."

Finn hoped she couldn't tell that what he really wanted was for her to leave so he could bury his face in Mom's clothes. Maybe he could pull them down from the hangers and just curl up in a nest of Mom's shirts until she came back. They'd still smell like her as long as nobody washed them, right? Finn sniffed a sleeve, and there it was: Mom's unique odor, a mix of vanilla and Spring Breeze laundry detergent, with maybe some cinnamon and grass stain lurking underneath.

And apples. Mom's clothes also smelled like apples.

"I . . . ," Natalie began, and Finn forced himself to turn around and look at her. She stood in the doorway, half in, half out of the room. "I want to help. And Chess and Emma don't trust me."

If they don't trust you, why would I? Finn wanted to say.

Most of the time, Finn said what he wanted to say as soon as he thought it.

But he'd never before thought it was possible that he'd never see his mother again. So right now he didn't trust his own brain. Or his own mouth.

I will see Mom again, he told himself. *I will. I will. I will. Soon.*

He was like that train in the book for little kids, chugging out, "I think I can. I think I can. I think I can. I can!"

He liked feeling like there wasn't room in his brain for any other thoughts besides that.

He ignored Natalie and began pushing clothes from one side of the closet to the other, even though he didn't really believe he would find a laptop behind or underneath them. He just liked the way moving the clothes set off more puffs of Mom smell.

He heard the doorbell downstairs and then Ms. Morales's powerful voice calling, "Natalie? Finn, Emma, and, uh, Chess? What's going on? This was supposed to be a quick stop, remember?"

Good thing Chess is downstairs, Finn thought. *He'll explain everything, and then Ms. Morales will understand why we have to stay here longer.*

Ms. Morales was a grown-up. A mom. Once she heard about the messages on Mom's phone, she'd probably say, "Why didn't you show me that right away? Of course that's a mistake. In fact, your mom just called, and she's on her way home right now. You won't have to spend the night at my house, after all!"

But Finn *didn't* hear the rumble of Chess's voice downstairs answering Ms. Morales. Instead, he heard Natalie's footsteps, headed out toward the landing.

"Mom, go back to the car before you start sneezing all over the place!" Natalie yelled. She was standing at the top of the stairs. "The kids needed a few things their mom didn't pack, so we're getting everything together. Just five more minutes, okay?"

"Are you *sure* everything's all right?" Ms. Morales asked.

"Of course," Natalie said. "Now, go away before your whole face swells up!"

"*Just* five more minutes," Ms. Morales said. Then she sneezed. "I'll be waiting in the car. Hurry!"

Natalie came back into Mom's room.

"You didn't tell her about the text messages?" Finn asked. "Wouldn't she—?"

"Help" was the word Finn wanted. No, that wasn't strong enough. He wanted Ms. Morales to solve everything. He wanted her to undo the text messages, make it so they'd never existed in Mom's phone, and so Finn, Emma, and Chess—and Natalie—had never seen them. He wanted Ms. Morales to fly to Chicago and back in the next five minutes and bring Mom home, just like that.

Sometimes it almost seemed like Mom had superpowers, taking care of everything Finn and Emma and Chess needed. Weren't all moms like that?

Natalie snorted.

"You do *not* want my mom to know about that text message," she said. "She'd make everything worse. Believe me. *She's* the one you can't trust."

Mom's far, far away, Finn thought. *I can't trust Natalie. She says I can't trust her mom, either. All I have is Emma and Chess.*

It was the most grown-up thing Finn had ever done, that he kept standing there peering into Mom's closet.

When all he really wanted to do was run downstairs, grab hold of Emma and Chess, and never let go.

SEVENTEEN

EMMA

Math, Emma thought as she descended the basement stairs. *Square roots. Prime numbers. Pi.*

Those were the most comforting things Emma could think of. They were constants. Two was always the square root of four. One, three, five, seven, and eleven were always prime. Pi was always 3.14, with an endless string of other numbers behind it.

Mom had always been a constant in Emma's life, too.

Yeah, well, she's still somewhere, Emma told herself. *She hasn't ceased to exist. And even if she thinks there's some reason she can't come home, we can find her and prove to her that she can.*

Emma picked up the plastic bag of dirty kitty litter and put it in the wastebasket by the bottom of the stairs, even though the kids were really supposed to put all litter bags directly into the trash can outside.

Mom will be so grateful when we rescue her, she's not going to get mad about a little kitty litter, Emma thought.

She regarded the main part of the basement: the one saggy couch that had been retired from the living room upstairs after Finn spilled grape Kool-Aid on it. The foosball table that could convert into a mini Ping-Pong table or a mini pool table. The bucket of Nerf balls. The Koosh dartboard. The tub of Legos. She remembered Finn's friend Tyrell asking once, "Isn't this your family room? Where's the TV?"

And Finn had said indignantly, "It's our *rec* room. Don't you think we'd *wreck* a TV if it was down here?"

That was when Mom explained that, really, "rec room" stood for "recreation room," and that a TV would distract her when she was working in the Boring Room, Mom's little closed-off office at the far side of the basement.

Why was a TV distracting when Finn and Tyrell screaming at the top of their lungs wasn't?

Emma stepped past the couch and the foosball table and went straight to the door to the Boring Room.

It was locked.

Sure, Mom, Emma thought. *Because of course that's going to keep Chess, Finn, and me out.*

She walked over to the couch and bent down to lift the little flap of fabric that covered the couch's legs. She felt around the couch's middle leg. From the front, that leg looked like a solid block of wood. But it had a notch carved into the back of it. Emma pulled a little metal key out of the notch.

Mom knows Chess, Finn, and I all know about this hiding place, doesn't she? Emma thought, sitting back up. They'd played hide-and-seek games with Mom where the hidden thing was a coin or a Polly Pocket—hadn't Mom herself sometimes hidden the coin or the doll in the couch leg for the kids to find? It was hard to remember, because those games seemed so long ago—maybe even before Emma started school.

But if Mom wasn't hiding this key from Chess, Finn, and me, then who was she hiding it from? Emma wondered.

Just that thought made Emma want to start reciting reliable things to herself again: *Fibonacci numbers. Multiplication tables. The Pythagorean theorem.*

"Hey, Emma! Come on up!" Chess shouted from the top of the stairs. "I found Mom's computer! And Finn and Natalie found the one she lets us use. So she must have taken the one from down there with her!"

Oh, good, Emma thought. *I don't even have to look in the Boring Room.*

This wasn't scientific or logical, but Emma was a little afraid of the Boring Room. Outside of the Boring Room, Mom was so *Mom*: always there instantly when one of the kids scraped a knee or wanted to show off a bike trick or was just exploding with a brilliant new idea. But if Mom was in the Boring Room, she kept the door shut. If one of the kids knocked, there was sometimes a long pause before Mom answered, "Yes? Do you need something?" And even if Mom answered immediately, Emma had discovered that it was possible to count to a hundred sometimes—sometimes even more—before Mom inched the door open, stepped out, carefully shut it behind her, and finally peered down at Emma with her usual amount of concern.

It was like the Boring Room made Mom *not-Mom*.

Those text messages on Mom's phone were really *not-Mom-ish,* Emma thought.

Just the text messages about Mom not calling them were not-Mom-ish. The one about Mom not coming back made it seem like she'd been swallowed up by someplace like the Boring Room, and she'd completely become the person she was in the Boring Room, not the person she was everywhere else in the world. And . . .

You're being silly, Emma told herself. *Not logical. Not like* your*self, either.*

She sat still for a moment, holding the key, and then she forced herself to walk over to the Boring Room door. It was like she had something to prove. If she could face the Boring Room, then she (and Chess and Finn) could figure out where Mom was and go rescue her.

Emma put the key into the lock and turned it. She heard the click that meant the lock had given way. Quickly, before she lost her nerve, she shoved the door open and reached for the light switch on the wall. The dim glow overhead revealed a room with blank walls, mostly empty bookshelves, and a desk and a chair that were so unremarkable that Emma could almost believe they came from a store called Amazingly Boring Office Furniture for the Home. That was a joke Mom had made once, and remembering that made Emma's eyes go a little misty.

Never mind that, Emma told herself. *Does anything in here look any different than usual?*

It was hard to tell, because when was the last time Emma actually looked into this room? She had vague memories of being a little kid playing with Finn out in the rec room while Mom sat at the desk in the Boring Room with the door open—maybe that was so long ago that Mom had needed to keep an eye on them all the time, even while she worked.

Emma could call up a fuzzy image in her mind from those days: Mom's eyes barely visible over the top of her laptop. . . .

Oh, duh, Emma thought. *Of course. The laptop's missing. It always sat right in the middle of the desk, and now it's not there.*

Maybe Emma's mind wasn't working very well right now. Maybe she was expecting too much, to think that her brain could work at all with the words of Mom's text message for next week still burned into her eyeballs: *I have to stay away for good, to protect . . .*

Emma reached for the light switch to turn it off again. But just shifting her position that much put her at a different angle; now she could see the edge of a piece of paper sticking out of the top of Mom's drawer.

A clue? Emma thought. And she wanted so strongly to believe that, that she left the light on and circled around to the other side of the desk. She pulled out the drawer, and the paper got stuck, smashed into accordion-style pleats. Emma gently eased the paper out, flipped it over, and smoothed it out.

The paper was a fuzzy copy of the back of Mom's phone, a reproduction of the crooked heart drawn on it. But it was *only* the heart; the words "We love you, Mommy" didn't show up.

Emma wanted to cry all over again. Nothing made sense.

Why would Mom have made a copy of that drawing when she always had her phone—with the original drawing on the case—right with her?

Except Mom didn't have the phone with her now.

She doesn't have this copy of that drawing, either.

Emma started to shove the picture back into the drawer. But then Emma saw what had been hidden in the drawer beneath the paper: Mom's work computer. The one she always used in the Boring Room.

So Mom went on a business trip and she didn't take her business computer with her? Or—any computer? Emma thought. *She left every single one of her computers at home?*

It wasn't exactly foolproof logic, but Emma was pretty sure she could make a deduction: Mom wasn't on a business trip at all.

EIGHTEEN

CHESS

The sun was still shining brightly when Chess stepped outside. That surprised him. It felt like the whole world should have gone dark while they were inside the house, like the sun should never come out again.

This was a feeling Chess remembered from when Dad died.

Mom isn't dead, Chess told himself. *I'm sure she's fine. And we have all her computers now. So we're going to find her. And everything will be okay.*

Still, Chess felt like his feet got ahead of him as he climbed down the porch stairs. His suitcase pulled him off balance, and his legs just didn't feel sturdy. It didn't help that Finn kept trying to walk so close beside him that the two of them might as well have been glued together.

It also didn't help that he could see how pale and drawn Emma's and Finn's faces were, or how they were weaving and stumbling just as badly as Chess.

"Don't say anything about any of this to my mom," Natalie hissed to Chess, Emma, and Finn as she turned to lock the front door. Evidently she'd taken the key from Chess while he wasn't paying attention. Evidently now she was slipping the key back into his hand.

Chess felt like there could be all sorts of things happening that he might have missed.

"Why shouldn't we tell your mom?" Emma asked Natalie.

Chess was aware enough to see Natalie bite her lip.

"Mom will go crazy," Natalie said. "She'll call social services and the police and the FBI and the TV news."

"Don't we want the police and the FBI helping us?" Finn asked, so innocently he practically chirped the words. "Don't we want grown-ups who know what they're doing finding Mom?"

Natalie shot a glance at Chess over Finn's head.

"Your mom said she wrote a letter that's *just for you*," Natalie said. "Don't you want to see that for yourself before anybody else sticks their nose in your business?"

Chess didn't know why Natalie kept looking at him like that. He kind of wanted to say, *Can't you tell I'm not really that much older than Emma and Finn? Can't you tell that when I saw that text message from Mom, I went back to being a four-year-old again?*

Chess, Emma, and Finn tripped down the driveway toward Ms. Morales's SUV. Somehow Natalie got ahead of them. She guided them into putting their suitcases into the back of the car. Then she yanked open both doors on the passenger side, one for her and one for the other three kids.

"That was stupid, Mom," Natalie complained as she slipped into the front seat. "Why didn't *you* pick up the suitcases before you picked up the kids? The bags were right beside the front door—you wouldn't have sneezed too much. And now these kids are homesick and missing their mommy, and it's all your fault!"

Chess helped Finn up into the SUV, into the middle row of seats again. Chess and Emma followed, as Ms. Morales answered Natalie, "For your information, young lady, I was *working* right up until I had to pick *you* up from school. Would you have preferred taking the bus?"

"No! Why would you even say that?" Natalie snarled back. "You don't understand *anything*! I've got all this home-work to do, and I just had to spend a whole hour helping that little boy find his lovey so he could sleep tonight. . . ."

Chess noticed that Finn was clutching a teddy bear that was missing an ear and an eye because he and his friend Tyrell liked to use it as a football. It wasn't Finn's "lovey."

"Natalie told me to bring this," Finn whispered in Chess's ear. "As a prop."

"If you spent less time texting, you'd have plenty of time to do your homework," Ms. Morales told Natalie, even as she started the car and pulled away from the curb. "Anyway, you weren't there an *hour*. It was barely twenty minutes."

"Right, and you still thought you had to come in and hurry us up?" Natalie moaned. "Mom, you are *so* embarrassing!"

And then, while Ms. Morales was peering right and left, preparing to turn onto the next street, Natalie spun around and winked at Chess, Emma, and Finn.

Oh, Chess thought. *Is she fighting with her mom on purpose? To distract attention from Finn's teary face and from the fact that all three of us are just numb and clumsy and stupid right now?*

Ms. Morales made the turn, and then Chess could see her eyes peering back at them in the rearview mirror.

"Kids, I'm sorry that my daughter is being so rude," she said. "I promise, we'll make this a fun night for you. We'll order pizza, and you can have any kind you want. And, well,

Natalie says *she's* outgrown it, but we still have a trampoline in our backyard, and . . ."

Chess's ears buzzed; he felt too dizzy to listen well. He kind of grunted when Ms. Morales paused and it seemed like she needed an answer, but he had no idea what he was agreeing to. Or disagreeing with. A grunt could mean anything.

And Mom's text messages? Could those mean something different than what we think, too?

He needed to see her phone again, to force himself to read the horrible words again. Maybe he'd just imagined them. Maybe he'd find an *April Fools!* or a *Psych! Got you!* or a *Hahaha! Just kidding!* right below.

But they'd stuffed Mom's phone and charger and all the computers into the suitcases, and Chess would have had to take his seat belt off and climb over the back row to reach them.

He knew that wouldn't go over very well with Ms. Morales. He didn't know if Natalie was right that they shouldn't tell Ms. Morales what they'd found. But he felt overwhelmed at the thought of saying anything. Even *uh-huh* or *hunh-uh* seemed beyond him now.

How well do Ms. Morales and Mom even know each other, if none of us remember Mom talking about her? Chess wondered. *What if Ms. Morales just decides that Mom is a bad person?*

He didn't quite understand what Natalie meant when she talked about Ms. Morales calling social services, but he could see why it would be a problem to call the police. What if *they* thought Mom was a bad person for leaving her kids behind and saying she was never coming back? What if they tracked her down just to arrest her?

Some time must have passed—fifteen minutes? Twenty?—and then Ms. Morales aimed the SUV into a long driveway that wound up a hill. The house at the top of that hill was easily three or four times the size of the Greystones' house, and Chess got a lump in his throat thinking about how Mom always called their house "a cozy Cape Cod." She had a way of saying those words that made Chess feel a little sorry for anyone who *didn't* live there.

"Is that your house, Natalie?" Finn asked, gaping at the mansion ahead of them. "It's enormous!"

Maybe he'd been chattering away all along—Finn talked whether he was happy, sad, worried, or (sometimes) even sound asleep.

"Yeah, Mom got the house in the divorce," Natalie said bitterly.

"Natalie!" Ms. Morales scolded. "Stop being so difficult! You don't have to tell the whole world everything!"

Beside Chess, Emma let out a sound that could have been a snort or a nervous giggle.

Oh. It was kind of funny—or ironic, anyway—that Natalie was getting in trouble for telling too much, when really she and the Greystones was keeping a gigantic secret.

They took the suitcases inside, and Ms. Morales pointed out where everyone would sleep. Chess couldn't keep the rooms straight—maybe Ms. Morales and Natalie had so many bedrooms that they could each use a different room every night of the week if they wanted.

"I'll give the kids a tour of the rest of the house while you're ordering the pizza," Natalie told her mother. Then, as she shepherded them down a hallway, she said in a softer voice, "Mom likes to eat dinner early and go to bed early. Because she gets up at five a.m. to exercise. So we'll meet at ten p.m. in her office, where she won't be able to hear us." She made her voice loud again, loud enough to carry down the hall to her mother. "And this is Mom's office!"

Chess thought time would drag until they could finally meet and pull out the computers. But evidently weird things happened when you were feeling completely numb and stupid. Ms. Morales made them play on the trampoline, and then they ate and did homework, and then she made them play Wii for a while, and then she made them play a long, boring game of Monopoly right before bedtime. And during all those times, Chess would just be sitting there thinking about Mom, and suddenly realize half an hour had gone by.

Finally they'd all brushed their teeth and Ms. Morales had tucked the younger two into bed and said to Chess, "Are you like Natalie, saying you're too old for a bedtime story?" and he shot out a panicked "Yes!"—and she left him alone.

And then it was time to creep back down the stairs, clutching the laptop that had been shoved into his suitcase. He was joined in the dark hallway by Emma and Finn, each bearing laptops of their own. Emma also held Mom's phone.

"Don't giggle," Chess whispered, because normally both of them would have. But now they looked up at him, their faces shrouded in shadows, and he could tell that tonight neither of them found anything amusing. Chess switched his whispered instructions to, "Don't worry. We're going to find out everything."

They tiptoed down to Ms. Morales's office. Natalie stood in the shadowy doorway and waved them in.

"Everybody's here?" she asked. "And you've got everything? Good. Now I can shut the door and turn on the light."

The four of them stood blinking in the sudden brightness. Chess's eyes took forever to adjust.

"Are you *sure* your mom won't hear us in here?" Emma asked, pushing a stray lock of hair behind her ear. She'd lost her ponytail rubber band on the trampoline, and her hair had puffed out again like so much dandelion fuzz. Chess was torn between wanting to smooth her hair down himself and wanting to snarl at Natalie, *Don't you dare say anything about Emma's hair being a mess! She's in fourth grade! Fourth graders don't have to care about stuff like that!*

But Natalie was moving briskly toward her mother's desk, a piece of furniture so vast and shiny that it seemed like it might have its own gravitational pull.

"I'm sure," she told Emma. "This room is soundproofed."

"Soundproofed? Why?" Finn asked, his eyes wide. "What does your mom *do*? I mean, besides making big pictures of her own face."

He pointed behind the desk, and Chess noticed a whole pile of signs leaned against the wall. They all held the words "For sale!" or "Sold!" along with Ms. Morales's picture.

"She's a Realtor," Natalie said, as if that was completely unimportant. "She sells houses. At least, that's the job we can talk about."

"Does she have another job you can't talk about?" Emma asked. "Can you tell *us*?"

Natalie tilted her head to the side, which made her hair stream down like silk.

"We told you everything *our* mom does," Finn said.

"Okay," Natalie agreed. "On the side, Mom's a private investigator. That's what she calls it. *I* call it a professional snoop. My grandmother called it being a busybody. Mom spies on men who are—" She glanced at Finn. "Let's just say they're not very good husbands. Mom gives the wives proof, so they have the upper hand in the divorce."

Chess thought about what Natalie had assumed about his mom—that she had a bad boyfriend, and that that was why she'd had to go away.

Mom didn't have a boyfriend. Chess would have known.

But she was talking on the phone to some man last night, he remembered. *Joe?*

Mom had not sounded like she was talking to a boyfriend. More like . . . a coworker? An employee? A boss?

Mom didn't have any coworkers, or employees or bosses, either. And she never used such a surly tone with clients. She was always nice to them.

She was always nice to everyone.

Chess saw that Emma was peering at the screen of Mom's phone.

"Can I—?" he whispered.

She handed it over, and Chess opened the call history. If he could find out who Mom had talked to last night, that would be a huge clue.

But the call history was empty.

So were Mom's contacts.

So were all her emails and text messages—except for the automatic ones she'd set up for Ms. Morales.

Natalie had stopped talking and was watching Chess

stare at his mom's phone. Chess gave the phone back to Emma.

"Let's talk about *our* mom," he said, and he didn't care that now *he* sounded rude. He slid the HP laptop he'd been carrying onto the desk. "This is the computer that Mom uses the most often. She doesn't usually let us use it to do homework or play games, so it's probably the one she'd write a letter on, if she didn't want us to see that letter until . . ." He had to gulp. "Until next week."

"Okay, you should start with that one," Natalie agreed.

"This is the computer Mom lets us use for homework and stuff," Emma said, putting the battered Dell laptop beside his and opening the screen.

"And this one's from the Boring Room," Finn said, adding the third laptop.

They powered up all three of the computers. Chess felt a gurgle of tension in his stomach like before a huge test, only much, much worse.

"How about if I look through your mom's phone while you three—" Natalie began.

"You stay away from Mom's phone!" Emma said, hugging it to her chest.

Didn't she know there was nothing on the phone worth seeing?

Chess didn't say anything.

"Okay, okay," Natalie murmured. Still, she hovered behind the three Greystones. It made Chess even more nervous.

Finn elbowed Chess.

"Do you know Mom's password for this laptop?" he asked. "Or Emma, do you?"

"No," Chess and Emma said together.

"Then I can't see anything," Finn said dejectedly. His shoulders slumped, and he looked like he might start crying again.

"Next time we go back to your house, we can look for your mom's password," Natalie said in the fake cheerful voice people used with toddlers. "Maybe she has it written down somewhere."

He's eight, *not three!* Chess wanted to yell at her. *Stop being so . . . so . . .*

"Patronizing" was the word he was looking for. But maybe he also meant *stop being so helpful.* Natalie was acting like this was her problem, too. And it wasn't. Now that she'd shown them the soundproof room, why didn't she just go back upstairs with her mom?

"Here, Finn," Chess said, stepping back. "Why don't you stand between Emma and me, and you can go back and forth between looking at both of these computers with us. You might see something we miss."

He shut down the laptop from the Boring Room and

maneuvered Finn between him and Emma. Oddly, Emma didn't move to the side to make room. She stood frozen, staring at her laptop screen.

Chess followed her gaze. She'd reached the desktop, with the background picture of all three kids at Halloween last year: Finn as a clown, Emma as a ninja, and Chess as a skeleton. Finn and Emma were totally cracking up, but Chess's face was hidden behind his mask. Though, actually, the image of all three kids was largely hidden, because they had so many files and games and shortcut links strewn about the desktop. It would be hard to find anything in that mess.

Then Chess saw that Emma had the cursor hovering over a file marked "FOR THE KIDS."

"Was this here before?" Emma asked.

"I never saw it," Finn said, but his voice was so hushed and scared he sounded like someone else.

Chess just shook his head.

Emma clicked the mouse. Chess started to object—did he want to warn his brother and sister that maybe he should read the file first; maybe he should protect them from whatever it was going to say?

A box appeared. Emma hadn't opened the *file*. She was only checking its properties.

"Mom saved this at four a.m.," Emma whispered. "Just this morning."

"So open it!" Natalie cried behind them.

Emma looked back over her shoulder.

"I—I'm afraid," she admitted.

Emma, afraid? Emma was *fearless*. Emma could face down math problems that made Chess's head hurt. And one time when she was only a third grader, Chess had seen her wade into a pile of sixth graders who were fighting, and she'd screamed, "Don't hit the little guy!" And then the kid who was being bullied just walked away.

But this was scarier than that. Chess himself felt like he'd forgotten how to breathe.

"We open it together," he suggested. "All three of us."

He put his hand over Emma's, and Finn put his hand on top.

Chess thought maybe it was actually Finn who had the courage to push down.

The file opened, and Chess blinked the words on the screen into focus:

Dearest Chess, Emma, and Finn,

I love you so much, and that is why I had to do this. I'm sure you have questions, and this letter will tell you everything you need to know. Only the three of you will be able to read it.

Eagerly Chess moved on to the next paragraph. But it was all gibberish.

He raked his finger down the touchpad, scrolling through the rest of the letter—page after page of more gibberish.

After the first three sentences, nothing in the rest of the letter made any sense.

NINETEEN

FINN

Finn stopped trying to read at the start of the second paragraph.

Those must be all third-grade words, he thought. *At least third grade. Good thing Emma and Chess are older than me and will know what they mean.*

But Emma and Chess were squinting harder and harder and harder.

"Is it . . . code?" Emma finally asked. "Or a cipher? I forget which is which—one is where each individual letter or number or symbol stands for a different letter, and one is where the whole word is replaced by a different word, which you can only figure out if you have the key to the code. Or the cipher. Whichever."

Finn could tell that Emma was doing what he did sometimes, where she was so upset she was just talking and talking and talking to keep herself from thinking about how upset she was.

If Emma was rambling on like that, she didn't understand either.

"Chess?" Finn whispered, tugging on his brother's arm.

"Mom wanted us to know about this," Chess said. He swayed a little. "But . . . I guess . . . she must not have wanted us to know *yet*. Not right away."

"And she thinks a little thing like a code is going to hold us back?" Emma asked indignantly.

That sounded more like the real Emma.

"Yeah!" Finn said. He reached up and patted Emma's head, and that gave him confidence again. There was a brilliant brain underneath all Emma's bushy hair. "Even I know *something* about codes. We talked about this at school. You always look for the *e*'s."

"You mean, you look for the most common symbol or letter in the code, and you can assume that that symbol stands for *e*, because *e* is the most common letter in English,"

Emma corrected. "And then you can work through the other common letters—*s? t? r?* We could always look it up, the use of all letters in order."

Finn was pretty sure that Emma was a genius. Maybe Chess was, too.

For all Finn knew, Natalie also might have an IQ that was as huge as her house.

He felt better already.

"So what do you think that first word is?" he asked, pointing at the screen.

"Um, Finn, this might take a while," Chess said faintly.

He stared at the screen. Emma stared at the screen. Finn looked back to see what Natalie was doing.

She was staring at her phone.

"I bet there are codebreaker apps," Natalie said, her fingers flying across the surface of her phone. "We could plug in that whole letter to some special site, and then—"

"Do we really want Mom's letter floating around out there on the internet?" Chess asked. Then he looked back at Natalie, too, and it was like the big kids were talking without even using words.

Usually Finn hated feeling left out and too young, but now he wanted to cheer, *Hurray! The three of you are going to take care of everything! You're even better than grown-ups!*

Natalie stopped typing on her phone.

"Oh, maybe not," she said. "I guess we would need to know what that letter says before we know if it's safe to use the internet to solve it."

"That doesn't make any sense!" Finn said, and he hoped the other three would laugh.

They didn't.

Emma and Chess went back to staring at the computer screen. Natalie shoved in beside them, which knocked Finn away, putting him at the wrong angle even to see the screen.

"I want to help, too," Finn said, pushing against Emma, which knocked her against Natalie.

"Hey!" Natalie said. "I'm trying to focus here!"

Chess looked down at Finn with a very Chess-like expression. Only Mom and Chess had ever looked at Finn that way: as though they really saw him, and understood that even though Finn could be loud and noisy and silly, he wasn't *just* loud and noisy and silly. In fact, Finn was sure that he had a quiet, still, serious part inside himself somewhere. Maybe *only* Mom and Chess could see it.

And now, with Mom gone . . .

"Finn, maybe we should take turns working on this code," Chess said. "Emma and I will start, and you and Natalie can look at Mom's work computer. See if there's anything strange on there."

"But that's just 'voices and stuff like that," Finn complained.

"Voices?" Natalie asked.

"*Invoices*," Chess corrected. "The bills she sends to her clients. Mom said she was going to Chicago. Maybe you can find out which clients she has in Chicago."

"Oh, that's a good idea." Natalie was using her fake voice again, the one that made Finn feel like she thought he was stupid.

"That's not as important as the letter!" Finn protested. "You're just trying to . . ."

Shove me away. Get rid of me.

That was what Finn wanted to say. But then Emma reached down and squeezed his hand twice, before giving him a nudge in the side as she looked up at Natalie with narrowed eyes.

And Finn understood.

Emma and Chess aren't trying to get rid of me, Finn thought. *They're trying to get rid of* Natalie.

Finn felt like a genius himself.

"Oh, all right," he said resignedly, as if he were still a little angry.

Natalie squeezed her lips together, like she was angry, too. But she moved over beside Finn and clicked the touchpad a few times.

"Your mom has ten customers in Illinois," she said as a

grid appeared on the screen. "What do you bet all those cities on that list are suburbs of Chicago? I think I've heard of
Evanston before. But . . . Buffalo Grove? Northbrook? Elm-
hurst? Wheaton?"

"How am I supposed to know?" Finn asked. "I've never
been to Chicago!"

Natalie let the cursor hover over the list of cities. A
moment passed. Natalie wasn't even looking at the list now:
She had her neck craned to look back at the code on the computer screen in front of Emma and Chess.

"Maybe we should look at the websites Mom made for
all those clients," Finn said. "You'll have to help me. Mom
never lets me use this computer by myself because she's scared
I'll mess something up."

Was that too obvious?

Natalie sighed and clicked on a link at the far right side
of the grid. A website came up advertising a landscaping
company. Finn scrolled through pictures of perfect yards,
the kind grown-ups had when they didn't have kids. None
of them looked like very good places to play.

Natalie gazed back at Emma and Chess's computer
again.

"That's the logo my mom uses on all her websites," Finn
said, pointing to a tiny purple butterfly at the bottom of the

page. "She likes butterflies because . . . because . . . what's the reason, Emma?"

"Rebirth," Emma said absently. She didn't take her eyes off her own computer screen. "Metamorphosis. Second chances."

"Yeah," Finn said. "She says it's not just because they're pretty."

"Huh," Natalie said.

What did Finn have to do to get Natalie's attention?

He clicked out of that website and tried one for a bakery.

"Oh, look," he said. "Don't these pictures make you want a doughnut? What kind do you think they are, Natalie? Maple bacon? That's *my* favorite."

If someone wanted to distract Finn, food was always a good topic. Maybe Natalie was the same way.

But Natalie barely flicked her eyes toward the doughnut pictures before turning back toward Emma and Chess's computer.

"And, see, here's my mom's butterfly logo again," Finn said, reaching the bottom of the bakery homepage. "She made this one a little more blue, and . . ."

And it wasn't at all the same butterfly logo as on the landscaper's page. But Mom had done both of these websites, hadn't she? Had she changed her logo and not even told the kids?

It was hardly the same as going off on a business trip and then setting up an automatic text to arrive a week later saying she was never coming back. That was just . . . unbelievable, in connection with Mom. But usually she was so predictable that even changing her logo seemed strange.

Finn clicked back to the landscaper's site. He zoomed in on both butterfly images.

It wasn't just the color that was different—so were the number and pattern of the dots. And the shape of the wings.

Finn made copies of both of the butterfly logos and pasted them into a new document.

He began opening other websites, one after the other, whether they were for businesses in Illinois or not. He copied and pasted every new butterfly logo he found into his own document.

Finally, when the variations just started repeating again and again and again, he stopped. He went back to the screen holding every single version he'd found: seven different kinds of butterflies, each one a different color. He zoomed in as close as he could on each butterfly without making every-thing go blurry.

The dots on the butterflies' wings weren't just in differ-ent places on each logo. They also contained patterns of their own, intricately drawn lines and angles.

Why go to the bother of drawing lines and angles inside

a dot, if those patterns weren't going to show up unless you enlarged the dot again and again and again?

Suddenly Finn knew why. He tugged on Emma's arm.

"Everyone, *look!*" he shouted. "I think this is a code, too!"

TWENTY

EMMA

Emma was stuck.

She was used to knowing answers instantly. She got in trouble for that sometimes in math class when the teacher would say, "Emma, honey, you have to show your work." And Emma would say, "The work was, I looked at the problem, and I knew the answer. How am I supposed to show that?"

Sometimes teachers told her she shouldn't say that in front of the other kids.

But the endless stream of letters and symbols and numbers in Mom's letter made no sense to Emma at all.

Not being able to understand made her feel itchy and weird and not like herself.

Or maybe she was already feeling itchy and weird and not like herself, because of Mom being away and saying she wasn't coming back.

Maybe Emma had felt itchy and weird and not like herself ever since . . . ever since she'd come home from school the day before and found out that kids with her and her brothers' names and ages had been kidnapped.

What if Mom *was actually kidnapped?* Emma wondered. *What if this is actually a ransom note, and we're never going to be able to rescue Mom because we're never going to be able to figure it out?*

It was a relief when Emma realized Finn was tugging and tugging and tugging on her arm, and shouting, "Would you *listen*? You have to look at this! I think it's a code, too! And there's not as much to it, so maybe it's easier to figure out!"

Of course Finn didn't know anything about codes. Emma had gone through a phase last fall where she'd checked out a lot of books from the library about codes and codebreaking, and she hadn't been able to get Finn or Chess to show any interest at all in writing secret messages back and forth in lemon juice, or substituting numbers for letters, or even using a mask decoder, which was the simplest thing of all. No one she knew at school was interested, either. So it had fallen to Mom to be the one Emma wrote notes to, saying things like, "H KNUD XNT." And when Mom wrote back, "J MPWF ZPV, UPP," Emma had been delighted, knowing they were both saying "I love you," using the same kind of code, just going in a different direction through the alphabet.

Oh oh oh.

Something amazing occurred to Emma. It was nowhere near as wonderful as figuring out Mom's letter would be, but now she felt all tingly, as well as itchy and weird.

Did I start checking out those code books on my own? Or was Mom the first one who picked up a code book and handed it to me and said, "I think you would like this"?

It was hard to remember exactly. Mom took Emma and Chess and Finn to the library a lot, and Emma always checked out a huge stack of books. Sometimes she chose her own books; sometimes Mom or Emma's favorite librarian, Mrs. Quinn, slipped them into her hands saying, "What about this one?" Sometimes it was even Chess or Finn asking that question.

But it *seemed* like maybe Mom had given Emma the first code book; it seemed like Mom might have said something like, "Sometimes kids who like math also like codes."

Had Mom been *preparing* Emma? Even way back last fall, had Mom been worried that some danger was coming, and she wanted Emma to be ready for it by learning about codes?

Emma didn't just feel tingly now. She felt like her heart was about to pound its way out of her chest.

She looked at the array of butterflies Finn had lined up on his computer screen. He enlarged one set of wings after another, showing the pattern hidden inside each dot.

"How can butterfly drawings be a code?" Natalie asked.

Something jiggled in Emma's brain. Something she'd read in one of the books about code.

"The guy who started Boy Scouts!" she shouted. "*He* did butterfly codes! When he was a spy!"

Natalie looked at her like she was crazy.

"Why would he do that?" Finn asked.

"Tell us about it," Chess said quietly.

"I don't actually remember his name," Emma admitted.

Chess reached for Mom's phone and typed in "Boy Scout founder spy butterflies."

"Lord Baden-Powell?" Chess said.

"I guess," Emma said with a shrug. "Anyhow, there was a war going on, or there was about to be a war starting, in, oh, *somewhere*—"

"Dalmatia?" Chess asked.

"Wherever that is," Emma said. "Anyhow, this lord guy pretended he was just a butterfly collector roaming around drawing pictures of the butterflies he found. But he was *actually* hiding spy drawings inside the butterfly pictures.

Drawings of all the military fortifications along the coast. So he could help his country's military know what to expect."

"You think Mom's helping the military?" Finn asked, going back to alternately zooming in and out on Mom's butterfly logos, growing and shrinking the dots and wings. "You think these are drawings of *forts*?"

"Only if the forts are built out of sticks." Natalie snickered. "How do you know you even have them in the right order? It's like there's every color of the rainbow there."

Emma felt tingly all over again.

"Natalie! You're brilliant!" Emma said, actually throwing her arms around the older girl's waist as though she were a friend, not a total stranger. "I bet it *is* a rainbow! Let's see, ROY G. BIV, red, orange, yellow . . ."

Emma took control of the touchpad on the computer Finn had been using. She moved the butterflies around, starting with the red one and finishing with the purple one—the one that might just as easily be called violet.

Chess patted Emma on the back, which felt like he was complimenting her. Finn squealed, "Those are the right colors!"

"So does your mom like rainbows, too?" Natalie asked, making a mocking face.

"It's like an inside joke for her and me," Emma said.

She was glad that neither Chess nor Finn said, "What are

you talking about?" Maybe they didn't even remember how disgusted Emma had been by some of the girls in third grade last year, who went around talking about rainbows and unicorns and butterflies and magic. And one night, when Emma was complaining at the dinner table, Mom had said very quietly, "Emma, it's possible to like rainbows and unicorns and butterflies and magic *and* math. Personally, I'd love it if the world were full of all of those things."

After that, "rainbows and butterflies" had become sort of code between Emma and Mom. It meant that Emma shouldn't get mad at other kids who didn't like math, and she shouldn't let anyone act like there was something wrong with her because she did.

Huh, code again, Emma thought.

"I still don't get it," Natalie said. "So you put the butterflies in rainbow-color order. So what?"

"So maybe, if we put all the dots together now . . . ," Emma began.

She enlarged all the dots from the butterfly wings one by one, until each dot joined with the one above, below, or beside it. Just as Emma hoped, the mysterious lines inside each dot joined, too.

"It makes a rectangle!" Finn shouted. "With . . . other shapes inside!"

"Is it . . . a map?" Natalie asked. "But what's it a map of?"

Emma jerked to attention. Her brain was working quickly again.

"Mom's office," she said. "The Boring Room." She pointed at one shape after the other. "See? There's the desk. There's the bookshelves along the walls."

"But what's that star over here?" Chess asked. "Is this a treasure map? Where *X* marks the spot? You were just down there—what's against the back wall of the Boring Room?"

Emma couldn't remember anything there but an empty bookshelf.

"I don't know if it's a *treasure* or not," she said slowly. "But I'm pretty sure that's where we're supposed to look."

TWENTY-ONE

CHESS

Chess reached for the doorknob of the Boring Room.

It was the next afternoon, and the three Greystone kids had convinced Ms. Morales that they *had* to stop by their house again to visit Rocket. Chess had been worthless all day at school—twice, his teachers had called on him and he'd had so little idea what they'd asked him that he wasn't sure if they were talking about language arts or social studies, math or science. Ever since about ten thirty last night, he'd been longing for this moment.

And dreading it, too. He had to force himself to carry through every action: *Now wrap your hand around the doorknob.*

Turn your wrist to the right. Push the door forward. . . .

"Is it terrible that I didn't lock the door of the Boring Room again last night?" Emma burst out behind him. She and Finn were crowded so close beside him that Chess's elbows knocked against them.

"Why didn't you lock it?" Natalie asked. At least she was a few steps back.

"I didn't think!" Emma wailed. It took a lot to make Emma wail. "I had too much else to think about! Why would Mom keep the Boring Room locked, anyhow? Why would it matter? And we *did* lock the front door of the house yesterday when we left, and that was still locked when we got here today, and there aren't any windows broken, so we know nobody would have come in here, so . . ."

Chess flashed his sister a warning look, hoping she'd get the message: *Don't talk about scary stuff like people maybe breaking into our house. Not around Finn. Don't scare Finn.*

Or did Chess really want to say, *Don't scare me?*

"Let's just see what's in this room," Natalie said. And Chess still felt weird about her being a Lip Gloss Girl (or a former Lip Gloss Girl?) and being in his house and even talking to him. But he liked how steady her voice stayed. He liked that she was older than him and knew things he didn't.

It made him feel a little bit less like that other Rochester—Rocky—in Arizona, who was probably still having to stay

135

brave for his little brother and sister. Unless they'd been found already.

Chess hoped they'd been found already.

The door creaked open. Chess reached in and turned on the light.

"Somebody did come in and steal everything!" Natalie cried, peering around.

"No, no—this is what the room looked like yesterday," Emma said. "Just the same."

"Mom keeps the Boring Room empty on purpose," Finn added fiercely. "If she had pictures and, I don't know, toys, it'd be too interesting, and she wouldn't get any work done."

"Oh," Natalie said.

But just that one word made Chess see the Boring Room differently. It *was* kind of weird how the room looked so abandoned, like someone had moved out everything but the heavy furniture. The room held nothing but the desk, an office chair, and three bookcases. Chess couldn't remember the Boring Room ever looking any different. But why did Mom bother having three bookcases in here for just—Chess looked around—two books?

Chess crossed the room and looked at the two books leaning forlornly against each other: an ancient-looking dictionary and a binder labeled "Computer Manual."

"Couldn't she just look that up online?" Natalie said,

right at Chess's elbow. The sound of her voice made him jump.

"Mom doesn't use the internet down here," Finn said, spitting out each word like a bullet. "That would keep the Boring Room from being boring! Why can't you understand that?"

"Didn't you say she designs websites?" Natalie asked. "Wouldn't she always need the internet?"

Chess froze. He'd never thought of that. But it was true: He couldn't think of many parts of Mom's job that didn't require the internet. Once or twice when their internet was down, Mom had had to go work at the library or Starbucks to have Wi-Fi.

Chess couldn't look at Natalie. It felt like she was saying Mom was a liar. No—it was worse than that. It felt like she was saying Mom lied about *everything*. Even little things, like the picture Mom had given Chess of his dad as a kid, telling him, "See this? You look exactly like your father did when he was your age. Same straight nose, same strong jawline, same handsome eyes. . . . This picture proves it."

It felt like, if Natalie saw that picture, she'd say, "It's so fuzzy! That could be anyone! You probably don't look anything like your dad. You just want to believe the stuff your mom says. Why can't you think for yourself, like I do?"

But Natalie would never see that picture, because it was

tucked away in a shoebox on the very top shelf of Chess's closet.

It wasn't actually a little thing.

Was thinking all this making Chess act strange? Desperately, Chess looked toward Emma for help.

Emma didn't even seem to be listening. She was peering intently at a paper they'd printed out the night before in Ms. Morales's office: the map of the Boring Room that came from putting together the butterfly spots.

"The spot with the X has to mean something," she muttered, drifting across the room. "And that spot is right about . . . here."

Her fingers brushed the wall above one of the empty bookcases.

"It's just a blank wall!" Finn said.

"The map is only two-dimensional," Emma said. "So the actual spot could be anywhere from the ceiling to the floor."

"I'll check the floor then," Finn said, rushing over to crouch beside Emma.

"I guess the ceiling's mine," Chess managed to mumble.

He brushed past Natalie, still without looking at her. To his surprise, she reached out and patted his shoulder, which made him feel slightly better and a lot weirder, all at once.

The ceiling of the Boring Room was lower than anywhere else in the house. But even standing on tiptoes, Chess still couldn't reach the top part of the wall. He pulled the desk chair over, positioning it a little off to the right from where Emma had pointed.

"Careful," Natalie said as he stepped up onto the chair.

What was wrong with Chess? He really wanted to snarl back at her, *What's it to you? Why do you care?* And maybe also, *Do you care?*

He kept his mouth shut and concentrated on reaching his hand toward the ceiling. Then he felt silly brushing his hand against the clearly empty wall.

"If there was anything to find here, wouldn't we see it?" he complained.

"Not necessarily," Emma said. "Maybe we need a magnifying glass. Maybe we need a microscope. Maybe we need to douse the wall with lemon juice or some other *reagent*."

Chess was not going to ask his little sister in front of Natalie what a reagent was. He hoped that Finn would do it for him. Or that Emma would just explain without waiting for anyone to ask.

But Natalie spoke next. "Um, guys, I'm not sure how long we have for searching before Mom gets suspicious and starts looking for us. If you think we need a magnifying glass or . . . something else . . . we should get it now."

Apparently Natalie didn't know what a reagent was either. And maybe she was embarrassed about asking, too?

"I don't know what we need," Emma said impatiently. "Not yet. Can't you call your mom and tell her we need more time with Rocket? Like, hours? Tell her he's really sad and missed us, and he needs us a lot!"

"Mom won't leave us alone in here very long," Natalie said. "Not when she thinks . . ." She glanced at Finn and fell silent.

Not when she thinks there's an angry boyfriend that Mom ran away from, Chess thought. *Not when she thinks there's danger.*

"I'm not finding *anything*," Finn complained.

Chess looked down. Finn was running his hands again and again in wide circles over the floor and the lowest portion of the bookshelf. Emma had started searching along the next two shelves of the bookshelf, and Natalie was feeling along the wall immediately above the shelves. When Natalie moved her hand over to the left, Chess stepped one foot onto the top of the bookshelf so he could reach farther.

But just as Chess sometimes forgot how tall he'd gotten lately, he also sometimes forgot how big his feet were. The rubbery front part of his sneaker jabbed too hard against the wall and bent like clown shoes. He had to dig his toes into the crack between the wall and the bookshelf to keep his balance.

And then the bookshelf shifted beneath his foot. It began to swing back away from the wall.

"Watch out!" Chess yelled at Natalie, Emma, and Finn.

Natalie jumped back, and Chess instantly wished she hadn't. Now there didn't seem to be any way to keep the bookcase from falling over on Emma and Finn.

"Catch it!" Chess yelled at Natalie, even as he himself fell backward against the chair, which also rolled backward. He scrambled to the edge of the seat and held out his hands, hoping he could at least stop the bookcase from hitting his brother and sister quite so hard.

The result was that he fell to the floor, so he was also in the path of the falling bookcase.

But the bookcase didn't move the way he expected; it didn't topple straight out from the wall. It moved at a slant, one side swinging out wide while the other tilted toward the corner of the room. Nothing made sense: The side that Chess had stepped on wasn't even the side that had separated the most from the wall.

Or—had it actually separated? Had the wall somehow come with it?

Tangled up on the floor, Chess couldn't make sense of anything.

But as soon as the bookcase stopped moving, Finn popped up and poked his head around the side of the bookcase.

"There aren't any books on this bookcase because it's not *really* a bookcase!" he cried. "It's a secret door!"

TWENTY-TWO

FINN

"Where's it go?" Emma asked breathlessly. "What do you see back there?"

"Um," Finn said. "It's too dark to see."

The darkness was awful. It was the thick kind that made Finn think of spiders and snakes. He wasn't afraid of creepy-crawly things, but the space that had opened up behind the secret door had damp air like he'd encountered in other people's basements—the kind that were full of centipedes and millipedes and pill bugs. The air had a strange smell to it, too—maybe the space behind the bookcase was full of *dead* centipedes and millipedes and pill bugs. Maybe dead rats and mice, too.

Maybe even dead humans? Finn thought. And then he decided he had to stop scaring himself.

"Where's the nearest flashlight?" Natalie asked.

"I'll find one," Finn volunteered, scrambling back from the edge of the bookcase.

It was a relief to be away from the darkness, away from the scary air. Emma and Chess were still jumbled up on the floor, their faces stunned and confused.

"Did you *look* for a light switch?" Emma asked.

"How can I look when there's nothing to see but darkness?" Finn asked, stepping past her.

"You use your hands," Emma said. "Look with your fingers."

"Why don't you?" Finn asked.

Emma being Emma, she actually stood up and walked over to the opening behind the bookcase. She ducked down and stepped into the darkness.

"Emma!" Finn screeched.

Emma turned around, but only to reach up and feel around on the other side of the wall.

What if something bites you? Finn wanted to shout at her. *What if there's a mousetrap back there, or, or . . .*

"Here it is," Emma said.

She must have hit a switch, because suddenly light glowed around her.

"Oh, good," Finn said. "I didn't know where the flashlights were, anyway."

Chess and Natalie were already rushing toward the opening. Both of them had to hunch over and touch their hands to the floor to duck through the secret doorway—it was really more like a half doorway. At least Finn only had to bob his head to the side and then back up again as he scrambled after them.

He stepped into the secret room and joined the others in looking around and around.

Despite the smell, the room he stood in now was clean and neat with no evidence of bugs, dead or otherwise. The walls were lined with shelves, and unlike the shelves in the Boring Room, these shelves were packed. Finn saw cartons of Campbell's soup and ramen noodles, and bundles of water bottles and peanut butter jars. He saw row after row of canned peas and tuna fish and pear slices, applesauce and mandarin oranges and corn.

"It's just a pantry?" Finn said in dismay. "We have something as cool as a secret room hidden under our house, and Mom just uses it to store food?"

"And old shoes?" Emma asked, pointing at a stack of shoeboxes Finn hadn't noticed.

Maybe they were full of spare *new* shoes—Finn saw that the picture on the side of the nearest shoebox was of the very same sneakers he wore on his feet.

"What if there aren't shoes inside?" Chess asked. He lifted the lid of the one of the boxes and said, "Ooooh . . ."

Finn rushed over beside his brother and peered into the box. Everything inside it was green.

"Money?" he said disbelievingly. "It's full of money?"

"Is every box like that?" Emma asked, lifting another off the shelf.

"Oh no," Finn said. "Oh no, oh no, oh no." Each "no" came out sounding more and more like he was crying.

"What's wrong?" Emma asked, grabbing another shoebox. "It looks like we're rich!"

"No," Finn wailed. He could barely get the words out. Or breathe. "It looks like Mom really did rob that bank!"

TWENTY-THREE

EMMA

"What are you talking about?" Emma asked.

"Tyrell and Lucy—yesterday—their bus was late because there was an accident, and they said they saw Mom running out of a bank carrying a big bag like she'd robbed it, and—"

"Mom would never rob a bank," Chess said decisively, like he was slamming a door. "Not *our* mom."

Yesterday we thought Mom would never go away and leave us behind forever, either, Emma thought. And for a moment, Emma was lost. She was so lost, it didn't seem like there was a single math fact that could save her.

Then Natalie said, "I'm pretty sure Chess is right. Your mom didn't rob a bank."

Emma, Finn, and Chess all whirled toward the older girl, who was rifling through one shoebox full of money after another.

"How do you know that?" Emma challenged.

"Because," Natalie said, "it looks like every single one of these bills is either a one or a five. If someone robs a bank, they take twenties, at least. Probably even fifties or hundreds."

"Why?" Finn asked with a forlorn sniff.

Emma knew the answer to this one.

"Bulk," she said. "You steal a million dollars in ones, you have to carry one million strips of paper. If you steal it in hundreds, that's still a thousand—no, ten thousand—bills, but that's a *lot* less than having to lug around a million one-dollar bills."

Oh yeah, she thought. *Knowing math* did *help.*

Having Natalie around had helped, too.

Natalie was still calmly scanning through shoebox after shoebox.

"If these people you're talking about—Tyrell? Lucy?— saw your mom carrying a big bag out of a bank, it was probably because she had a lot of ones and fives," Natalie said. "Not because it was a lot of money altogether."

"But why would Mom want all this money here?" Chess asked. "Or all this food and water?" He tilted his head back, looking up at the shelves that stretched toward the ceiling. "Our whole family wouldn't eat this much food in a year!"

"Was your mom a Doomsday prepper?" Natalie asked. "Did she talk all the time about how society was going to fall apart, and how it would be everybody for themselves, and the only people who would survive were the ones who prepared ahead of time?"

"*No,*" Emma, Chess, and Finn said, almost as one.

"Yeah, I guess that's stupid," Natalie said. "Because if she were a Doomsday prepper, she wouldn't want cash. She'd have gold bars, or silver, or something like that. Things you could barter with. I'm pretty sure the Doomsday preppers think paper money will be worthless when society collapses. Okay, then, this is just a panic room."

"A what?" Finn said. "How do you *know* this stuff?"

"Don't you guys ever go online?" Natalie asked. "Or watch TV?"

"Mom let us watch *The Lego Batman Movie* the other night," Finn began. "And—"

"Just tell us what a panic room is," Emma said through gritted teeth. She hated not knowing things.

"Okay," Natalie said, shrugging in a way that made her

hair ripple down her back. "Panic rooms are what rich people have in their houses, where they can go and be safe and lock themselves in if someone breaks in. Or if someone is trying to kidnap them."

"But we're not rich!" Finn protested. "Unless you count having shoeboxes full of one-dollar bills."

"*I* wouldn't count that," Natalie said.

Emma wanted to add, *And nobody would want to kidnap us!* But her memory nagged at her: She'd thought the same thing before, after the kids in Arizona with the same names and ages as Emma, Finn, and Chess *had* been kidnapped. They probably hadn't expected it, either.

Emma gazed around again at the well-stocked shelves.

But Mom expected something. *She was preparing for* some *threat or danger. . . .*

Emma remembered what Mom had said the day they'd learned about the kidnappings in Arizona: "You don't have to worry about being kidnapped. I promise. I'll do everything I can to prevent that."

Had Mom set up this whole room after that? Had she gotten all the money and all the food and water the next day, before leaving?

And did she dig out a whole other part of our basement and build these walls and shelves in that time, too? Emma wondered. *That's so not logical! It'd be impossible!*

Anyhow, why would she have done all that work and then . . . just left? Without even telling the kids what she'd done?

"So I wonder . . . ," Natalie began.

"What?" Chess asked.

"I don't know if your mom's a Doomsday prepper or if this is just a panic room, for some reason," Natalie said. "I don't even know your mom. But either way, I think there'd be more hiding places, even inside the panic room. Like, maybe for other secret things that are more valuable than food or one-dollar bills? Or . . . weapons? Those Doomsday preppers always have lots of guns."

"Let's look!" Finn said enthusiastically.

Guns? Emma thought. *What would we do if we found guns?*

"Maybe there's something hidden behind these shelves," Natalie said, tugging on the wood frame of one that held boxes of granola bars. "Chess, what did you do to get the bookshelf back in your Mom's office to move?"

"I'm not sure," Chess admitted with a gulp.

His face looked pale, as if he was just as distressed as Emma at the idea of guns.

"I'll go look," Emma said.

She ducked back out of the secret room and peered down at the empty bookcase/door, which still hung completely open. To her surprise, Chess followed her.

"Chess, you didn't know Mom had this secret room down here, did you?" Emma asked.

"What? *No,*" he said. He held up his right hand. "Scout's honor."

Emma believed him.

"So when you opened the door . . ."

"I was just standing on the top of the bookcase," Chess said. He peeked toward the secret room, then back at Emma. "Well, I kind of kicked the wall, too, but that was by mistake."

He brushed his fingers against a scuff mark on the wall.

"And then?" Emma said. "Is that when the shelf moved?"

"Yes," Chess said. "Er, no, first I tried to dig my toes in to keep from falling. And that's when the shelf moved and I did fall."

"Then maybe it's something right where the bookshelf and the wall meet," Emma suggested. She felt along the back of the shelf. "Oh!"

Emma's finger brushed a tiny button that looked like nothing more than a small defect in the wood. The shelf began to move back toward the wall.

"Stop! Stop! Stop!" Emma screamed. She jammed her body between the shelf and the wall.

Chess tugged on her arm, trying to pull her away.

"What are you doing?" he yelled. "You'll get hurt!"

"No! Finn and Natalie will get trapped!" Emma yelled back at him, keeping her shoulder wedged in place.

The bookshelf-door ground to a halt as soon as it touched her arm. It sagged a little, half-open, half-shut.

"Did we break it?" Chess asked.

"I—I don't know," Emma whispered.

Then Natalie and Finn were there, peeking out from the secret room.

"What's all the shouting about?" Natalie asked irritably.

"We found the button that makes the bookshelf move," Emma told her. She looked at the awkward way the shelf tilted. "But now maybe it's stuck."

"Worry about that later," Natalie said, tossing her hair over her shoulder. "Come see what we found."

"It's a lever!" Finn said excitedly. "We can all try it together." He scrunched up his face. "Do you think we're really going to find guns? Remember how Mom always said she wanted to protect us from guns?"

Emma didn't answer. She didn't admit how shaken she still was by the thought of Finn and Natalie being trapped in the secret room. What if the button had stopped working after that, and Emma and Chess couldn't get Natalie and Finn out?

We would have told Natalie's mom, Emma thought. *She would have figured out how to rescue them. And they would have had plenty of food and water. And money.*

But what if there wasn't enough air in the secret room when the door was shut? What if the lights automatically turned off?

Stop it! Emma told herself.

She turned back toward the bookcase door, to reassure herself that it was still open and there was nothing to worry about. Their cat, Rocket—whom they'd totally ignored, ever since arriving at the house—was just poking his head curiously into the doorway.

"Scat!" Emma yelled at him. "You be safe!"

Rocket turned tail and ran away. Chess looked curiously down at Emma.

"Are you okay?" he muttered.

"Sure," Emma said.

And then Natalie was showing them the lever.

"At first Finn and I thought it was just part of the top of this shelf, but it sticks out a little," she said.

"And even though it's the same color as the wood, it's actually metal," Finn added.

"And if you pull it—?" Chess asked.

"Let's see," Natalie said.

She reached up and eased the handle down. At first nothing happened. But then the floor jerked—forward a little, back a little, then steadily forward. It made Emma think of a merry-go-round starting up.

"The whole room moves?" Finn crowed delightedly. "Even the walls?"

Emma felt dizzy. The room *was* rotating, faster and faster and faster. It was like a merry-go-round where you didn't even have a horse to hang on to.

Emma grabbed the side of one of the shelves. The lights blinked off and on and off again.

"Where's it taking us?" she shrieked.

"I thought . . . I thought it would just open a secret compartment!" Natalie cried.

"Hold on!" Chess commanded. He grabbed Finn's arm and Emma's shoulder. Emma reached one hand back and clutched his hand.

And then the spinning stopped.

"What *was* that?" Finn asked.

Nobody answered him. Emma glanced back over her shoulder, back toward the opening where she'd seen Rocket's face just a few moments ago. But now there wasn't an opening anymore, just row after row of solid shelves blocking the way out.

"The door's gone!" she cried. "The door's gone, and now we're *all* trapped!"

TWENTY-FOUR

CHESS

"Emma, Emma, Emma," Chess said, patting his sister's shoulder. "It's not gone. It just moved. Or—we moved, so it looks like it's in a different place."

He pointed off to the left, where a thin sliver of light spread across the floor like an arrow pointing toward a crack in the wall. He was still getting oriented himself. The overhead lights had gone out and come back on and flickered again, and now they were on only dimly, like emergency lights leading out of a burning building or a crashed airplane.

Okay, maybe those aren't the best comparisons to make. . . .

The floor beneath them gave a shudder, as if it were considering starting up again.

"Let's get out of here!" Emma cried, running toward the sliver of light and the opening. "Rocket! Rocket, are *you* okay?"

"Emma . . . ," Chess began.

But Finn and Natalie ran after her, as if they were just as spooked.

Chess dashed for the door as well, because Emma had infected him with a sudden fear: What if the door closed and he got stuck in the secret room all by himself?

But what if the door closes after we're out and we never get it back open again? he thought. *What if there's some secret in the hidden room that we need so we can figure out how to find Mom?*

Just before he stepped out, he bent down and grabbed a can of green beans from the nearest shelf. He wedged the can against the doorframe, so even if the door tried to shut on its own, the can would keep it propped open.

Then he slammed headfirst into Natalie's back.

"Oh, sorry," Chess mumbled. "I wasn't looking where I was . . ."

Natalie surprised him by clutching his arm.

"Didn't we leave the light on in your mom's office?" she asked.

Finn and Emma grabbed on to Chess as well. Chess

blinked, trying to make out the familiar furniture of the Boring Room: the desk, the chair, the bookshelves. His eyes adjusted a little to the strangely dim light, but he couldn't get them to see anything but blank floor and empty walls.

"L-light switch," Emma said, daring to step away and stride toward the opposite wall.

She hit the wall, and Chess braced for the bright overhead light of the Boring Room to come back on.

A lightbulb flickered and sizzled then steadied, but only sent out a low-wattage glow.

Chess looked down at swirls on the floor—swirls of dust on an otherwise empty concrete floor.

"This isn't your mom's office!" Natalie cried. "We ended up in somebody else's house!"

TWENTY-FIVE

FINN

"Ian? Mr. and Mrs. Han? Mrs. Childers?" Finn started calling out the names of all the closest neighbors he could think of.

"Shh," Emma said, grabbing his arm warningly. "We don't know *whose* house we're in."

"Right," Finn said in what he thought was a very reasonable tone. "So we should make as much noise as possible, so someone will come down and tell us. Also, so no one thinks we're sneaking around doing something wrong. Like stealing stuff. The Hans live on one side of us and Mrs. Childers lives on the other, so whichever way that room spun us around, we—"

"Finn," Chess said sharply. He walked over to the doorway that led out from the little room they were in, into what Finn guessed had to be the room beyond. Chess opened the door a crack, then looked back at the others. "Do either the Hans or Mrs. Childers have a totally empty basement?"

"No, silly," Finn said, laughing. "Ian Han has more toys than we do in his basement. And Mrs. Childers . . . remember that time she paid us to move her Christmas ornaments down into her basement? Well, she wanted to pay us, but Mom said it was enough that she fed us Christmas cookies. Even though they were kind of stale. And . . ."

Emma pushed past Finn and Chess, and shoved the door leading into the next room completely open. Finn saw a space like the wide-open part of the Greystones' basement, with tiny half windows at the top letting in murky light.

The light shone down on nothing but a bare concrete floor.

"This basement doesn't even have carpet," Emma said. "Don't the Hans and Mrs. Childers have carpet?"

Natalie turned side to side, facing first one direction, then another. She pointed, and her lips moved silently. Then she looked up at everyone else.

"The main part of your basement was on the side that faced the street," she said. "So if we're not in the house to the left or the right, on the same street as you . . . what do you know about the house *behind* yours, on the next street over? Behind your backyard, I mean?"

"There's not a house right behind ours," Chess said. "There's a bunch of trees."

"If it weren't for all those trees, it'd be a great place to play football," Finn said. "*That's* how much space there is before you get to the next street over."

Emma walked out into the main part of the basement and squinted up at the tiny windows.

"Nothing but bushes," she muttered. "At least, that's all we can see from here." She whirled back toward the others. "It felt to me like we were just spinning, but what if the secret room is on some sort of track? Like . . . a trolley? Could it have carried us all the way to the street behind ours?"

"I guess," Chess said. But he had his whole face smooshed up into a squint, like he was really saying *None of this makes any sense*.

"I'll find out where we are," Natalie said, yanking her phone from her back pocket. Her thumbs flew, then she looked up, squinting just as hard as Chess. "That's weird. I don't have service down here."

"Then let's go upstairs!" Finn raced for the stairs. He

glanced back to see that nobody else was following him. He paused on the bottom step. "What are you waiting for?"

"Finn . . . ," Chess began. He pointed back toward the door they'd come through. "Maybe we should just go back to our house. Through the secret room. We probably still have time to pet Rocket a little before Ms. Morales gets worried about us."

"What if we go back through the secret room and it spins again, and we end up somewhere else?" Emma asked. "Or . . . we get stuck?"

"Why can't I get my phone to work?" Natalie grumbled. She waved it in the air and held it up toward the nearest window, as if that would make a difference.

Something surprising occurred to Finn.

"Are you all scared?" he asked. "Just because you don't know where the spinning room took us? Does it scare you that much when you don't know stuff?" He jumped up to the next higher step. "You should all remember what it's like to be a second grader. There's *lots* of stuff I don't know or understand, and I'm fine!"

That wasn't entirely true—if he thought about Mom being gone, he didn't feel fine at all. But he was fine with the spinning room. He was fine with being in a strange house.

As far as he was concerned, the mystery of it all was a great way to keep his mind off missing Mom.

"Here," he said. "I'll make it easy for you. Catch me!"

He dashed up the rest of the stairs and burst through the door at the top crying out, "Hello? I'm lost! Whoever lives here, can you tell me where we are?"

As soon as he was through the door, Finn poked his head around the corner and looked around.

"You all are worrying about nothing!" he called back over his shoulder. "This whole house is empty! We're not bothering anyone!"

It *was* a little creepy to see the expanse of bare floor before him. And why wasn't there more light? Instinctively, Finn gazed toward the place where he'd see the nearest window if he'd come up the basement stairs in his own house.

Oh. There was a window, but it was boarded up, covered with plywood. The only reason any light crept into the house at all was because the plywood was cracked.

Natalie shoved her way up the stairs behind Finn.

"What's with the windows?" she asked. "Nobody would be able to sell a house with the windows boarded up. Who does that?"

"None of our neighbors," Finn said. "No one on our street."

"So *is* this house on the street behind yours?" Natalie asked.

"Let's see," Finn said. He crossed the room before him,

which seemed to be about the same size and shape as his family's living room. He reached for the doorknob of the front door. It was stiff and hard to turn, so by the time he managed to wrench it open, not just Natalie but even Chess and Emma were clustered right beside him.

The door opened in, so everybody had to step back.

Finn saw a crumbling porch first; then a weedy, overgrown yard; and then the tall fences blocking off the houses on either side. The fences soared so high that probably even Chess couldn't see over them.

They also had rusty, spiky wires lining the top of them.

"Do you recognize where we are now?" Natalie asked, turning from Finn to Emma to Chess. "Does anything look familiar?"

Chess's face had turned stark white. Emma's eyes had grown so big it seemed like they'd taken over her face.

It fell to Finn once again to do all the talking.

"I've never been here before in my life! None of us have!"

TWENTY-SIX

EMMA

Logic, Emma told herself. *Sense. Facts. Think about those, and you won't panic. We can't be that far from home.*

But even the air seemed to be conspiring against her, making her think otherwise. The weather had been clear and sunny when she and the others had stepped into their own house just—what? Ten or fifteen minutes ago? But the threat of a storm had apparently blown in, just in that short amount of time. The sky now was full of low, ominous clouds, and the air felt murky and thick. It was the kind of air that made it hard for people to breathe if they had asthma. Emma had

had a problem with that when she was little; she was just lucky that she'd outgrown it.

Was it coming back now?

Stay logical, Emma reminded herself again. *Stay calm.*

She made herself take a deep breath of the nasty air.

"This *could* be the street behind ours, and it's just changed a lot since the last time we were over here," she said, trying to force the doubt out of her voice. "We don't come this way very often because none of us have friends in this direction, and we always go the other way to get out of the neighborhood. And, you know, there are all those trees in the way, so we never really see what's happening on this street. . . ."

"Oh," Natalie said. "That makes sense. I'll just look at the GPS location on my phone, and . . ." She peered intently down at her phone, then back up. "Ugh! It's still not working!"

"Maybe if we walk out to the street, we'll see something familiar," Emma suggested, stepping out onto the porch. Finn and Natalie—who was holding the phone up in the air again—followed close behind.

"I think we should go back," Chess said. He remained right on the threshold, the door open behind him.

Emma's stomach clenched at the thought of going back through the strange house, back through the secret room— and maybe even back through another round of spinning.

She *really* wanted to see something familiar and figure out where they were.

And then we can walk back to our house through our own back-yard. And tonight back at Ms. Morales's house, we'll figure out the code behind Mom's letter, and we'll know how to rescue her that way, and we'll never have to go into that secret room again. At least, not without her being with us, telling us how to work it. . . .

Emma reached back and tugged on Chess's elbow, throwing him off balance.

"Come on, Chess," she said. "Where's your spirit of adventure?" This was something Mom said sometimes; it was amazing that Emma could speak the words without starting to cry. "I just want to look and see if we can find any street signs. Nothing's going to happen if we walk down this driveway for a minute!"

Chess toppled forward, barely missing stepping on Natalie's heels.

Maybe Chess's long, gangly arms caught the edge of the door somehow; maybe there was a breeze that Emma hadn't noticed. But as soon as Chess was out of the way, the door swung shut behind him with a loud bang.

Chess jumped, knocking his shoulder against the scarred wooden door.

"Oops," Emma said.

Chess reached back and twisted the doorknob. It didn't budge.

"We better hope we see something familiar," he muttered. "Because this door's locked now. We *can't* get back to the secret room!"

TWENTY-SEVEN

CHESS

"I'm sorry," Emma said.

Chess shook his head, unable to choke out any words.

Why is this so hard? he wanted to scream. *I just want Mom to be home and everything to be normal. I don't want to have to think about secret rooms or letters written in code or the fact that we were down to having only one parent, and now she's gone, too. I just want to be an ordinary sixth grader, with an ordinary life. . . .*

He might as well wish that Dad was still alive.

"If we stick together, everything will be fine," Natalie said, as if she could tell he was about to lose it. But even she had a tense look around her eyes, like she was fighting against squeezing them shut and pretending none of this had happened. "Maybe if we go out to the street, my phone will work. Sometimes there are dead zones in certain houses. Mom says she sees that all the time when she's selling houses, and sometimes the buyers even ask for lower prices because of that. . . ."

"*I* wouldn't buy a house where a phone wouldn't work!" Finn agreed.

Don't let Finn see how upset I am, Chess thought. *Don't let Finn see how scared I am. Don't let Finn see how confused I am, how I don't understand anything. . . .*

"Lead the way," Chess said to Natalie. He waved his arm out to the side as if he were just being a gentleman, letting her and the others go first.

Really, he just wanted to walk behind Finn and Emma so they couldn't see his face and Chess wouldn't have to stiffen it into a confident, cheerful, unconcerned mask. He wasn't sure he was capable of doing that right now.

Natalie stepped down from the crumbling concrete porch, followed by Finn and Emma together, with Chess bringing up the rear. A short sidewalk led over to the blacktopped driveway, and both the sidewalk and the blacktop were just as crumbly as the porch, with large patches of rocks and dirt showing through.

"What a mess," Natalie said. She covered her mouth for

a moment, as if she'd said something wrong. "I mean, your house is nice, and the other houses on your street are, too, and if this is just one street away, it's not fair that the people who own this house let things get so run-down. That makes it so you wouldn't get as much money if you sold your house."

"We're not selling our house," Emma said.

Oh no . . . If Mom really doesn't come back, would we have to sell our house? Chess wondered. *Would we have to be adopted by some family we don't even know? Would we maybe even be split up, me and Finn and Emma all going separate places?*

Chess's stomach twisted, as if someone had grabbed it and tried to squeeze it down to nothing.

"Mom would never let anyone sell our house!" Finn agreed with a little laugh, as if the whole idea was ridiculous. "Mom . . ."

From behind, Chess saw the exact moment Finn's shoulders sagged, as if a terrifying idea had just hit him: What could Mom do to prevent someone from selling the house if she wasn't even there? If she never came back?

"Hey, Finn," Chess said too loudly. "How long do you think it took to build those huge fences on either side of this house? Do you think they used different-colored boards on purpose? Would you do that, if we decided to build a fence around our house?"

"I don't like fences," Finn said sulkily. "They make it so you can't *see*."

Chess caught up to Finn and put his arm around his brother's shoulder. Ahead of them, Natalie stepped past the corner of the nearest fence. She pulled Emma alongside her and asked, "See anything familiar now?"

"Umm . . . ," Emma began, turning her head right to left to right again, looking up and down the street.

Natalie dipped her head toward her phone screen once more.

"Searching, searching, searching . . . ," she muttered.

Chess shepherded Finn out past the fence as well. Chess could have sworn every street in their neighborhood had sidewalks, but there wasn't one here. He stepped directly from the crumbling blacktopped driveway out into the street. He immediately tightened his grip on Finn's shoulder and looked both ways for cars.

"Watch out!" he warned Natalie, who was still peering at her phone.

She looked up, but Chess's caution was unnecessary. There weren't any cars. The only movement on the street was a group of five boys headed toward them.

Chess squinted, hoping he'd recognize someone from school. Maybe one of them would even be able to tell Chess the name of this street and how to get back home. But these boys all looked older, maybe even high-school age. One or two of them had the beginnings of beards. They all wore matching dark blue and orange, as if they were all on the same elite sports team. They also all moved with the same intimidating swagger. It reminded Chess of certain boys he tried to avoid at school, the ones who went around in packs, challenging other kids to fight.

Only, these boys had a lot more muscles. They looked like they actually *could* fight. Not just threaten to.

"Don't say anything to those boys," he whispered to Finn. "Just . . ." What did Chess know about dealing with menacing older boys? Nothing. He gulped. "Just let them walk on by."

But the boy at the front—the tallest and most muscular— was looking their way. Even at a distance, Chess could see amazement flow over the boy's expression.

"Natalie?" the boy called. "Natalie *Mayhew*?"

"Is that someone you know?" Chess hissed at her.

Natalie squinted toward the older boys.

"I don't *think* so," she whispered back. Then she raised her voice and called back to the boy, "Uh, hi . . ."

The boys came closer.

"It *is* Natalie," the guy in the front called out excitedly. Was he the leader? As if on command, all five boys stopped a few paces away. The four behind the leader slouched, seeming not so much menacing now as idling, waiting for their next command.

"Yeah, it's me," Natalie said, shrugging. "So what?"

Chess felt oddly proud of her. Of course. She'd been a Lip Gloss Girl; she'd practically run the whole elementary school. She could hold her own even against a group of stupid high school boys.

"So what are you doing in *this* neighborhood?" the leader asked.

Natalie glanced down at Emma and Finn. Somehow her gaze also took in Chess, making him feel both smaller and younger.

"Babysitting," she said scornfully.

Chess slid from feeling a little younger than Natalie to feeling like he was practically a baby.

"*You* babysit?" the leader asked, narrowing his eyes at Natalie. "You?"

Natalie fixed such a withering gaze on the leader that he seemed to shrink an inch or two.

"My mother's making me," she said. "Do you *know* my mom?"

"Yes, yes, of course," the boy immediately behind the leader began babbling.

The leader shot him an annoyed glance, and the other boy shut up.

"I thought maybe you were helping scope out the neighborhood," the leader told Natalie. He stood taller, puffing out his muscular chest even more. "Because, you know. This is where the criminal was found. You heard the news, right?"

"What news?" Emma dared to pipe up.

Chess was torn between being proud of her courage and wanting to beg the leader, *Please don't hurt my little sister. Please. She doesn't know any better. She doesn't even see that you're a bunch of bullies, and you probably run this whole street, and . . .*

But the leader perked up, like he was excited about getting to tell.

"I don't know how you could have missed it," he said. "I thought *everybody* knew. There are signs up about the criminal on practically every corner. They caught her yesterday. You know she'd been on the run and in hiding for eight years? But the government set a trap. They spread the news that her children had been kidnapped—or maybe they really did kidnap her children. I don't know. Anyhow, she showed up, thinking she could rescue her kids and—boom! I heard there was a SWAT squad waiting over there, and there, and there. . . ."

He pointed up and down the street, toward one tall fence or hedgerow after another.

"And there's going to be a public trial and sentencing this

174

weekend. On Saturday," the leader continued. "Of course everybody'll go."

Chess's whole body felt tingly and strange. Maybe he was about to faint.

Kidnapped children, he thought.

Had the *government* kidnapped those kids in Arizona who had the same names and birthdays as Chess, Emma, and Finn? Or had the government *pretended* to?

And was Mom connected somehow?

Eight years . . . eight years ago was when Dad died. . . .

"What did . . . did . . . ," he started to stammer out, because he needed to know what the criminal had done, what made her a criminal. He wanted to know her name, too, because he thought that might prove that Mom *wasn't* involved, that this really didn't have anything to do with her.

He didn't want it to have anything to do with the kidnapped kids from Arizona, either.

But before Chess could say another word, he heard a furious shout behind him.

"Natalie Maria Mayhew! Just *what* do you think you're doing?"

TWENTY-EIGHT

FINN

Finn swiveled his head toward the loud voice. A figure loomed in the doorway of the house they'd just left. The *open* doorway.

"Ms. Morales!" he cried, running back toward her. "You found us! And—you unlocked the door!"

Out of the corner of his eye, he saw the boys they'd been talking to take off running, as if they were terrified of Natalie's mother. Or, maybe, of any adult.

A grown-up! A mom! She'll fix everything, Finn thought. *All she had to do was show up, to get rid of those scary boys!*

But Ms. Morales's face was like a storm cloud.

"Natalie! I asked you to explain—"

"Stop it, Mom!" Natalie yelled back. "Why do you always think everything is my fault?"

"Because I left you in charge," Ms. Morales said. "You were supposed to *only* go into one house, the Greystones', and visit a cat for five or ten minutes, and let me know *immediately* if there was any problem. And then you don't answer your phone, and nobody answers the door when I go in after *half an hour,* and I find you've led the kids through some secret tunnel, and *trespassed* in an empty house, and Lord only knows who it belongs to, and—*achoo!*"

She stopped seeming quite so fierce when her first sneeze was followed by six more.

"Rocket!" Finn burst out, because he saw the cat rubbing against Ms. Morales's ankles and her high-heeled shoes.

"Get him—*achoo!*—away from me!" Ms. Morales commanded.

Finn stepped back into the empty house and scooped up Rocket. He held the cat off to the side, away from Ms. Morales.

"I will, I will," Finn promised. "But listen, nothing about that empty house was Natalie's fault. We—"

"I saw four sets of footprints in the dust," Ms. Morales huffed. "Of varying sizes. Don't try to lie and pretend you weren't here."

"No, I mean, yes, we were," Finn said. "But it was *my* fault. I'm the one who led everyone else through the empty house."

"And I'm the one who didn't want to go back through the, uh, tunnel," Emma admitted, right behind him.

"And I opened the door to the tunnel," Chess said, stepping up onto the porch with Emma.

Only Natalie was still out by the street, peering off into the distance.

"Natalie, if you go chasing after those boys, so help me, I'll—" Ms. Morales began.

"I'm coming, I'm coming," Natalie grumbled, turning back toward the house.

Ms. Morales looked down at the cat in Finn's arms. Rocket waved his paws, struggling to be put down.

"Your cat might run away if we take an outdoor route back to your house, right?" Ms. Morales asked Finn, her voice a little gentler than it had been when she was yelling at Natalie.

"Maybe," Finn said. "Mom says cats think for themselves. They do whatever they want."

Ms. Morales sniffed.

"All right, quick," she said. "Everyone back in this house and we'll go back through the basement tunnel. But don't touch *anything*. You didn't damage anything already, did you?"

"What's there to damage?" Natalie asked, catching up to the others.

Ms. Morales didn't answer. But as soon as everyone was back in the house, she slammed the door *hard*.

They all made a silent procession back toward the basement stairs, except for Ms. Morales sneezing twice more, and complaining, mostly just to herself, "How could anybody sell a house like this, with that *stench* everywhere?"

Finn realized that the bad smell he'd noticed in the secret room wasn't just there; it was in this house and out in the yard, too. He'd just kind of gotten used to it.

It's like something dead and rotting mixed with lots of dirty stuff and . . .

The words that came into his head were "and with something evil," but Finn didn't like those words. Not when Mom was away and Ms. Morales was mad at Natalie.

"You were really smart to find us," he said to Ms. Morales, because sometimes when Mom was mad, it cheered her up to hear a compliment. "We really didn't know *where* we'd ended up."

"Thank the cat, not me," Ms. Morales said stiffly. "I followed him."

They all climbed back down the stairs and went into the little room that was shut off from the rest of the basement the same way the Boring Room was in the Greystones' basement.

"Did the, um, tunnel spin when you went through it?" Emma asked Ms. Morales.

"Spin? Of course not," Ms. Morales said. "But I could barely see anything. I had to use the flashlight on my phone. See?"

She switched it back on as they ducked back into the secret room. Or the panic room. Or the tunnel. Finn wasn't sure what to call it now. Behind them, Chess switched off the light in the empty basement. Somehow the lights that had been on before in the secret room were gone now, so Ms. Morales's phone flashlight was the only glow around them. Finn stepped a little closer to her.

"At least your phone works," Natalie said sulkily. "Mine completely blanked out. Honest—I didn't hear you call. Not once."

"Really, Natalie? Really?" Ms. Morales said. "Try your flashlight—I bet your phone's working now."

A light sprang on behind Finn.

"Uh-huh," Ms. Morales said.

"You never believe anything I tell you!" Natalie accused. "Even when I'm telling the truth!"

"So you're admitting that sometimes you lie?" Ms. Morales said. "How am I supposed to know the difference?"

Finn wasn't used to being around kids fighting with their parents. Or, really, anybody fighting.

"Rocket doesn't like hearing people yell," he said, and it was weird how injured his voice sounded.

"Sorry, Finn," Ms. Morales said. She patted his shoulder and made her voice soft and gentle. "What would you like for dinner tonight? Mac and cheese, maybe?"

But Finn saw the look Ms. Morales shot Natalie. Even in the dim glow of the phone flashlights, he saw the looks Emma and Chess exchanged.

It felt like everyone was keeping secrets from him.

TWENTY-NINE

EMMA

This doesn't make sense, Emma thought, silently trudging behind Finn and Ms. Morales.

The secret room that had spun them around and somehow joined the Greystones' basement with the mysterious house really did feel more like a tunnel now. Emma started counting her steps as soon as they entered the tunnel—right after Chess pulled the door to the empty house's basement shut tight behind them. She made it up to thirty-two. Then she lost count because she started distractedly thinking, *Surely we didn't walk thirty-two steps before. Surely there wasn't that much distance between our basement and the empty house. Surely the secret room didn't spin us that far forward, when I didn't even feel like we were moving forward at all. . . .*

It wasn't like Emma to lose count of anything. But there was almost a haze in the air, as if the overcast, about-to-storm sensation from outside had seeped down into the tunnel as well. It felt like it had seeped into her mind, too.

Why did it seem like there weren't even shelves lining the walls anymore?

Science, math, facts, logic, Emma told herself.

Fact: Walking in the narrow glow from a flashlight—or even two flashlights—had the effect of making everything outside that glow seem eerie. Walking with a flashlight worked that way anywhere. If nothing else, it made everything outside the flashlight glow hard to see.

Fact: Emma, Chess, Finn, and Natalie hadn't exactly explored the secret room thoroughly before Natalie hit the lever, the room spun, and then they fled into the empty house. So there might be huge sections of the secret room that they hadn't seen. Some of those sections might not have had shelves. Maybe there'd been . . . a bend in the room. An entire corner they hadn't even seen.

So why weren't they turning any corners now?

They reached the half doorway that led back into the Boring Room. As Finn, Ms. Morales, and Natalie ducked under and stepped through, Emma caught a glimpse of

Mom's desk. It was all Emma could do not to run over and throw her arms around the desk, because it was finally something familiar, something she recognized.

The desk was there. Mom wasn't.

Emma didn't hug the desk.

Mom, we're going to figure all this out and find you, Emma thought, as if she really believed she could communicate with her mother telepathically. *We are. Don't worry.*

Emma caught up to Natalie. Ms. Morales and Finn were already out of the room, headed for the basement stairs. Chess was still a few steps behind.

"Ten o'clock tonight?" Emma whispered to Natalie. "Same place?"

Natalie gave a sharp nod.

"Absolutely," she said. She narrowed her eyes. "We've got a *lot* more to look up and figure out."

THIRTY

CHESS

"Would you mind helping your brother and sister do their homework?" Ms. Morales asked Chess as soon as they got back to her house. "Natalie and I need to have a little talk."

"Uh, sure," Chess said.

Finn and Emma did not need his help with homework. Sometimes when Chess was stuck on a math problem, Emma helped *him*.

But Finn, Emma, and Chess all plopped their backpacks down beside the huge table in the kitchen and began taking out folders and books. Ms. Morales held on to Natalie's arm and steered her past them toward her office.

"Seriously, Mom?" Chess heard Natalie grumble. "Are you sure you don't want to put me in handcuffs, too?"

Behind Ms. Morales's back, Emma gave Natalie a thumbs-up and made a zipper motion across her lips. As soon as Natalie and Ms. Morales were in the office and Ms. Morales shut the door, Emma scampered after them.

"That office is soundproof, remember?" Chess called softly. "It's not going to work to press your ear against the door. Besides, you'll get caught."

Emma's shoulders sagged and she stopped following.

"But I want to know *everything!*" she complained, slouching back toward the table. "Can we really trust Natalie? Did Mom tell Ms. Morales anything she's not telling us? Has Ms. Morales heard anything new from Mom besides those stupid automatic texts?"

"*I* trust Natalie," Finn announced, his pencil hovering over a worksheet. "And Ms. Morales, too. They're nice."

Finn would probably think a murderer was nice.

Or was it that even a murderer would be nice to Finn?

Chess patted the back pocket of his jeans.

"Natalie . . . gave me something," he said slowly. He wasn't sure what to do. "In the car. She said it was . . . in case her mom is so mad she sends Natalie to her dad's and Natalie doesn't get a chance to say goodbye. Or to see us again at all. But I think maybe . . . maybe . . ."

"Just tell us what you're talking about!" Emma demanded. She put her hands on her hips and whipped her hair over her shoulder sort of like Natalie always did.

Chess dug out a pair of wireless earbuds and held them up for Finn and Emma to see.

"Natalie wants you to listen to music?" Finn asked.

"No," Chess said. He pushed his hand a little deeper into his pocket and pulled out the other object Natalie had given him: a phone. "She says her mom keeps burner phones around just, well, just in case someone needs them. So she gave me one. She said she'd set hers to call me if there's something she wants us to overhear. And with these earbuds . . ."

"The earbuds mean she'll call you and we can listen *secretly*! Without Ms. Morales knowing!" Emma's eyes lit up. "Ooo, *I* like Natalie, too! I like the way her brain works!"

But is Natalie really trying to help us—or just trying to get back at her mom? Chess wondered. *Is it really a good idea for us to hear whatever Ms. Morales is going to tell Natalie?*

Still, he handed one of the earbuds to Emma. He stuck the other in his own ear.

"None for me?" Finn said, making a pouty face.

"Sorry, Finny," Chess said. "There are only two. Anyhow—"

"I know, I know," Finn said. "I'm too young. It might scare me. Don't you know I'm brave? Don't you know I want

187

to help get Mom back as much as you and Emma do?"

It hurt the way he said that—as if he'd already grown up too much. Already Finn had changed from the eager, bouncy, silly boy he'd been two days ago. Even his face seemed less rounded and babyish, his cheekbones more noticeable than his dimples.

You're imagining things, Chess told himself. He wanted to tell Finn, *Don't think I'm babying you. I'm not even sure I'm old enough to deal with all this.*

But he just said "Sorry" and ruffled his brother's hair. Then he held a finger to his lips, because the phone in his hand began vibrating. He hit the button to answer, and he heard a burst of sound from the earbud. At first, it was just an indistinct noise, but he twisted the earbud slightly in his ear, and then he could make out words.

"But I didn't do anything wrong!" Natalie was protesting to her mother. Her phone was probably buried in her pocket but set on the speaker function—that was why everything sounded so muffled.

Chess double-checked to make sure he had the phone in his own hand set to mute any noise he, Emma, or Finn might make.

"Natalie, you *know* every woman I help is someone in a dangerous situation," Ms. Morales said. "That means we need to be extra cautious about . . ."

Chess hoped Emma was listening closely to hear what they needed to be extra cautious about, because he blanked out for a moment.

So even Ms. Morales realizes Mom is in danger?

Then he remembered what Natalie had said the day before, thinking that Mom was running away from a dangerous boyfriend. That was probably all Ms. Morales meant. Chess knew she was wrong about that danger.

". . . I trusted you to help these kids, to be aware of issues they wouldn't understand, and this is what you do? Sneak away to a dangerous area to meet up with a bunch of older boys?" Ms. Morales was asking.

"Mom, I did not walk through that other house just to go meet those boys!" Natalie said, and even through the earbud, Chess could tell she was gritting her teeth. "I wasn't looking for them! They said hi, I said hi—it was a one-minute conversation! I don't even know them!"

Chess noticed that she didn't tell her mom that the boys had known *her*. That they'd called her by name.

"And you had little kids watching you—were you *trying* to show the Greystone kids that it's okay to talk to strangers?" Ms. Morales asked.

"Mom, it wasn't like that!" Natalie protested. "We were lost! My phone wouldn't work! We—"

"And it never once occurred to you to just turn around

and walk *back* through the tunnel to the Greystones' house?" Ms. Morales asked, her voice rising with incredulity.

"Mom, that tunnel wasn't . . . the secret room wasn't . . . Did *you* know Mrs. Greystone had that secret place— whatever it was—attached to the basement of her house? At first I thought it was just a panic room, but . . . didn't it seem really, really weird to you?" Natalie asked.

"People have panic rooms all the time," Ms. Morales said stiffly. "There are houses I've driven by for years, and I didn't know they had panic rooms until the owners listed the house to sell."

"And those panic rooms you've seen—are they like the one the Greystones have?" Natalie asked, her voice rising. "Are they connected to a completely different house on a completely different street?"

"Well, no . . . not that I've ever seen before," Ms. Morales admitted.

"How well do you even know Mrs. Greystone?" Natalie challenged, and Chess felt that something had changed. Now it was Natalie interrogating Ms. Morales, not Ms. Morales interrogating Natalie.

Good for you, Natalie! Chess thought, even as he listened more intently.

"How well do I know . . . Mrs. Greystone was in PTO with me for years," Ms. Morales said. "She was always quiet, but she was one of those people who, if she volunteered to do something, she did it. On time, and the right way. And she didn't complain about it, or ask a million questions that were so annoying I started wishing I'd just taken care of everything myself."

Chess felt a little proud of his mom.

"And that was enough to make you volunteer to take care of her kids for who knows how long?" Natalie challenged. "Didn't you ever think that she might be tangled up in something really strange and awful, and—"

"Yes, I *did* think she might be tangled up in something really strange and awful," Ms. Morales countered. "And that's why I offered to help. Because I don't think it's something that's her fault at all. I pray you never learn this directly for yourself, Little Miss Superior, but lots of times people—especially women—get caught up in awful situations they didn't cause, that they need help getting out of. Think about it. Why would I help someone who doesn't need it?"

"Mom, I put up with you inviting all sorts of people into our house. People you trust just because they're women and children," Natalie said. "There was the kid who broke my laptop, the one who stole my favorite jeans—"

"That you might have lost yourself," Ms. Morales interrupted.

Natalie just kept talking.

"And, you know, that woman who cried all the time."

"She had good reason to cry," Ms. Morales said, her voice tense.

"Don't you think the Greystone kids are different than the others we've had here?" Natalie asked. "Not as . . . scared all the time, maybe?"

Chess thought about the careful way Ms. Morales had shepherded the three of them through the school parking lot, as if she was hiding them from some unknown danger. As if they were supposed to understand. He *hadn't* been scared then.

But he was now.

"Some people hide things better than others," Ms. Morales said. "I wouldn't have pegged Kate Greystone as the type to get involved with a dangerous man, either. But there was always something about Kate. Something . . . mysterious. And sad. She never talked about her husband or her past."

"See, Mom? Not everyone goes around telling anyone who will listen what a scumbag their husband used to be," Natalie said. "You should learn from that, and—"

"Natalie, Kate Greystone isn't divorced," Ms. Morales said. "Her husband died. Years ago. Before they moved here."

Moved? The word caught oddly in Chess's brain. Everything had changed after Dad died. There'd been a period of time when it felt like the sun burned out, like nothing Chess ate had any flavor, like he spent weeks doing nothing but lying on his bed, staring up at his ceiling. One morning he'd awakened, and the ceiling he opened his eyes to was different: smooth and white and peaceful, instead of swirled and shadowed and cobwebbed. And he got up, and he remembered going to find Mom and hearing her explanation: "Do you like our new house? I didn't want to disturb you kids any more than I had to, so I brought you here while you were sleeping. Do you like your new furniture? Everything is new. It's a new start. I promise you, we'll be happy here. Everything will be better."

Had Chess been too busy thinking *Nothing could be better without Dad* to ask any questions? Or to listen to anything else Mom said that day?

Chess's mind worked strangely thinking about anything from the time surrounding Dad's death. Maybe it was just because he'd only been four; maybe it was because Mom never talked about certain memories. Maybe he'd been too sad to remember everything.

But Chess was pretty sure they'd just moved from one house to another, not from one town to another.

So why did Ms. Morales make it sound like we moved from an entirely different place?

Now that he thought about it, wasn't it weird that Mom

193

had moved them in the middle of the night? Without warning them ahead of time?

Or had Mom warned them, and Chess just didn't remember?

"Don't forget anything," Mom had told him just a few days ago—practically the last words she'd spoken to him before she vanished.

But what if he'd already forgotten something important?

What if he hadn't remembered what he was supposed to from the very beginning?

THIRTY-ONE

FINN

"Finally," Finn exploded as soon as he stepped out into the hall. It was 10 p.m. exactly—Finn had watched the numbers change on the digital clock in his room.

"Shh," Chess said, falling into step with him and looking around nervously. Then he crouched beside Finn. "Listen, Finn, it's really late for you to still be up, and this is the second night in a row. . . . Maybe you should just go back to bed and get some sleep. Emma and I can tell you everything we find out in the morning."

"Except you wouldn't tell me *everything*, if you thought it was going to scare me," Finn said. He could feel his lower lip start to jut out, like he was just a sulky little kid. He forced himself to keep his lip in, stand up straighter, and stare Chess right in the eye. "I want to help, too. I . . . I have to."

Chess's face was shadowed; it wasn't possible to see how he was going to answer.

"Finn comes with us," Emma said, stepping between her brothers. "We don't leave him behind."

And then she ruined everything by adding, "Even if he falls asleep in one of those chairs down in the office, he stays with us."

I won't fall asleep, Finn told himself. *I'll never sleep again, if that's what it takes for me to help find Mom.*

But he couldn't help himself: He let out a jaw-cracking yawn.

He hoped it was too dark in the hall for Emma or Chess to notice.

The three of them tiptoed along, with Natalie joining them right at the top of the stairs. She held two laptops under her arm.

"Extras," she whispered. "So we'll all have something to work on."

Natalie isn't saying I should just go to sleep! Finn thought, and he climbed down the stairs walking alongside her.

But when they got to the office, the other three kids went right to work, and Finn wasn't sure what he should do.

He stood in front of one of Natalie's laptops—he wasn't tall enough to reach it if he sat down—and he stared at the Google drawing of the day, which seemed to be a bunch of men and women staring at a computer. It was probably something about computer history that Finn didn't know about, but he wasn't going to ask the others.

Mom would just tell me, he thought. *If Mom were here, she would have known I didn't know, and I wouldn't have to ask, and . . .*

Finn couldn't let himself think about how everything would be better if Mom was there.

He sneaked a peek at the computer Emma was working on: She had Mom's letter full of gibberish up on the screen and she was muttering to herself, "Substitution code? Is the key maybe part of the code? Would it be numerical, since Mom would *know* I'd look for a number pattern?"

"Hey, Emma," Finn said. "Why don't you email me Mom's letter, and then I can work on it over here? Maybe I'll see some clue to help you."

It took Emma a million years to turn her head toward Finn. Sometimes she got like that when she was thinking hard.

"Hmm?" she said slowly. "Oh, um, Mom put some sort of coding on this letter so we *can't* email it anywhere. Or copy it. Or print it out. I already tried to email it to myself, to have a backup copy, and it wouldn't work. *Maybe* I could do some extra research to figure out how to unlock all that, but . . ."

But Emma thought it was more important to work on solving the code herself.

And maybe she was right. Finn didn't know much about codes.

Finn turned toward Natalie, who had called up a picture of the Greystones' house on her computer. She tugged on Chess's arm.

"This is your address, right?" she asked.

You could have asked me! Finn wanted to shout at her. Instead, he just said quickly, before Chess could answer, "It is. Why?"

"I'm looking around the area on Google Street View to figure out exactly where we ended up today," Natalie said.

"How does that help us find Mom?" Finn demanded.

"Well, if we find out who owns the empty house that's connected to yours by that tunnel, then maybe we'll know who might have, uh . . ."

Finn saw Chess put his hand over his mouth. Was Chess signaling Natalie to be quiet, so she didn't scare Finn?

Finn had to prove he was brave enough to hear anything.

"You think our mom was kidnapped?" Finn asked, trying so, so hard to keep his voice from wavering on the last word. "Maybe by someone from that other house? Or by the 'criminal' those boys were talking about?"

"I don't know what to think," Natalie said, spreading her hands wide, as if to show how much she didn't know. "I can't find anything about some fugitive criminal being caught, or about any kidnappings around here. I thought it might help to find the address of that house we were in, but there's no house on any street near yours that matches what it looked like."

"That doesn't make sense," Finn protested. "Do you know about Google Earth? Where it's like you're looking down from above? Just look for the fences that were around that house!"

Natalie ran her finger over the touchpad, making the view on the screen race up and down the Greystones' street. All the houses there looked exactly like they should: totally familiar.

"I don't know, Finn, maybe the Google pictures of the other street were taken so long ago, those fences weren't built yet," Natalie said.

"But those fences looked really old," Finn said, remembering the mismatched, faded wood. "Like, even older than *me*!"

"Yeah . . . ," Natalie said absently, switching to a broader view of the neighborhood.

Finn glanced toward Chess again, hoping his older

brother noticed how Finn had had that whole conversation with Natalie without falling apart at the thought of Mom being kidnapped.

But Chess still had his hand over his mouth.

Then Finn saw what Chess had written in the search box on his computer: "Andrew Greystone obituary."

Finn's stomach twisted.

"You're looking up something about our dad?" Finn asked Chess, and this time he had no control of his voice. "Why? What's an oh, obit . . . uh . . ."

"Obituary?" Natalie finished for him, snapping her head toward Chess's computer. "You mean the news story from when he died? Let's see."

But Chess had already X-ed out of that screen.

"Never mind. It was just . . . something I wondered about," Chess said. He seemed to be breathing hard.

"You mean, you're looking for who all is listed as survivors? So maybe you can find relatives you haven't met who might have more info about your mom?" Natalie asked. "That's smart."

"Uh . . . something like that," Chess muttered. "But it doesn't matter. I can't find anything. I guess maybe eight years was too long ago."

"Try looking up some other relative," Natalie suggested.

"Maybe one who died after your dad?"

"All our other relatives died before Chess was even born," Finn said, and his voice came out too loud this time, as if, even though they were in a soundproof room, he was trying to wake Ms. Morales.

He really wouldn't mind if she did wake up, and came down and took care of him.

But the other kids would be mad.

Natalie and Chess kept talking about dead people. Finn stared at his own blank computer screen, the picture of the unknown computer programmers seeming to taunt him about everything he didn't know, everything he was useless at helping the other kids find out.

I might as well be asleep, he thought. *Or, no—I might as well be kidnapped myself, like those kids in Arizona who started this whole mess. . . .*

He knew it wasn't fair to blame the kids in Arizona for their own kidnappings—and it wasn't like that was even connected to Mom's business trip or her weird texts. But hearing the news of their kidnappings had been the start of everything weird; it had marked the first day that Finn felt strange about anything.

I bet those kids were rescued a long time ago, and we didn't even bother looking it up, he thought. *If I found out that they're home*

*safe, and back with their parents . . . well, that would be like proof
that we're going to find Mom again, too, and everything's going to be
okay.*

Painstakingly—because he hadn't really learned how to
type yet—he keyed in "Rochester, Emma, and Finn" and
added the words "kidnapped" and "news."

The first headline that came up said, "Gustano Parents
Beg for Kidnapped Children's Safe Return."

Okay, that did not make Finn feel better.

He reached for the laptop, ready to close out the whole
screen and pretend he'd never seen it. But maybe he was too
tired to operate a computer properly. His finger dragged
across the touchpad, bringing to life a video that took over
his whole screen. Instinctively, he slammed the lid of the laptop down, shutting off his view.

But that didn't shut down the sound.

"Please, we just want our children back," a woman's
voice cried out.

Finn froze. On either side of him, Emma and Chess
snapped their heads toward Finn's computer.

"Is that *Mom*?" Emma said.

"How do you have a recording of Mom's voice?" Chess
asked.

Emma reached past Finn and lifted the laptop lid again.

And there on the screen was Mom's face.

THIRTY-TWO

EMMA

"Does Mom have an identical twin she never told us about?" Emma asked.

She was so glad her brain supplied that explanation, because otherwise, she would have had to believe she was hallucinating. The woman in the video on the computer screen looked and sounded so much like Mom. It was hard to believe it wasn't Mom—a version of Mom, anyway, who had gotten her hair cut a lot shorter, so it curled around her ears like a pixie cap, and who'd been out in the sun a lot more, so her skin was tanner, maybe even a little leathery.

A version of Mom, maybe, who lived in Arizona.

"You say that woman looks like your mom? She's identical, even?" Natalie asked. She squinted at the computer screen in front of Finn, her eyes scanning the words at the bottom of the news report. "But . . . she's the mother of some kids who were kidnapped way out in Arizona?"

"Kids who have the same names and birthdays as us," Finn informed her. He turned to face Emma. "If you think this is Mom's twin . . . does that mean we have *cousins* with the exact same names as us? Can that happen?"

"And Mom never told us any of this?" Chess asked. His voice came out sounding wild, like even calm, easygoing Chess was on the verge of panic. "That day when we saw the news about those kids being kidnapped—wouldn't she have *said* we were related? That she knew them?"

"There's a lot Mom never told us," Emma said. And this was another fact. But it wasn't a comforting one.

"I don't understand anything!!" Finn complained. The corners of his mouth trembled, and his eyes filled.

Quickly Emma slid her arm around Finn's shoulders.

"We'll figure this out, Finny," she said. "We'll figure this out, and we'll rescue Mom, and, and those other kids will be found, and . . ."

Chess wrapped his long arms around both Finn and Emma. But he didn't say anything else.

Natalie took a step toward the three Greystones, then looked at all of their faces and took a step back.

"Mothers!" she said.

"Our mother had a logical reason for whatever she did, whatever secrets she kept," Emma said. "I'm sure of it. And she left us a letter to explain. . . ."

"In a code you can't figure out," Natalie said scornfully.

Emma couldn't look at Finn to see if his eyes were still swimming with tears, or if the tears had started rolling down his cheeks. Because if she looked, it might make her eyes flood with tears, too.

Really, there wasn't anything Emma could look at right now.

She squeezed her eyes shut.

"Maybe . . . maybe you and your family are like, I don't know, *royalty* from some other country," Natalie said. Her voice was soft now, like someone telling a fairy tale. "And your mom and her twin sister went into hiding, to keep you safe. In totally different states. But they gave you and your cousins royal names to keep the connection alive—that's why they're the same. And . . ."

Maybe Natalie meant her little fantasy story to be comforting. Maybe she thought Emma had gone through one of those little-girl phases where she wanted to be a princess, like all the other girls when Emma was in kindergarten. Maybe Natalie thought Chess and Finn had secretly seen themselves as knights and noblemen.

First of all, Emma wanted to say, *I dressed up as a scientist in a lab coat for Halloween in kindergarten, when the other girls were wearing princess crowns. And secondly—do you think there's any ending to that story that doesn't put Mom and Finn and Chess and me in danger, too?*

Emma couldn't say that in front of Finn.

Maybe she wasn't capable of saying it aloud, regardless.

"What does the kidnapped kids' dad look like?" Chess asked. "Did you find any pictures or video of him?"

Curiosity was enough to make Emma open her eyes again.

Chess thought about their dad a lot more than she did. Emma knew that. For her, their dad was like the unknown in a math problem that you didn't have to solve for. She didn't know that much about algebra yet, but it seemed that sometimes there were x's and y's both in a problem, and you only needed to find the value for one of them. She didn't have a single memory of Dad from when he was alive, and he was gone now, and nothing would bring him back. And Emma had Mom and Chess and Finn, and that was all she needed.

Except, she didn't have Mom anymore, either.

And apparently the Arizona kids' dad was still alive,

since she'd seen the word "parents" at the bottom of the computer screen.

Chess began fast-forwarding through the video of the Mom-twin. (The Mom-clone? The Mom-double? The Mom-who-wasn't-Mom?) Emma hadn't really wanted to listen to any more of what sounded so much like Mom's voice, weighted down so heavily with worry and fear. But the sped-up video made the resemblance seem even clearer: That was exactly how Mom tilted her head when she was upset. That was exactly the way Mom's face developed twin worry lines on her forehead—and then the worry lines erased—when she was trying to sound more optimistic and cheerful than she actually felt.

Maybe Emma hadn't fully understood before that there were times when Mom was only *pretending* to look and act and sound optimistic and cheerful?

The camera angle shifted in the video, zooming out, then zooming in again on a dark-haired man standing next to the Mom-who-wasn't-Mom. The tagline below said, "Arthur Gustano, father."

"He's not as tall as Daddy was," Chess murmured, and Emma wondered if he knew that he'd said "Daddy," not "Dad."

"*You* were a lot smaller eight years ago," Natalie said, almost apologetically. "So it's not really—"

"That man is only a little taller than his wife," Chess said. "And our dad was a lot taller than Mom. I know that. From pictures I've looked at . . . recently."

"Yes, but you don't actually *know* that that woman is the same height as your mom," Natalie said. "I mean, okay, sure, you say she looks and sounds like your mom, but even if they're twins—or just sisters—then—"

"Shut up," Finn said.

And this was crazy. Finn never told people to shut up. He never sounded that fierce and hurt and angry.

He turned his head side to side, peering back and forth between Emma and Chess, like they were the only other ones in the room.

"Is that what our daddy looked like or not?" Finn asked, his voice trembling.

"Chess?" Emma said, even though she'd seen plenty of pictures of their father before and should have been able to answer.

"No," Chess said decisively. "I mean, brown hair, brown eyes—yeah, that's the same. Or similar. But this guy's nose is bigger and his face is blockier, and his hair's straighter. And *listen*. His voice isn't anywhere near deep enough."

Chess even remembers what our dad sounded like? Emma thought, and she felt a stab of something that might have been jealousy.

The man on the screen inclined his head toward his wife.

"Nobody who hasn't gone through this could imagine what a nightmare this is," he said. "How could anybody be so cruel? Our children are innocent! They—"

Some heartless news reporter in the crowd in front of the man called out, "But is there any reason you can think of that someone would be trying to get revenge on you and your wife? Any reason that—"

"There is no reason for any of this," Mr. Gustano snarled. "Are you asking if my wife and I have ever done anything that would lead to our kids being taken? *No.* We are ordinary, law-abiding American citizens. We're *blameless.* Our kids are blameless. But nobody could deserve this horror. My kids should be in school right now, drawing pictures in art class and playing tag on the playground and . . . and . . . not . . ." He looked straight at the camera. "Please, if you can hear this, if you have any humanity in your hearts at all, don't harm my children. Just let them go. Let them come home."

He buried his face in his wife's shoulder. She stared out at the reporters, then it felt like she was staring out at Emma, Chess, Finn, Natalie, and anyone else who might be watching. And her steady gaze was so much like Mom's that Emma got chills.

"That is all we have to say," the Mom-twin snapped, then gently guided her husband out of the camera's range.

Emma shoved the laptop sideways, toward Natalie.

"Natalie, you have to find out everything you can about those kidnapped kids and their parents," she said. "Finn, Chess, and me—we can't watch anymore. It's too hard. And we need all three of our brains for figuring out Mom's code."

"Even mine?" Finn asked. He sniffled. "You really think I can help—"

"Help solve this?" Emma asked. "Finn, I *know* we can do this together. Because we have to. There isn't any other choice."

THIRTY-THREE

CHESS

Emma sounds like Mom, too, Chess thought. *She sounds exactly like Mom when she's telling all of us what to do.*

A memory tugged at Chess's brain, one that was so painful and from so long ago that he could only reassemble bits and pieces of it. Maybe it wasn't even real. Or maybe he just wanted to convince himself it hadn't happened. He could remember lying on the floor—playing with his red toy car again, maybe. Only, was it *after* they'd gotten the news that Dad had died? This wasn't part of his usual memories about Dad's death. Maybe it was a few days later. Maybe he'd stopped playing. Maybe he'd been screaming and pounding his fists on the floor. Or just lying still, too sad to move. And then Mom was there, picking him up. And he'd cried to her, "I want Daddy back! Make him not dead!"

And Mom had murmured, "Oh, Chessie, I want that, too. But we don't have that choice. It's not possible." She'd smoothed back his hair and hugged him close and whispered, "Other choices, though . . ."

The next thing that had happened was that Mom laughed. It had startled Chess, and somehow, even though he was only four, he'd understood that the laugh wasn't a happy one. But he'd been too young to understand what a laugh like that could mean instead, and that had frightened him.

He hadn't understood Mom's next words, either: "What am I talking about? I *have* to do this. There isn't any other choice."

There isn't any other choice. He heard the words the way Mom had said them eight years ago, and the way Emma said them now, and the tone was exactly the same. Both of their voices were full of determination—determination fighting with fear. With the determination winning.

It was that similarity that had jarred loose Chess's memory.

"We're all like Mom," Chess said dazedly. "All three of us. We're *all* . . . well, not Mom-twins, but . . . mini-Moms, anyway."

Emma, Finn, and Natalie all snapped their heads toward Chess. All three of them looked puzzled, and Chess realized their conversation had moved on while he'd been stuck in the past, stuck hearing echoes of Mom's voice in his head. He flushed, realizing how dumb he sounded. He expected Finn to protest, *What are you talking about? I'm not like Mom! I'm not a girl!*

But Finn, for once in his life, wasn't rushing to talk. He just looked up at Chess, so trustingly, as if he thought Chess had figured out something big, and he was waiting for Chess to explain.

Ohhhh . . . Maybe I did just figure out something big, Chess thought.

"Mom says we're the only ones who will be able to read her letter," he said, pointing to the computer screen Emma had been poring over before they'd heard the voice like Mom's. He stretched out his arm so his fingers brushed five words in particular in the few lines that were understandable: *Only the three of you . . .*

"Because you're the ones she's mailing that letter to," Natalie said with an annoyed flip of her hair over her shoulder. "She's only sending it to you three, so—"

"No," Chess said. Somehow he found that he didn't care anymore that Natalie had been a Lip Gloss Girl in charge of everything at school, and nobody ever challenged her.

"That's not what this means. She wants us to be the only ones to know what's in this letter, and so she put it in a code that only we can read. Because we're the only ones who would know the key."

"You mean, it's going to be something with math," Finn said glumly. "Because Emma's a math genius. Mom knows Emma can solve any math puzzle. I can't help, after all."

"No," Chess said again. Would he have to disagree with everyone until he got them to understand? He saw Emma recoil, and he tried again. "I mean, yes, Emma's a math genius, but so are other people. If it's just some tricky math answer, we could send it to the head of, I don't know, MIT, and *he* could solve this."

"Or *she*," Emma said. "Do you actually know if the head of MIT is a man or a woman?"

"I don't," Chess admitted. "There are lots of things I don't know. But ever since . . . since Mom left, all three of us have been saying things like, 'Oh, Mom would never do that,' and, 'We know Mom loves us. She . . .'" The words stuck in his throat, but he forced them out. "'She would never abandon us unless she thought she had to.'"

"You're saying we're all experts about Mom," Emma said, finally catching on. "And you think that's what's going to matter, solving this code."

Chess saw Natalie start to open her mouth, and just from

the way she twisted her face, he knew she was going to say something like, *But you didn't know she was going to vanish!* Or, *You didn't know she had a look-alike twin in Arizona! (If that's even a twin. You don't know for sure.)* Or, *You didn't know she had a room that spins and a secret tunnel under your house! You're not very good experts!* And Chess was going to need to stop her from saying any of that.

But before Natalie or Chess could speak, Finn said, "I know Mom smells like apples. Some guy—or woman— from MIT wouldn't know *that*."

And the way he said it—Chess's heart squeezed. Finn could just as easily have said that Mom smelled like sweat and grass and gasoline when she came in from mowing the yard, or like pumpkin pie when it was Thanksgiving, or like rosemary-mint shampoo when she'd just washed her hair. But all that would have been true of lots of moms.

Their mom did smell like apples. Even when she hadn't been around apples. It was just how she was.

Chess saw Natalie shut her mouth. He stopped watching her and turned back to Emma.

"I didn't always pay much attention when you kept talking about codes all the time last winter," Chess said. "But wasn't there one kind where you had to know a quote from the Bible or a line of poetry or some other phrase, and that's how you could figure out the solution to the code?"

"You think that's the kind of code Mom used," Emma said. Her eyes lit up. "And you think that the key to this code is some phrase that Mom says all the time, that only the three of us would know."

"Yes." Chess felt triumphant, almost as if they'd already solved the code and found Mom.

"Then you don't actually need me at all," Natalie said, bitterness in her voice. "Because I wouldn't know any of that. Don't mind me—I'll just be over here listening to parents sobbing about their kidnapped kids."

And you think that's a tougher job than listening to Emma, Finn, and me talking about our missing mom? Chess wanted to shout at her. *Or than being us, trying to remember everything we can about Mom, when we already miss her so much?*

But something weird happened. Natalie caught Chess's eye, and it was almost like she understood what he wanted to shout.

"Sorry," she muttered.

Chess felt a little dizzy. He wasn't used to having anyone understand him except Mom, Emma, and Finn.

"I'll start saying stuff Mom says," Finn said excitedly. "Is someone going to write it all down? She says, 'I think Captain Underpants is really funny, too.' She says, 'Sure, go ahead and jump on the bed. You only get to be a kid once.' She says . . ."

"Finn, Mom does *not* say you're allowed to jump on the bed!" Emma corrected. "She just pretends not to notice. But that thing about only being a kid once . . . that's a good one. I'll try it as the decoder." She reached for a piece of paper from Ms. Morales's desk and started writing. "What else can you think of? '*Everybody* should know how to clean a toilet,' maybe? Or, 'It's okay to mess up. Nobody's perfect'?"

Chess caught Natalie still watching him. He realized he'd winced at every Mom-phrase Finn or Emma quoted.

"I'm really sorry," Natalie repeated. "Sorry that you think you have to, to *dwell* on everything like this. And that . . ."

"We're going to find our mom!" Chess interrupted before she could finish. "It's going to work! It is! All right?"

And somehow, even though he hadn't meant to, this time he really did shout at her.

THIRTY-FOUR

FINN

Finn woke up in a different place than where he'd fallen asleep. Again.

It was his third morning at Ms. Morales and Natalie's house, and the past two nights, no matter how much he'd tried to stay awake and help the older kids solve the code, each night Emma had started going on and on about matching up letters, and, "No, no, *this* is how you test for whether that's the right phrase. . . ."

And the next thing Finn knew, he was waking up in the bedroom Ms. Morales had assigned him, rather than the office, where he'd fallen asleep. Probably Chess had carried him up to bed each night, and Chess was so tall and strong and nice that he probably hadn't even asked Emma or Natalie to help.

Finn stretched, his left hand clunking against the wall that he kept forgetting was there, because his bed back home sat in the middle of the room, not off in a little alcove like this one.

And this bed had a comforter covered in weird red flowers, which would be about the last comforter design in the world that Finn would have chosen. But he wasn't going to complain about that to anyone, not when there was so much else going wrong.

Like Mom being away. And not calling us. And . . .

Finn's eyes flooded, and he balled up his fists and pressed them against his eyelids until the tears went away. He wasn't used to having to stop his brain from thinking about whatever it wanted to think about. But over the past few days, he'd learned that he couldn't think about Mom during school or around Ms. Morales. He couldn't think about the kids in Arizona either. Why had the kids in that family vanished, when in Finn's family . . .

Finn scrambled up out of bed to distract himself, so he wouldn't have to dig his fists into his own eyes again. *Take off your pajamas, put on your clothes, don't think about how Mom always has you pick out a shirt the night before, and Ms. Morales didn't. . . . Don't think about how Chess, Emma, and I have been working on solving Mom's code for two nights straight, and we're still stuck. . . .*

Finn wasn't sure he buttoned and zipped everything properly, but he left his pajamas in a heap on the floor and raced out of the room like he was scared his own thoughts would chase him. He wanted to find Chess or Emma, but when he passed their rooms, he could see that his brother and sister were still motionless lumps in their beds.

Natalie, then . . .

Natalie had to get up earlier, because middle school started before elementary school.

Her room was totally empty, but he could hear someone walking down the stairs.

I'll sneak up on her and then jump out and surprise her, Finn told himself. *That's a normal thing for me to do.*

It was weird how he thought about his every action now, too. Before Mom went away, he'd just done whatever he wanted, mostly without thinking. But now he always had to ask himself, *Am I acting like myself?*

The alternative to acting normal was jumping up and down and screaming, *I want my mommy back! Mommy, come and get me! Now!*

He couldn't do that, because what if he did, and it *still* didn't bring Mom back?

Finn made himself concentrate on tiptoeing silently down the hallway, then down the stairs behind Natalie.

None of the stairs in the Morales house gave off a friendly little *squeeeak* like the stairs back home. So Natalie didn't hear him. She didn't turn around.

I could be a spy, Finn thought. *I'm good at this. Mom would be proud.*

That last part made him gulp hard, and not exactly silently. But Natalie didn't seem to notice because she was stepping into the kitchen, where a coffee maker gurgled, and Ms. Morales had a TV turned on low, some announcer talking about stocks or bonds—boring grown-up stuff.

"Did you sleep well?" Finn heard Ms. Morales say in a fake, hearty voice, and Natalie snapped back, "Does it matter? Would you let me go back to bed if I didn't?"

Finn decided he wasn't ready to talk to Natalie and Ms. Morales yet this morning. He'd keep being a spy.

He pressed his back against the wall separating the kitchen from the dining room, and stood still. On the other side of the wall, Ms. Morales sighed.

"I know you still love me," she told Natalie. "Someday when you get past being thirteen years old, and you're not so angry about the divorce, you're going to thank me for just smiling back at you when you're like this."

Natalie made a sound that was halfway between a snort and a harrumph.

"And . . ." Maybe Ms. Morales was leaning in closer toward her daughter, because Finn had a harder time hearing. "I do need your help, Natalie. I still don't know when Kate Greystone's coming back, and she's so vague in all her texts—when she even answers my texts. I'm starting to get worried. I told her to take as much time as she needed, but . . ."

"What do you want me to do about it?" Natalie snarled.

"You're not allergic to cats," Ms. Morales said. "You don't have to take Benadryl for days and *still* be all foggy-headed after being around a cat for five minutes. That means—"

"That maybe I got *something* good from Dad's side of the family?" Natalie asked.

Maybe Ms. Morales made a face at Natalie. Her voice got a little louder, but other than that, Ms. Morales kept talking as if Natalie hadn't said anything.

"That *means* that you can take care of the Greystones' cat for me this afternoon," Ms. Morales said. "If we're going to have those kids stay with us for more than just a few days—and it looks like we are—I don't think it's a good idea for them to keep going back to their house so often and getting upset all over again. I'll pick you up after school, you can take care of the cat, then we'll get the kids when their school day ends, and we'll tell them, I don't know, maybe that their mom wanted me to take them to—what's that place that's like Chuck E. Cheese's, except for older kids? Dave and Buster's? That should keep their minds off missing their mother for another night."

"Oh, so you want me to clean up cat poop and lie to a bunch of little kids," Natalie said. "Great, Mom. Thanks."

"It's only a white lie," Ms. Morales protested. "I'm sure Kate does want me to keep her kids happy while—"

"What about the tunnel under that house?" Natalie demanded. "Aren't you afraid I'll sneak through it again to meet boys? The ones I don't even know, but—"

"Natalie, I'm *trusting* you. I'm giving you another chance to act responsibly." Finn could practically hear the frown in Ms. Morales's voice. "Because I know you *are* capable of being trustworthy and responsible."

"Thanks for the vote of confidence." There was a thud that might have been Natalie slamming the refrigerator door.

"I do want you to stay out of that tunnel," Ms. Morales said, and her voice was hesitant now. Maybe even scared. "You're right—it does worry me. I tried to find out about the design of that house—I looked for building permits filed at the courthouse and everything. But there's nothing. It doesn't make sense. I think I'm missing something."

Finn held his breath. If he'd been Natalie, he would have spilled everything right there. He would have opened his mouth, and the whole story of the automatic text messages and the coded letter and the website butterflies and the secret lever in the panic room would have tumbled out, whether he wanted it to or not. Even now, even though Ms. Morales wasn't *his* mom, he was tempted to round the corner into the kitchen and tell all.

But Natalie was just yelling at her mom.

"Yeah, Mom, you're missing a *heart*, because of how you treated Dad. And me. You always treat me like you think I'm going to make the same mistakes you made and ruin my life like you did and . . ."

Natalie came dashing out of the kitchen and smashed directly into Finn.

And then Ms. Morales was there, too, right behind Natalie, bending down to take Finn by the shoulders and say in the fakest, heartiest voice of all, "Oh, Finn, we didn't hear you get up. Did you just come downstairs?"

Her eyes begged him to say yes, and Natalie's gaze was as intense as lasers. Finn was pretty sure Natalie was trying to say, *No matter what you heard, don't tell Mom anything! Lie if you have to!*

"I just got here," Finn mumbled obediently. Then,

because he thought anybody could have told he was lying, he added a normal-Finn line, "Is it breakfast time yet?"

"Almost!" Ms. Morales said, her voice flooded with fake cheer. "Just give me a few more minutes!"

"Hey, Finn," Natalie said too loudly. "Why don't you come outside and wait for the bus with me? Then when the bus comes, you can go back inside, and Mom will have your breakfast ready."

"Th-that's a good idea," Ms. Morales said, as if she was stunned that Natalie had suggested it.

"Okay," Finn said.

Natalie slid a yogurt container, a granola bar, and a water bottle into her backpack and hoisted it to her shoulder. Finn trailed after her, out the front door.

As soon as the door shut behind them, Natalie asked, "You heard everything, didn't you?"

"Yep."

Natalie reached down and unbuttoned and rebuttoned two buttons of Finn's shirt. Evidently he had done it wrong.

"Mom's not really that much of a monster," she said apologetically. "It's just, she's the one who asked for the divorce, and that just . . . just . . ."

"I don't think your mom's a monster," Finn said. "At least you *have* your mom."

Emma or Chess would have immediately hugged him and said, "We will, too! Soon! We're going to get our mom back!" Natalie just kind of froze.

And somehow, this morning, Finn liked that better.

"I didn't think you took the bus," he said as they started walking down the long, long sidewalk toward the street. "I thought your mom drove you."

"She does, except when we have other kids staying here," Natalie said. "Which . . . probably makes me selfish that I get mad about that."

"Sorry," Finn said.

Natalie laughed. "You could make it up to me by telling Mom you're craving carne asada. She also always serves really boring meals when we have kids here, and that bugs me, too."

"Is that food?" Finn asked. "I bet I would crave it, if I knew what it was! I like food!"

And then Natalie really did hug him. A little bit.

"I don't mind having *you* around," she said. Finn didn't know if she meant that about just him, or about Emma and Chess, too. He decided not to ask.

"Nothing happened after I fell asleep last night, did it?" he asked. Which was a stupid question, because he'd made Emma and Chess promise to wake him up the instant they solved the code. In the bright sunlight, with Natalie, it was possible to ask a little more. "Or . . . maybe . . . did someone find those kids in Arizona?"

Somehow it seemed like if the kids in Arizona were found, it would be a sign that he and Chess and Emma would get their mom back, too.

"No . . . ," Natalie said. She kicked at the mulch that lined the sidewalk. "But, Finn . . ."

"What?" Finn said. She wouldn't look at him. "You know something! Tell me!"

Natalie's face twisted and untwisted, like she was trying to decide.

"Okay," she said. "I haven't said anything to Emma or Chess, because they're all 'We've got to solve the code! That's all we can think about!' And they're already upset. You know I've been using earbuds, so none of you have to hear . . . what I'm working on."

Finn knew what she wasn't saying: *So you don't have to hear the voice that sounds like your mother's but isn't.*

"But I have been looking at everything I can about the kids in Arizona and their parents," Natalie went on. "And— did you see that the mother's name in Arizona is also Kate? Just like your mom's. For some reason, it wasn't in the original news coverage. But that woman in Arizona looks almost exactly like your mom *and* has the same first name."

"No," Finn said. His mind couldn't take that in. He

wasn't going to ask if that other mom had the same birthday, too, just like her kids had the same birthdays as Chess, Emma, and Finn. He couldn't. His voice turned accusing. "Are you sure you read it right? Or heard it right?"

He tried to think if he'd seen or heard the Arizona mother's name before, either on his mother's laptop that first day while she stood in their kitchen, or on the laptop he used in Ms. Morales's office two nights ago. He'd been too distracted both times.

"Finn, I'm sure," Natalie said. "And . . . I used facial recognition software that Mom has on her computer. Emma helped me get a photo from your mom's phone and I took a screenshot of the other woman. And that software thinks your mom and the Arizona mom are the same person exactly."

Finn absorbed that. Wouldn't facial recognition software think identical twins were the same person?

But why would identical twins both be named Kate?

He thought of a better question.

"Which one?" Finn asked. His voice cracked. "I mean, does the computer think my mom is Kate Gustano, or that the Arizona mom is . . . is Kate Greystone?"

He could barely even say his mother's name.

"I'm not sure," Natalie said, squinting at him thoughtfully. "That software doesn't give an identity by name, it just says they're the same person. But maybe if I can find a better program, like what police use, then . . ."

"My mom's not a criminal!" Finn protested.

"That's not what I'm saying." Natalie patted his shoulder. "I just . . . I have a theory. But you and your brother and sister aren't going to like it."

"Try me," Finn said. He puffed out his chest a little, hoping that made him seem older and better prepared for whatever Natalie was going to say.

"Well, sometimes grown-ups who say they're just traveling a lot for their jobs actually have . . . two different families, in two different places," Natalie said. "They lie. I mean, usually it's fathers who do this, not moms, and if the birthdays aren't lies, too, then either you or those kids in Arizona are adopted—and now that I'm saying this out loud, it sounds kind of crazy, but—"

"Natalie, my mom travels for her job maybe once or twice a year!" Finn exploded. "Just one or two days at a time! She's almost *always* with us, except . . ." He couldn't say it, but surely Natalie understood that he meant, *Except now.* "My mom doesn't have another family! She doesn't lie! She isn't a criminal! You can stop thinking about any theories that make her a bad person!"

"Okay," Natalie said softly.

And then she hugged him again, almost exactly like

Chess or Emma would. As soon as she let go, Finn turned around, to face away from the street. If the bus came now, he wouldn't want anyone on it to see how close he was to tears. But now he was facing the house. Something moved in the huge picture window in the front—it was Ms. Morales stepping off to the side, behind the drapes.

She'd been watching them. And it was funny: When Mom watched out their front window while Finn, Emma, and Chess were waiting for their bus, it always made him feel safe and secure. Loved. Protected.

Having Ms. Morales watch him and Natalie now—and dart behind the drapes so he didn't see her—just scared him more.

What was Ms. Morales afraid of?

What if it was something that even a grown-up couldn't protect him from?

THIRTY-FIVE

EMMA

"Ten thousand failures," Emma muttered.

"Huh?" Chess said, swiveling in his chair beside her. They were back in Ms. Morales's office for their third night in a row of trying to solve Mom's code with her own words. "You think we've already tried that many possibilities?"

"No, I'm trying to remember a Thomas Edison quote." Emma tapped her pencil against her jaw. "Something about how he didn't fail ten thousand times, he just found ten thousand ways that didn't work. Or took ten thousand steps to success, or something like that."

"Oh," Chess said.

He didn't look any more encouraged than Emma felt. Back *before*—that was how Emma had started thinking about everything in her life up to the last moment she'd seen her mother—Emma had loved reading and hearing and thinking about inventors and scientists and mathematicians who'd overcome all sorts of obstacles on their way to some brilliant new breakthrough. The obstacles made their stories even more exciting.

She'd never known how exhausting all that failure was.

How discouraging.

And, really, Edison had tried so hard just because he wanted to beat other inventors, and be more famous. It wasn't *his* mother's life on the line.

I don't know that my mother's life is on the line, either, Emma reminded herself. Even exhausted and discouraged and scared, she wasn't going to start treating something like a fact if she wasn't sure.

But this *felt* like a life-and-death issue.

Mom loves us so much, she wouldn't go off and leave us like this if it weren't incredibly, terribly important, Emma told herself.

If this wasn't life and death, it was really, really close.

That was why Emma had been working on her mother's code as close to around the clock as she could. She'd carried notebooks full of notations to school with her, and worked on the code every time the teacher looked away. She'd worked through recess and lunch.

"New project, Emma?" her math teacher, Mrs. Gunderson, had asked fondly as Emma walked to gym class scratching off letters and symbols in her notebook. "Is this going to be the one that wins the Nobel Prize?"

Emma liked Mrs. Gunderson—she liked anyone who liked math. But it was amazing how close Emma had come to breaking down into tears at that moment. She wanted to shout back at Mrs. G.: *This isn't some cutesy little-kid-pretending-to-be-a-mathematician project! This isn't the kind of thing I used to do! This is REAL!*

Would Mrs. G. have used that tone with Katherine Johnson at NASA when Katherine Johnson was calculating how to get John Glenn up into space and back down again without crashing?

Would Mrs. G. have smiled so patronizingly at the Enigma codebreakers during World War II who were trying to figure out how to stop Nazi subs from sinking Allied ships?

Even way back in the 1940s, those codebreakers had had early versions of computers to help them. Emma was pretty sure there was a way to set up a secret computer program to test various keys to Mom's code, but it seemed like it would take too long to figure that out.

Or to make completely sure it was private and secure. Mom always made a big deal about that.

"'Anytime you put something online, you have to ask yourself if you want the whole world to see it,'" Emma said aloud, quoting Mom. "That's another saying we should test."

"Are you sure it isn't, '*Whenever* you put something online . . .'?" Chess asked.

And that was the problem with Mom's sayings. They weren't *exact*. Sometimes Mom had said "Anytime," and sometimes she'd said "Whenever." That meant Emma needed to try both versions, writing out the complete phrase, and then listing, *a, b, c, d, e* . . . etc. above each letter.

And what if the key to the code was actually "Every time you put something online . . . "?

Maybe Emma was wrong about everything. Maybe Chess was, too, and they weren't even trying the right approach.

Emma's pencil snapped against her paper, sending the tip spinning into the air.

"Maybe you should take a break," Natalie said from across the room, where she had twin earbud cords snaking out of her hair down to her laptop. She also had Finn curled up beside her, with his head drooping against her arm—he'd fallen asleep an hour ago.

"No," Emma said stubbornly. "We have to solve this."

"Well then, at least take some time to look at the books I brought from your mom's office," Natalie tried again. "Maybe that will help."

"No, thanks," Chess said, and Emma was glad that he spoke for both of them. She would have left off the *thanks*.

It bugged Emma that Natalie had been at the Greystones' house without Chess, Emma, and Finn. Ms. Morales had had Natalie take care of Rocket because, Ms. Morales said, that gave them more time to have fun with their special Friday-night treat: a trip to Dave & Buster's.

Emma hadn't had fun at Dave & Buster's. Ms. Morales had insisted she leave her notebooks in the car, so Emma had been reduced to writing potential code keys on napkins and awards tickets, and stuffing them in her pocket.

Surprisingly, this had also proved that she was better at Skee-Ball when she didn't look while throwing the ball than when she did.

But all afternoon, anytime Ms. Morales was out of ear-shot, Natalie had made a big deal about how she'd smuggled out the two books from the Boring Room bookshelves: the dictionary and the old computer manual. It was like Natalie thought *she* had to be the one who provided a way to solve Mom's code.

"I thought they might be important," Natalie had said. "I looked up codes online, and there's one type where you can use a dictionary or some other book."

"Right—if the person who made the code gives you a page number and another number that tells you how far down on the page the key word is," Emma retorted, almost as if they were arguing. "Mom didn't leave us any numbers!"

Now Emma did at least reach across the desk and absent-mindedly rifle her finger across the pages of the dictionary. Just because it was Mom's. Then she moved her hand to trace the crooked-heart picture on the back of Mom's phone.

"What you should have brought us was the heart picture from inside Mom's desk," Emma told Natalie. "*That* might have been a clue."

"You said it was just a copy of the picture on Mom's phone," Chess reminded her. "Do you think the *original* picture is a clue? Finn drew it on Mom's phone case three years ago! How could it be a clue?"

"I don't know!" Emma snapped back at him. "Doesn't it feel like we don't know anything?"

Chess stared back at Emma. His eyes looked watery, as if he might be on the verge of crying.

Or maybe it was just that Emma was seeing him through watery eyes.

"We're all tired," Natalie said, in a surprisingly gentle tone. "I don't think we're going to figure out anything else tonight. Tomorrow's Saturday. Why don't we all just go to bed, and then tomorrow morning—"

"No!" Emma and Chess said together, both of them shouting at Natalie.

Natalie jerked her head back at the force of their words. That must have yanked her earbud cord out of her laptop, because suddenly Mom's voice surrounded them: "—I'm sure they're taking care of each other. Ever since they were born, I've told my kids, 'You'll always have each other.' I'm an only child myself, so—"

Natalie scrambled to plug the metal tip of her earbud cord back into its port, and the Mom voice went silent.

"Sorry!" she cried. "I'm so sorry! There's a new interview with the Gustano parents out tonight, and I was listening to that, and . . . I guess this destroys our theory about your mother and Mrs. Gustano being twins, right? I mean, if she was telling the truth about being an only child, and—"

"Play it again," Emma said.

"Emma, we don't have to torture ourselves," Chess said. "We can let Natalie—"

"Play it again!" Emma insisted.

Natalie fumbled with the laptop.

"I'm not sure I'm rewinding to the right place, but—"

Mom's voice sounded again: "—since they were born I've told my kids, 'You'll always have each other . . .'"

Emma flipped over Mom's phone and, fingers flying, punched in the code and opened the texting app.

"Mom told us the code key from the very beginning!" Emma cried. "We've had it all along!"

"What are you talking about?" Natalie asked.

Emma pointed at a clump of words on the screen of Mom's phone. Natalie was too far away to see, but Chess leaned in close, then away.

"Emma, it hurts to look at that text message, Mom saying she'll never see us again, ever," he began, choking on his own words. "Do you really think . . ."

Emma tapped the sentence that began *Tell them . . .* , and Chess went silent. Meanwhile, Emma was counting.

". . . twenty-four, twenty-five, TWENTY-SIX! It's perfect! With the apostrophe and the period, 'You'll always have each other" has exactly twenty-six characters, just like the alphabet, and that is something Mom says all the time, and if she'd only wanted to remind us of that, she would have said, 'Tell them *they'll* always have each other,' so this has to be it! It has to!"

"Try it," Chess said.

Dimly, Emma was aware that Natalie eased Finn's head onto the arm of the couch and left him behind to come over and watch Emma writing down letters. Dimly, Emma heard Natalie ask Chess as he stood up and leaned in to watch, too, "Do you think this will explain the Gustano kidnappings, too, or just your mother going away?"

Dimly, Emma heard Chess mutter, "Let's see if it works at all, first."

It will work, Emma told herself. *This time I know it!*

"You'll always have each other" wasn't a perfect code key, because some letters duplicated—there were four *a*'s, three *l*'s, and three *e*'s, and so that meant anytime Emma encountered one of those in the coded message, she had to write down a variety of choices, and then go back and figure out which was correct from the context. She decided to focus on just one sentence at a time.

"Yes!" she screamed. "It makes sense! It's real words!"

"Let us see!" Natalie demanded.

Emma kind of wanted to show only Chess first, but she was too excited to care. She slid her arm back, revealing the deciphered words in a sea of cross-outs and false starts.

Only then did the meaning of the sentence before her start to sink in:

How much do you know about alternate worlds?

THIRTY-SIX

CHESS

"Alternate . . . worlds?" Chess repeated numbly.

Natalie was typing on her phone.

"I got the definition," she said. "They're parallel universes. Places that could be almost completely identical to our world, or very, very different. And there's something about how they go along with theories of quantum mechanics, blah, blah, blah . . . an infinite variety of worlds existing alongside ours, but—"

"We know what alternate worlds are!" Emma exploded.

She was breathing hard, her eyes wild, her cheeks flushed, her hair held back only by a pencil she'd stuck behind her ear two hours ago and clearly forgotten about. She looked feverish, or maybe even delirious.

For himself, Chess only felt dizzy and confused. He knew what the word "alternate" meant. He knew what "worlds" were. Together, the two words were harder to grasp.

"Maybe if we . . . translate more of the code . . . ?" he began.

"Good idea," Natalie said.

Emma opened her mouth, shut it, and picked up her pencil again. She held one finger beside the computer screen, inching the fingernail forward to touch every letter.

"So that becomes a *w*, then an *e*, then . . . ," she muttered.

Chess knew he should offer to help his sister; maybe he should suggest they take turns with alternating words?

Oh, alternating. Alternate . . .

Chess felt dizzy again. His thoughts weren't making sense. He kept his mouth shut.

Emma dropped her pencil and held up the paper she'd been writing on.

"Mom's next sentence is 'We all came from an alternate world, and I had to go back,'" she announced. "Could that be right?"

She sounded like she doubted her own ability to read.

"'Two parallel universes might start with only one difference separating them,'" Natalie read from her phone. "'Some scientists theorize that a new universe might split off every time anyone makes a decision, creating a separate world for each possible choice. Then the differences multiply. Or they might be erased. So if you walk into an ice-cream shop, there might be one universe created where you pick chocolate ice cream, one where you choose vanilla, one where you choose strawberry. . . .'"

"Nobody ever chooses vanilla or strawberry!" Emma protested, as if that actually mattered.

Maybe not in this universe, Chess wanted to joke. He was seized by an awful desire to laugh. He wanted Emma to shout out, *Ha, ha! This was just a joke! Did you think I was serious? Mom's coded messages actually says . . .*

He couldn't think what he wanted Mom's coded message to say. He didn't even know what was possible.

Were alternate worlds possible?

"Why are we talking about ice cream?" Chess asked. "Mom did not leave us because of ice cream!"

"We don't know that!" Emma said, waving her hands helplessly at Chess. "Any little decision could change anything!" She blinked, dazed, as if struggling to go back to being her usual, logical self. "Like ice cream . . . This isn't about Mom, but here's how it could be a big deal. Say you pick vanilla instead of chocolate, and so the scooper guy has to go back to the walk-in freezer that much sooner to get a new tub of vanilla, and that's where he is when a robber comes in with a gun, and so he isn't shot and killed. . . . Or maybe it's the other way around, and he *doesn't* go back for the next tub of chocolate ice cream as quickly, and so he's still at the counter when a robber comes in, and that's why he dies . . . just because of ice cream! So now there are two different worlds created from that one little decision, one where the scooper guy is alive, and one where he's dead. And, I don't know, maybe he was supposed to become president someday, but because he's dead in the one world, that means —"

"Can we stop using examples where people die?" Chess asked quietly.

Natalie looked up from her phone. Her gaze felt too sharp, too focused.

"We already know the difference between this world and, um, the other one," she said, as if that was supposed to make everything better. But then she bit her lip. "Part of it, anyway."

Chess could only stare at her. Even Emma stopped raving about ice cream.

"It's your mom," Natalie said. "Your mom and that woman in Arizona."

Emma clenched the arms of her chair so tightly that it seemed like she might leave dents.

"Explain," she whispered.

"Well, I don't know if this is what split the worlds, or just a, a consequence," Natalie said. "But . . . what if your mom and that Arizona mom are different versions of the same person?"

Chess recoiled. Mom was not a "version" of anyone. She was fully herself, totally unique. She was *Mom*.

Chess waited for Emma to start shouting about that—he *wanted* her to start shouting at Natalie. But Emma just gulped and held on to the chair even tighter. Now the color seemed to have drained from her face.

"Your mom and that Arizona mom look almost exactly alike," Natalie said. "They sound alike. They use some of the same expressions—'You'll always have each other'? And . . . they're both named Kate."

Chess hadn't known that part, but at this point, he didn't even care.

"So maybe, before the worlds split, your mom and the other woman were totally, one hundred percent the same person," Natalie said. "But the worlds did split—somehow. I'm a little fuzzy on how that could have happened. Maybe it's like . . . I don't know. Copying a picture on your phone, and editing the two versions differently?"

"Maybe the worlds split before Mom or that other woman were even born," Emma interrupted. Her breathing was more ragged than ever. "So they were always separate.

Did you ever think of that? Our mom is not just a copy!"

Chess wanted to cheer Emma on. But he felt too paralyzed to speak.

"Okay, okay," Natalie said, her hands out as if she were backing away from a dangerous animal. "You're right. We don't know *when* the worlds split. Maybe that's in the rest of the letter. But we *do* know there are two worlds, and two Kates. And one world's Kate marries a man named Arthur Gustano in Arizona. And the other marries a man named . . . what was your dad's name?"

Neither Emma nor Chess told her it was Andrew. Natalie kept talking anyway.

"Each woman still ends up having kids named Rochester, Emma, and Finn, on the exact same dates," she added. "So . . . is that the only really big difference between the two worlds? Who your mom married? And then did that lead to all the other differences? What state they lived in, and . . . ?"

And the fact that those other kids got kidnapped, and we didn't, Chess thought. *That's different, too.*

He couldn't quite follow what Natalie was saying. But he couldn't forget about the kidnappings.

What if that was *why* Mom wanted them to be in this world, instead of wherever they'd started out?

How could she have known ahead of time that the kidnappings were coming?

Chess sat down, because he was afraid he might fall over instead.

"It isn't possible to travel between two different alternate worlds!" Emma shouted. "All of this is just . . . hypothetical! Alternate worlds are just hypothetical!"

"Maybe they figured it out in the other world?" Natalie said. "Maybe you three and your mother were the first to make this kind of trip?"

Emma pressed her hands over her ears, like she was trying to shut out Natalie's words.

"This is not what I expected," she muttered. "It doesn't . . . I can't . . ."

Emma's brain must have been spinning as badly as Chess's. His thoughts were completely out of control.

"You have to translate the rest," Natalie said.

She sounded calm. Or at least, calm*er*. Natalie mostly just seemed excited to have finally solved the mystery. It wasn't her mom who was missing, in a completely different world. So of course Natalie could act like this was just a matter of deciphering code.

Natalie seemed to notice that neither Emma nor Chess were reaching for a pencil.

"I'll do it," she said.

Chess and Emma both watched dazedly as Natalie tilted

the computer screen so she could see the coded message better.

"*A*'s and *e*'s and *l*'s are tricky, because they could be lots of different letters," Emma explained weakly, pointing to her own scribblings.

"Got it," Natalie said.

She snatched up a pencil. Chess blinked, then felt amazed that he was capable of that much movement.

"We said we'd wake up Finn as soon as we solved the code," Chess told Emma. "As soon as we had an answer."

"Do we really have an answer yet?" Emma asked. "Do *you* understand this well enough to explain it to Finn?"

No, Chess thought.

He made no move toward his little brother. He just sat there watching Natalie scrawl letters onto paper. Emma unfroze a little, starting to point out to Natalie, "If that *h* translates into a *t*, that makes that word 'this.' And that word's got to be 'old' . . ."

Chess couldn't have begun to translate any code right now. His brain still felt like an echo chamber: *Alternate worlds. Mom says we're from an alternate world. So Emma, Finn, Mom, and I don't belong here at all?*

It was true that he'd always felt different from the other kids at school. But he'd always thought that was because he was the only kid he knew whose father was dead. The only kid he knew who'd had to comfort his crying mother when he was only four, and sad himself.

The only kid he knew who'd had to become a father figure for his little brother and sister, when he was barely older than them himself.

Chess glanced over at Finn, draped across Ms. Morales's office couch and still soundly asleep. One arm dangled off the edge of the couch, and his mouth was open; that made it look like he was both reaching for and calling out to Chess.

"I think we still have to wake Finn," Chess said, finally answering Emma's question out loud.

He got up and stumbled toward the couch. He slid his arms under Finn's neck and knees and lifted.

"Finny?" he said softly, cradling his brother against his chest. "Finn? We've got good news. . . ."

He didn't actually know yet if it was good or not. It didn't feel that way.

"Mmm," Finn murmured, which could have been the start of saying *Mom . . .* or just a protest at being disturbed.

Chess carried Finn back to where Emma and Natalie were working. Finn snuggled his face against Chess's neck, as if he thought this was just a new place to sleep. His legs dangled awkwardly. Chess was tall for his age and Finn was small for his, but it still wasn't comfortable for a twelve-year-old to carry an eight-year-old.

"Finn?" Chess said. "You need to wake up and—"

"What? Did we mess up somewhere?" Natalie cried, stabbing her pencil against the paper. "None of this is making any sense now!"

"That would be an *a*, that would be a *b*—oh no!" Emma clutched her head, smashing her hair down. "You're right, Natalie. It looks like Mom changed the code for the next section! We can't read the rest! Not without figuring out another key!"

"But you got some of it?" Chess asked hopefully.

"This," Natalie said, handing him a page full of scratch-outs and crooked letters. Natalie's calligraphy-like printing mixed together with Emma's mad-scientist-style scrawl; even the pretty lettering got messier and messier, the farther he looked down the page.

Chess shifted the weight of Finn's drowsy body to the side and hesitantly began: "'I don't . . .'" He got stuck on the next word, because it had too many scratch-outs and erasures. Emma snatched the paper from his hand.

"Here, I'll read it," she said, her voice harsh. Chess didn't think she was really mad at him, though. "Mom wrote:

"'I don't know how old you are, reading this. I see you

as eight and ten and twelve, but maybe I made this code too hard, and you are older now. Maybe even much older. So it is hard to know how to explain.

"'The world the four of us came from was a dangerous place. Your father and I were part of a group trying to make it better by exposing the lies of the people in power. But powerful people like to stay in power, and the truly evil ones will do anything to keep control. Our leaders made it illegal to criticize them—or even to reveal the truth about what they were doing. We thought we could do our work in secret, and eventually the truth would win. But then they killed your father, and—'"

"Wait—what? 'Killed'?" Chess interrupted. His legs collapsed beneath him. Still clutching Finn, he almost missed the chair. "*Killed*? Dad's car wreck wasn't an accident? And Mom never told me?"

His ears rang; his vision seemed to go in and out.

"Chess, you were—what?—*four* when it happened?" Natalie asked gently.

Chess tightened his arms around Finn, who was still soundly asleep. He resisted the impulse to cover Finn's ears, so he wouldn't hear. And Finn was eight.

"But . . . now," he managed to say. "Now I'm twelve, and Mom—"

"And Mom is telling you now," Emma said. Her gaze was so steady.

So much like Mom's.

Weakly, Chess lifted his hand, motioning for Emma to continue.

She cleared her throat, and read on in a husky voice:

"'. . . killed your father, and I knew I had to leave. To save the three of you. But I couldn't just abandon everyone else I cared about, everything I knew, everything I could help with. So I made a bargain . . . a dangerous one. I kept up my work from here. But I thought the three of you would be safe. I didn't think anyone could follow me to this world.

"'But some of our enemies did. Just now.

"'I'd always known I should never attempt to find my doppelgänger here in this world. I tried very hard to make sure that our paths never crossed. That was part of the reason I worked so hard to keep my own name and face and identity out of any public records. If you looked up the records for our house, it wouldn't even say that I'm the one who owns it.'"

Chess looked over at Natalie, whose face flushed. Evidently she'd known that already. What else had she tried to look up about Mom, only to find . . . nothing?

Emma was still reading Mom's words:

"'I tried to keep you kids' identity private, too. That's why I always signed the forms saying your names or pictures couldn't be used on the school website; that was why I was always so careful about what I let you do online. I tried to keep all of us as invisible as possible. Just in case.

"'It never occurred to me that my secrecy would endanger my doppelgänger. But I covered my tracks too well. So when the bad people came, they found her and her family, not me. They thought she *was* me. After all, our fingerprints matched, other details matched—I'm sure they thought the details that didn't fit were just part of my attempts to hide. Those kids in Arizona were kidnapped because of me, because the bad people thought those kids were the three of you. The bad people must have thought that was the only way to lure me back.

"'I know it's a trap. But I can't leave those innocent kids in danger, because of me. I can't leave those other parents grieving. I think I know a way to rescue the kids without endangering myself. I have to try.

"'I've always kept a supply of food and money—all in small bills that wouldn't be traced—to share with people suffering back in the other world.'" Emma glanced up. "That's—"

"What we saw in the panic room," Natalie finished for her.

"Go on," Chess urged, because he couldn't care about canned food and dollar bills when he felt such dread rising inside him. The word "killed" still echoed in his ears.

And if that's what they did to Dad, then Mom . . . Mom . . .

Emma peered back to the paper in her hand. Chess noticed that her hand was shaking.

"Let's see, '. . . suffering . . . ,' oh, yes. 'Cash is important in that world, because so much is done in secret. I thought if I had a lot more money, I could hire some of the people I'd helped, to turn around and help me rescue the Gustano kids. I had to cash out your college savings—'"

"That's what Finn's friend saw her carrying out of that bank!" Natalie exclaimed. "Hear that, Finn? Your mom didn't rob a bank!"

Finn barely grunted in his sleep. Emma glared at Natalie.

"We already knew that," Emma practically snarled. "*We* never thought she was a robber."

Chess didn't care about banks or money, either.

"That's not the end, is it?" he asked. He had to steady himself by holding on to Ms. Morales's desk.

"She goes on to say, 'I'm really sorry about the college accounts. I'll figure out how to build them up again when I get back,'" Emma said. Her eyes flickered; she was reading ahead. "But, Chess—"

"She says she's coming back!" Chess blurted, and to his

own ears, he sounded as young as Finn. He fought to regain control. "That's all that matters."

"Oh, Chess," Emma said. Her face had gone mournful and still, like stone.

Chess waited, unable to speak. Finally Emma lowered her head and read in a choked voice:

"'If I've been gone long enough for you to get this letter and decode and read this, that means I was wrong, and I failed completely. I'm so sorry. You must never try to follow me, because . . .'" Emma gulped, and finished in a whisper.

"'Because it's too late.'"

THIRTY-SEVEN

FINN

Finn heard the word "never." He heard the words "too late." They slipped into a dream he'd been having about playing Trouble and Jenga and other games with Mom. Part of the time they were playing in their regular house, and part of the time they were playing in the abandoned house he'd found after going through the secret tunnel with Chess, Emma, and Natalie.

And then Finn was waking up, lifting his head from where it bobbed against Chess's shoulder.

Maybe Chess had jerked back suddenly, and that had jolted Finn awake.

"What's too late?" he mumbled sleepily.

He opened his eyes to see Chess, Emma, and Natalie staring back at him in alarm.

"Never mind," Chess said, pressing Finn's head back toward his own shoulder. "Don't worry about it. Shh, shh, shh . . . go back to sleep."

Being told to go to sleep always made Finn wider awake.

He kept his head up and shoved Chess's hand away. He saw Emma slide a piece of paper behind her back.

"What's that?" he asked. He started squirming his way out of Chess's grasp to reach for the paper. "Emma! Did you solve the code? And you were going to surprise me? That's great! You're a genius!"

"Finn, it's . . . complicated," Emma said. She kept the paper away from him.

"We're still trying to understand it ourselves," Chess said. "It may not be something you need to . . . know. Yet."

Was anything more annoying than big kids and adults telling little kids they weren't old enough to know something?

"But it's something about Mom, right?" Finn said. He told himself it was because he'd just awakened that he sounded so whiny and, well, little. Babyish.

"It's scary," Natalie said, as if that settled it. "You don't want to know. We'll take care of things. Emma, Chess, and me. We promise."

Finn slid down to stand on his own two feet. He leaned away from Chess, to gaze toward the laptop and the papers on the desk behind Emma and Natalie.

"What are al-ter-nate worlds?" he asked, because those were the words he could see.

Emma sagged back against the side of the desk.

"We have to tell him that much," she said. "It's not fair otherwise. Finn, they're places like our world, with a few differences. Or, there could be lots of differences, but they all start with one different decision, and . . ."

For such a smart person, Emma never explained things very well. Or maybe Finn's problem was that he'd been asleep a moment ago, and his brain wasn't fully awake yet. He blinked, still not entirely sure he was really with Chess, Emma, and Natalie in Natalie's mom's office, rather than with Mom at home. Or in the boarded-up, abandoned house from his dream.

That dream . . . I was in both our house and that other house in the dream, but it was almost like . . .

It was almost like the two houses had been the same. In the dream, Finn sat in the same places to push down the bubble over the Trouble dice; the rays of the sun hit at the same angle over Mom's shoulder as she pulled out the wooden Jenga blocks.

"Oh!" Finn shouted, so loudly that Chess winced. Chess had started to bend down, so Finn's mouth was right by Chess's ear. Finn tried to speak a little more softly, going on, but his voice still rose in excitement. "You mean like how our house is built just like the house we found when we walked through the tunnel, only we live in our house, so it's got furniture and everything, but nobody lives in that other house, so it's empty? Is that how you mean two places can be the same but different?"

"Finn, that other house was just—" Chess began, but Natalie interrupted.

"Guys—he's right! He's exactly right!" she said. "I just realized—I think that other house did have the same floor plan as yours, at least, what we saw of it. The windows were boarded up, but they were in the same locations, the basement stairs came out at the exact same spot on the first floor, the kitchen was in the same place—believe me, my mom has dragged me through enough empty houses she's trying to sell. I *know* houses. But . . ." She stopped looking so excited. "Lots of neighborhoods have cookie-cutter houses, because it's cheaper for builders to just use the same design over and over again. It doesn't mean anything."

"How many of those houses are connected by a secret

tunnel?" Emma challenged. "One that you reach by going into a panic room and flipping a switch and making it spin? Where you feel disoriented the whole time you're in the tunnel? This has to be *why* that tunnel didn't make sense, and we couldn't find that house on any online map. Finn, you just solved everything! When we went to that other house, we were in an alternate world! And we just have to go back to find Mom and rescue her!"

THIRTY-EIGHT

EMMA

Emma grabbed Finn by the shoulders and started jumping up and down, like kids on the playground whose team had just scored a goal or a touchdown or a home run.

"I did?" Finn said. "We do?"

He didn't even sound awake yet, but he joined her in jumping and dancing around. His hair flopped up and down, side to side—even his hair was dancing.

Emma reached out, ready to pull Chess and Natalie into the celebration, too. But Chess pulled back.

"Emma, Mom said *not* to find her. She says it's too late," Chess moaned. "We did all this work for nothing. Mom sent

us that letter for nothing. Or just so we didn't always wonder, I guess."

Emma stopped dancing. But only for a moment. Then
she started jumping again.

"We got the letter early, remember?" she asked.

Now all the other kids stared at her.

"Mom was sending us that letter in the *mail*," Emma
argued. "Maybe she even gave it to somebody and said, 'Don't
mail this until next week,' so it wouldn't get to us very fast.
She didn't know Finn and Rocket were going to find her
phone in the dresser drawer that very first day, which made
us search her computers right away. I bet she just left this
letter on her laptop as a backup, in case the letter got lost in
the mail. She knew we would search and search and search."

Especially me, Emma thought. *Mom knew I would never
give up.*

She glanced at the coded portion of the letter they hadn't
translated yet, the part that required finding a different key
to break the code. Had Mom made that code even harder?
Was that her way of making them wait until they were older
to know what it said?

Maybe that wouldn't ever matter. If—no, *when*—they
got Mom back, they could just ask her directly.

"We're smarter—and luckier—than Mom thought, so
we *can* go and rescue her," Emma told Chess.

Chess was still shaking his head.

"It's dangerous," he said. "Mom wants us to be safe. And we really don't know. . . . We don't know anything about the alternate world, if that was the alternate world, except that Mom says it's a dangerous place. And all we saw was that empty house and the tall fences and . . . and those boys Ms. Morales got so upset about. . . ."

"And the boys said there was a criminal who'd been trapped and captured because of some kidnapped kids!" Emma said. Everything was falling into place in her mind. "Just like Mom said the bad people from the alternate world used the kids from Arizona as a 'lure,' and she had to rescue them. Chess—that criminal who was captured in the alternate world—what if that's actually *Mom*? Not that she's really a criminal, but if they have bad laws . . . The people from the alternate world think the Gustano kids are hers. And . . ." Now the ideas in Emma's brain were working like a tidal wave, everything flowing together and growing by the minute. "And those boys told us the 'criminal' was going to be tried and sentenced on Saturday! We *know* she'll be safe until then. But after that . . ."

"Saturday's tomorrow," Finn said solemnly, as if he was the only one who could have figured that out.

Chess's expression was still so doubtful, it seemed he didn't even trust the days of the week.

"But we don't even know where or what time on Saturday," he argued. "Or—"

"But can't we find out?" Natalie asked. Emma whirled to look in the older girl's direction. Natalie had one eyebrow cocked, and the beginnings of a smile on her face. "Those boys said there were signs with information about the criminal on practically every street corner."

Emma reached out and hugged Natalie.

"You're right! You're right!" Emma said. "So we get your mom to take us back to our house and we go through the tunnel and we walk around to look for a sign. And that will tell us where to find Mom. It's simple!"

THIRTY-NINE

CHESS

It wasn't simple.

Chess fell asleep Friday night feeling like he had a weight pressing down on his heart, and he woke up Saturday morning feeling like the weight had done nothing but grow overnight.

Mom wants me to keep Emma and Finn safe, he thought.

But how could they *not* try to rescue Mom, if there was any chance that was possible?

Chess slipped out of bed and tiptoed into Emma's room. She was still sound asleep in the dim morning light—four late nights in a row had taken their toll. He thought he'd have to quietly rummage through her suitcase to find what he wanted, but one ray of sunlight came in through the blinds and showed him exactly what he was looking for: Emma had Mom's cell phone clutched in her hand, pressed against her cheek.

It looked like she'd fallen asleep trying to call for help.

Chess blinked, and another image slipped into his head: Emma at two or three, clutching her "lovey." Other little kids might have had a blanket or a stuffed animal as their lovey, but Emma had carried around a piece of paper like it was her favorite thing ever. And of course *her* favorite "lovey" paper had been covered in numbers.

Numbers written in Dad's firm script.

Chess froze, even as he held his hand out toward Emma. He hadn't thought about Emma's paper lovey in years. It didn't seem fair that he could remember that so well, when so many of his other memories felt so slippery. He shook his head, trying to clear it. Dad was dead, and Mom was in danger, and what was Chess supposed to do now?

Chess reached down and gently tugged Mom's cell phone out of Emma's grasp. Emma stretched out her fingers, still reaching for what she'd lost, and she let out a soft, distressed, "Unhf . . ."

But she didn't open her eyes.

I'll bring it back, Chess wanted to tell her. *Just give me a minute.*

Chess tiptoed back into his own room.

As soon as he was inside the doorway, he typed the unlock code into the phone. He'd watched Emma do it enough times now that he knew it, too.

"Okay, Joe," he whispered, as if he could talk to the unknown person he'd heard his mother argue with on the phone in the middle of the night, right before she went away. "It'd be really great if you tried to call back. Right. Now."

The phone stayed silent and dead in his hands. He opened Mom's call history, and it was just as empty as before. He checked her texts—avoiding the row of fake ones she'd set to send out automatically—and her email. Unless the message from the pediatrician's office about Finn's eight-year-old checkup had a hidden meaning, the phone contained nothing new, nothing helpful.

Why had Chess thought that it might, just because another eight hours had passed since the last time he'd looked?

"Think we should wake up Finn and Emma and start Operation Let's Trick Mom?" Natalie's voice from the hallway made Chess jump.

"Natalie . . . Maybe . . . Those two get grumpy when they don't get enough sleep," Chess said. And even though he'd been at Natalie's house for days now—and talking to her and everything—his voice this morning came out sounding like he was still that flustered fifth grader who didn't know what to say when a sixth-grade girl said he was cute.

Or maybe he just sounded like he wanted to believe the only thing his little brother and sister needed protection against was not getting enough sleep.

"Do you think . . . ?" he began to ask Natalie. But he couldn't even figure out how he wanted to finish his sentence.

"That your mom's going to call you on that phone and tell you everything's going to be okay?" Natalie finished for him. "From a totally other dimension—or alternate world, or whatever it's called? *No*."

Without even thinking about it, Chess tightened his grip on his mother's phone. The rigid edges cut into his hand.

"Maybe we should tell *your* mother what we found out," he said.

"About your mom being in an *alternate world*?" Natalie's voice cracked with incredulity. "She'd never believe us. She'd ground me for lying and, I don't know, have the three of you committed to a mental institution. She didn't even believe me when I told her I didn't know those boys on the other street Wednesday afternoon. When they literally weren't even from the same *universe* as me. We didn't talk about this last night, but don't you think those boys acted like they knew the Natalie Mayhew from their world? Do you think the other Natalie Mayhew is just like me or not? Am *I* one of the differences in that world?"

It kind of freaked Chess out to hear her talking about the alternate world like it was a fact. And—like it was something fun to speculate about.

"You—You're older than us," Chess stammered. "You've got to see. . . . This isn't just a game."

"No, it's about getting your mom back," Natalie said, her voice ringing with certainty. "And maybe those kidnapped kids, too. I *hope* we can rescue those kidnapped kids, too. This'll probably be the most important thing any of us do in our entire lives. We'll be heroes!"

Her eyes glowed, and her face was flushed with excitement. Maybe it wasn't a game to her, but it wasn't something she was afraid of, either.

Maybe that was because she wasn't a coward like Chess.

Or is it just because her parents are only divorced, not dead and in danger like mine? Chess wondered.

He let out a sigh that did nothing to relieve the pressure he felt on his lungs and heart.

"You wake up Finn," he said. "I'll get Emma."

"Operation Let's Trick Mom, here we come!" Natalie drummed her fingers against the wall, ending with a dramatic thump. "Mom doesn't have a clue what's about to happen."

"Neither do we," Chess whispered.

But Natalie was already gone, racing for Finn's room.

FORTY

FINN

Maybe I should be an actor when I grow up, Finn thought as he buckled his seat belt in Ms. Morales's SUV. *I am really good at this.*

Over breakfast, he'd made himself start thinking about how much he missed his mom. And then, even though Ms. Morales had gone out special that morning and gotten the exact kind of bagels and cream cheese Finn loved best, big globs of tears had started to form in his eyes. Then his lips began to quiver, and he'd pushed his plate away, claiming, "I'm not hungry." (When, duh, anyone who knew Finn would know that he was always hungry. Especially when he was really happy, because this was the day they were getting Mom back!)

And then Ms. Morales had started fussing over him—"Oh, do you want me to fix you eggs instead? Or something else?" And Finn had let loose with a loud wail: "I just want my mommy!"

He'd started listing all the things he missed about her, finally getting down to the smell of her clothes. And even though Chess missed his cue to say, "Yeah, sometimes when Mom's away, the only thing that makes Finn feel better is sitting in her closet, breathing in that smell," Natalie picked up on it, and pretended that she'd noticed Finn getting calmer in Mom's closet, and wasn't it better to try that than to have to listen to a hysterical eight-year-old over breakfast?

Maybe Finn and Natalie would be famous actors together someday.

After they got Mom back.

So now Ms. Morales was driving all four of the kids back to the Greystones' house. And even though Natalie was pretending to argue with her mom about going along ("Don't you know I have homework to do before I go over to Dad's this afternoon? Don't you know I have a life of my own, even if you keep trying to ruin it all the time?"), every time her mother looked away, Natalie kept turning around and winking and waggling her eyebrows at Finn, Emma, and Chess.

Finn sniffled and reached for Emma's hand, just in case Ms. Morales looked in her rearview mirror. Chess put his arm around Finn's shoulder. And maybe Chess was kind of good at acting himself, because the one-armed hug felt exactly like it did when Chess was really trying to comfort Finn.

Soon they were pulling up in front of the Greystone house. Ms. Morales turned to face Finn.

"You can sit in your Mom's closet for a little while," she said. "While Chess gets the poster board he needs for his science project and Emma gets the next book she wants in that series she's reading. Harry Potter, wasn't it?" These were excuses Chess and Emma had added for needing to go along to the house with Finn. Ms. Morales kind of had an odd gleam in her eye—maybe they'd piled it on a little thick? Was she getting suspicious?

Finn gulped in air, ready to distract her.

"I miss—"

"Yes, yes, we know," Ms. Morales said quickly. "You didn't let me finish. What I was going to say was, when you come back out, why don't you bring some shirt with you that smells especially like your mom? So you don't have to come back here the next time you want to, uh, sniff it?"

Like Natalie made me bring that teddy bear to act like it was my "lovey," that first day? Finn thought. *Ms. Morales is going to think I'm a total baby!*

Finn could live with that, if it got Mom back.

"O—kay," he said, making sure he paused in the middle of the word to sniffle again. And then he drew out the *aaay* part as if he was leading into more tears.

Chess, Emma, and Natalie all helped him out of the SUV, making it look like it took three of them just to make sure he could walk upright.

They got to the front door, and Finn was *really* happy about being just a few steps away from no longer having to walk all stooped-over and sad. As soon as they were in the house, he could run just as fast and excitedly down to the basement as he wanted. But then, just as Chess started pulling out his key, Natalie took an abrupt step back, almost falling off the front porch.

"Oh no," she said. "Ohhh no."

"What's wrong?" Finn asked. He glanced over his shoulder. "Your mom's staring at her phone right now. You don't have to keep acting mad."

Natalie didn't exactly look mad anymore. She stared at the doorframe looking more like she'd just seen a ghost. Was she still acting or not?

She brushed a finger against the crack between the door and its frame.

"It was right here . . . ," she murmured. "I'm sure of it."

"What are you talking about?" Chess asked.

Natalie teetered on the edge of the porch.

"Somebody's been here," she said. "Since yesterday. Somebody's been in your house."

FORTY-ONE

EMMA

"Explain," Emma said. "How do you know that?"

She was not going to freak out about anything until she had all the facts. And then . . .

Well, get all the facts, and then see what you want to do.

"I left a piece of tape on the door," Natalie said. "I got the idea from what the chaperones did on our Cedar Point trip the last day of sixth grade—they put tape over everyone's hotel room door, so they'd know if anyone tried to sneak out. Or, at least, they *told* us that's what they did."

Emma almost got distracted thinking about how weird life must be in sixth grade. Almost.

"You tried to tape someone *in* our house?" Finn asked. "You thought a piece of Scotch tape would trap them there?"

"No," Natalie said. "I put the tape there after I came out, when I knew the house was empty. Just so I could see if someone came in or out while we were away. Like . . . if someone came back through the tunnel and out your front door."

Now that they knew the tunnel led to an alternate world, that idea was scarier than ever.

"Was it windy last night?" Emma asked. "Or stormy? Maybe the tape just blew away."

She hadn't been paying attention to the weather; all she'd been able to think about last night was Mom's code and the alternate world. She was so focused, she wasn't even sure what the weather was like *now*. (She glanced over her shoulder. The sun was out.)

Finn, Chess, and Natalie all made doubtful faces, as if none of them had been paying attention to the weather either.

"So there," Emma said. "Not seeing the tape—that doesn't prove someone was here. If the tape had still been there, still stuck to the door, that could have proved that no one opened the front door after you. But the proof doesn't work in both directions."

"I . . . guess," Natalie said, as if the words were being dragged out of her.

Chess opened the door, and they all stepped through. But Emma didn't race down to the basement the way she'd been planning. She stepped cautiously, looking around constantly. Would she notice anything amiss if someone had been there searching the house? The middle drawer of the coffee table stuck out just a little—maybe an eighth of an inch—but for all Emma knew, maybe it had been like that before.

"I, um, put tape over the door in the basement, too," Natalie said. "The one that leads to your Mom's office. What you all call the Boring Room."

"Well, let's go look at *that*," Finn said, with only a little of his usual bounce.

It took a lot out of him, pretending to cry for the past half hour, Emma told herself. *That's the only thing that's wrong.*

All four of them trooped down the stairs. Chess reached over and turned on the basement light.

"Meowr?"

It was only Rocket standing and stretching on the basement couch, but Emma jumped. She was pretty sure the others did, too.

Finn recovered first.

"You'd tell us if anybody sneaked into the house, right, Rocket?" Finn asked, bending down to pet the cat. "You're a good guard cat, aren't you, boy?"

Natalie walked toward the Boring Room door.

"None of us locked that door after we came back from the alternate world, did we?" Emma asked. She'd been too spooked to think about it herself. And besides, she hadn't wanted Ms. Morales to know about the key and its secret hiding place in the couch leg.

Nobody answered Emma. Nobody said anything as they watched Natalie run her hand across the top of the frame around the door leading to the Boring Room.

"This tape's gone, too," she said.

"There's no wind in the basement," Finn said, unnecessarily.

"But maybe it just fell," Emma argued. "Maybe it didn't stick very well, and then Rocket started playing with it—you know how he's always carrying ponytail rubber bands away when Mom or I drop them on the floor?"

"It was good tape," Natalie said. "I stuck it on there *hard*. And now it's completely gone. Like someone saw it and took it. *Not* your cat."

Emma still wanted to argue: *But this isn't* absolute *proof, is it? You can't be one hundred percent sure! There's a—what's it called?—margin of error, right?*

"We have to tell your mom," Chess said heavily, turning to Natalie. He sounded like an old man, maybe someone speaking with his dying breath.

Natalie lifted her chin defiantly, mimicking the same kind of head toss she constantly gave her mom.

"She wouldn't let us back into the house then," she said. "Not until the cops have examined every inch of the house. You think cops are going to believe anything we tell them about an alternate world?"

"What if the cops keep us out of the house for hours and then we really are too late going to rescue Mom?" Finn asked, in the same sorrowful, little-kid voice he'd been using all morning with Ms. Morales. Only this time, it was entirely real.

"Here's what we do," Emma said, surprised she could find her own voice. "We go into the alternate world, we find a sign on the nearest street corner that gives the information about Mom, and *then* we bring it back and show it to Ms. Morales. And tell her everything."

She saw Chess hesitate. And then she saw his shoulders slump—not as if she'd won the argument, but as if they'd both lost.

"Okay," he said. "We'll do that."

Natalie opened the door to the Boring Room, and they repeated the procedure from their last trip through the tunnel. Chess pressed the button hidden at the back of the bookcase— just with his finger this time, not his shoe. The doorway to the panic room/secret passageway/tunnel to the alternate world opened up, and Emma reached in to turn on the light.

"Should we leave the door open or shut?" Natalie asked.

No one answered. But no one pulled the door shut behind them, either.

"The lever was above the peanut butter shelf, right?" Finn asked.

It was like they were all trying to be brave, all trying to prove that they weren't worried about what was going to happen next.

"We should pay attention to everything," Emma suggested. "Count the number of times the panic room spins, or how many turns the tunnel takes, if it's nothing but a tunnel now, not a place that spins like it was the first time we went through here, and—"

And the room was already spinning. Emma had to grab a shelf to hold on once again, but this time she made sure she was facing the exact spot where the door back out to the Boring Room had been.

Watch for the door, she told herself. *Count how many times it passes.*

The spinning made her eyelids want to close, but Emma reached up with her free hand and held her right eye open.

Surely we've made a complete rotation—why haven't I seen the door yet?

A moment later, she thought, *Did we maybe pass it, and I forgot to count? So let's just say it's been one, uh . . .*

Emma couldn't quite remember what number came after one.

The room spun faster.

Are we going forward? Sideways? Backward?

Emma thought those words, and then wasn't entirely sure what they meant.

And then the spinning stopped, and Emma was facing a door once more. They'd left the door back into the Boring Room wide open, with the lights on bright. And this door was open just a crack and barely lit. Did that prove anything?

Emma sensed rather than fully saw the others starting to unfreeze and let go of the shelves they'd been holding on to.

So there are *shelves at this end of the tunnel now?* Emma wondered. *Even though they weren't here when we came back going the other direction with Ms. Morales? And* she *never felt the room or the tunnel spin at all, in either direction. . . .*

Emma wanted so badly to figure out how the tunnel worked. Maybe the spinning *opened* the tunnel, and then the section of the room with shelves snapped back to being part of the Greystones' house again? And maybe the tunnel stayed open if . . .

"Everybody okay?" Chess asked, in such a grim voice

that Emma could tell he was thinking, *Mom isn't. She's in danger.*

Emma forgot about figuring out the tunnel and took a wobbly step toward the door.

"It *smells* as bad as before," Finn said, wrinkling up his nose. "Maybe worse."

"Burning rubber?" Natalie said, sniffing the air. "Dead mice? Formaldehyde?"

"Everything horrible, all at once," Chess said, as if he were ending the discussion. "Let's get this over with."

He went through the door first, stepping out into darkness. After he switched on the light, the others followed, and Natalie started to shut the door behind them.

"No!" Emma exclaimed. "Last time Chess put a can in the doorway to prop it open. We have to do everything the same!"

The others watched her grab a can of peaches from a shelf and wedge it into the doorway. Nobody said anything.

Do I feel so terrible now just because I'm worried about Mom and I don't really understand the alternate world? Emma asked herself. *Or is there something about this place that really messes with your mind?*

Maybe it was just the trip through the spinning room that had thrown her off. If that really had been a journey between alternate dimensions, no wonder she felt disoriented.

Emma rubbed her forehead and shoved her hair back from her face.

One, she told herself. *Two, three, four, five, six, seven . . .*

At least she could remember how to count now.

I should have stayed up all night and figured out how to translate the rest of Mom's code, she told herself. *That probably explains everything we want to know.*

All they had to do was grab a poster and go back to Ms. Morales. Maybe if Ms. Morales decided to call the cops, there'd be cops who could help with the code. Maybe they'd figure it out in a matter of minutes. Emma was only a little girl—why had she thought she could do anything?

Stop that! she told herself. *What's wrong with you?*

She grabbed Finn's hand, then Chess's.

"Come on!" she said.

She saw Natalie put her hand on Finn's shoulder.

All four of them walked through the empty basement and up the stairs in a clump, almost like a single creature—an amoeba, maybe. The first floor of the house was still empty, the windows still boarded up.

"It is like our house," Finn whispered, peering around, his eyes wide. "Our house without us, and without Mom and without Rocket, and really, really sad. . . ."

They burst out of the house, and Emma wanted to gulp in fresh air. But the air outside smelled just as bad, only bad in a different way.

More like burning rubber, less like rotting dead mice? she thought.

Still, it was a smell that beckoned Emma forward, as if a smell could whisper, *Come see. You have to find the source, to destroy it. So you don't have to live with this forever. You have to look now. . . .*

"We should prop this door open, too," Chess said firmly, and Emma saw that he'd carried a can of corn up from the basement.

"Good thinking," Natalie said.

Were her teeth chattering? Was Natalie that scared?

"Check your phone," Emma suggested.

Natalie barely glanced at the screen.

"No signal," she whispered.

Chess left the can in the door, and they all inched forward: off the porch, down the driveway. . . .

"Do you feel like . . . like we're going through patches of fog?" Emma asked. "Only it's patches of feelings? Hope, fear, hope, fear . . . And it goes along with how strong the smell is?"

"Yes!" Natalie said.

"I thought I was the only one feeling that!" Finn said. "I

thought I was going crazy!"

"Shh," Chess said. He pointed. They'd reached the end of the driveway and the edge of the tall, faded, multicolor fence. And out in the street, people were walking by in clumps.

"Is that . . . Mrs. Childers?" Emma whispered. The white-haired woman, who'd been their friendly, chatty next-door neighbor for as long as Emma could remember, walked by without even looking at them. Though maybe it wasn't her after all—her face seemed to have extra lines and wrinkles, as if she'd started frowning and squinting all the time. She was a lot thinner, too. And she was wearing a shirt that was bright orange and navy blue, the same colors as the jackets of the teenaged boys they'd seen before.

Did the high school change its school colors, and nobody told me? Emma wondered.

The Mrs. Childers they knew wouldn't have bothered dressing in a sports team's colors any more than Emma would.

How different could people be in this world?

"I don't think anybody is going to know us here," Chess whispered back. "If anybody remembers us, it would be from when we were really little kids, and we didn't look the same. . . ."

"Except for Natalie," Finn chimed in.

Natalie flipped the hood of her sweatshirt over her head,

hiding her hair and the top part of her face.

"Maybe we should get away from standing in front of this house," Natalie said. "Just in case."

Without even discussing a direction, they all turned and started following Mrs. Childers and the other clusters of people. None of the people around them were talking. Many of them were wearing the same shades of orange and blue as Mrs. Childers, but their grim expressions made it seem more like they were headed to a funeral than to a sporting event.

Is there anyone in the crowd who doesn't *look afraid?* Emma wondered. Even the littlest children—also mostly dressed in orange or blue—cowered against their parents' shoulders. One toddler actually seemed to be trembling with fear. *No, wait, now everybody looks angry. And . . . now it's back to fear again. . . .*

Was it possible for lots of people to have their feelings controlled all at once? Maybe by a smell?

But who's doing it? Emma wondered. *And why?*

"There's a sign on that pole, up on the corner," Chess murmured. "But I can't see. . . ." He took two long strides forward, breaking off from the others.

Emma stretched out her legs to catch up with him. Beside her, Finn and Natalie did the same. Finn was almost running.

"It's—" Finn began, and Emma clapped her hand over

his mouth so he couldn't give them away.

It was Mom's face on the sign.

Good, Emma told herself. *That's what we wanted. Now grab the sign and run back to the house, back through the tunnel or the spinning room, whatever takes us back to Ms. Morales. . . . That's all you have to do!*

But it was so terrible to see her beloved mother's face under the dark, nasty words "CRIMINAL CAUGHT!" It was indisputably Mom—and her name, "Kate Greystone," appeared directly below, along with the words "Enemy of the People." But this was a picture of her mother Emma had never seen before. Maybe it had just been taken, after she was captured—or maybe it was altered. Everything strong about Mom's face looked defiant and ugly. Everything hopeful looked mocking.

She still looked like Mom, but she also looked like a criminal. Or an enemy.

Emma dropped her gaze, forcing herself to read the rest of the sign:

PUBLIC TRIAL AND SENTENCING
ALL MUST ATTEND
SATURDAY, MAY 9
10 A.M.
PUBLIC HALL

Emma's eyes darted back to the time: 10 a.m.

"Natalie!" she whispered. "Check your phone! What time is it?"

Natalie didn't move fast enough. Emma reached over and yanked the phone out of Natalie's sweatshirt pocket. She hit the button to light up the screen.

The clock numerals glowed in white: 9:45.

"We don't have time to go back to Ms. Morales!" Emma gasped. "We have to go rescue Mom *now*!"

FORTY-TWO

CHESS

"Cover for me," Chess said, reaching for the sign on the pole. "Don't let anyone see."

Emma grabbed his arm.

"Didn't you hear me?" she demanded. "There isn't time for that plan! That sign doesn't matter now!"

Even with Emma tugging on him, Chess kept moving his arm forward.

"Here's what we do," he said. His voice came out sounding deceptively calm and steady. "You and Finn take this sign back to Ms. Morales. Tell her everything. Natalie and I will go rescue Mom."

The plan seemed so clear and perfect in his brain. Finn and Emma would be safe this way. They'd be with grown-ups. Maybe even cops. But as Chess yanked on the paper sign, he also turned to glance at Emma.

And she couldn't have looked more betrayed and hurt if Chess had balled up his fist and smashed it into her face, full force.

"You don't think we can help," she whispered.

"You'd still be helping," Chess said. He held out the sign to her. "Just in a different way. By getting Ms. Morales to help."

"No," Finn said. He crossed his arms over his chest.

"Right," Emma said, mimicking his stance. "I say no, too. You can't make us go back, Chess."

Had they been taking lessons all week from how Natalie treated her mother?

"Don't you understand?" he began.

What was he going to tell them? *Dad died in this horrible place. He was* murdered. *Do you want that to happen to us? We're just a bunch of kids; what can we do to rescue Mom? Don't you see how even Natalie is terrified, too? Did you see how she had her phone primed to call 911 the whole time we were walking through our own house, in case someone was still there, and jumped out at us? And now there's no way to call 911? And maybe the police here are the bad guys, if they arrested Mom?*

"We understand that we have to rescue Mom," Emma said. "Don't you wish you could have done something to rescue Dad before he died?"

She understood enough. She'd found the one thing to say that would change Chess's mind.

"I—" Chess began. He looked down at the poster in his hand. It didn't seem real. There wasn't enough time. Why hadn't they figured out a way to come last night, as soon as they knew about the alternate world?

Because we didn't want to believe any of this was real . . .

To the others, he settled for saying, "We don't even know where this 'Public Hall' is!"

"I think we can just follow everyone else," Natalie said. "'All Must Attend.'"

She was reading from the sign.

Chess stuffed it into the pocket of his windbreaker—his dark green windbreaker, which looked out of place in the midst of so many people wearing navy blue and orange. At least Natalie's sweatshirt was black, which sort of blended in. But Emma's T-shirt was maroon, and Finn's was a bright yellow. They might as well be wearing signs that spelled it out: "We don't belong here."

Or maybe, "Arrest us, too."

"Fine," he told Natalie, biting off the word in a way that made her wince. He tried to soften his voice, but it came out more like a bark. "Let's walk fast."

He couldn't understand what Emma had meant about going through the patches of feeling—fear, hope, fear, hope, fear. . . . For him, as they moved forward in a group—trying not to be too conspicuous about passing other groups ahead of them—he felt more like he was on a constant downward slide into despair.

We don't even have a plan, he thought. *We can't have a plan because we don't know where Mom is being held or how many guards are around her. We don't know anything about this public hall or how a trial and sentencing works here. And maybe I don't understand anything about alternate worlds. I thought there were supposed to be similarities beyond the design of one house and people with the same names being in both worlds. Nothing looks familiar around us— nothing!*

This last part, Chess realized, wasn't entirely true. The houses they passed were all fenced off or hidden behind towering hedges, so he could barely see any of them. But when they turned a corner, he saw a small pond off to the right. It was the same size and shape as the retaining pond in his own neighborhood. But the pond back home had lilac and forsythia behind it, with picnic tables, a small playground, and a winding bike path off to the side.

This pond looked muddy and dark, surrounded by nothing but sparse blades of dying grass. Any picnic tables or playground equipment that might have once stood nearby had been swallowed up in dense, thorny-looking bushes and trees.

Why is it different? Chess wondered. *What happened here?*

Had Mom seen all this when she sneaked back to this world to try to rescue the three other kids named Rochester, Emma, and Finn? Had she understood what the alternate world was like? Had it been this bad back when Chess's family had lived here?

Chess remembered that the boys who'd recognized Natalie had said "the criminal" was captured by SWAT teams right on the same street as the abandoned house. No matter how much Mom knew or understood, her plan had failed before she even got off the first block.

So what hope is there for us kids? he wondered.

He kept walking forward anyhow.

After they'd gone six or eight blocks, the scenery changed even more: The street opened out into a wide boulevard with imposing buildings on either side. Maybe as the neighborhood Chess knew was falling apart, this part of the town had turned fancy, more like a big city. These buildings were steel and glass and hard to tell apart; they all held enormous banners that swept from their lowest to highest windows. The banners were orange and blue, and maybe they were just for some holiday that existed in the alternate world but not in the world Chess knew. Maybe they were supposed to be festive, like the decorations people put out for July Fourth, Halloween, or Christmas. But these banners were too stiff and formal to seem cheery. They made Chess think more of military flags, as if some invading army had taken over and wanted everyone to know.

Chess wanted so badly to get away from this strange, unfamiliar street. But so many people surrounded them now that he and the others could no longer dart ahead as a pack, slipping beyond the rest of the crowd. He felt Emma slide her hand into his; when he glanced over his shoulder, he saw that she was also holding on to Finn's hand, and Finn was holding on to Natalie's.

"You lead," Emma whispered, and Chess nodded. They had to thread their way through the crowd single file now, and holding on to one another was the only way to keep from being separated.

If we get out of here alive, I'll have to thank Natalie for being at the end, and making sure Finn doesn't get pulled away and swallowed up by the crowd, Chess thought.

Maybe it counted as hopeful that he could even think *If we get out of here alive. . . .*

Soon the crowd grew so thick that Chess could no longer see where they were going. If he craned his neck, he could squint up at the murky sky. Otherwise, he couldn't see past the steel-and-glass buildings with their blue-and-orange banners, or the blue-and-orange clothes of most of the people around him. So he was surprised when he slid his foot forward and clunked it against a marble step. Then there was another one.

"Stairs!" he called back to Emma, Finn, and Natalie. "Be careful going up the stairs!"

Others beside him were talking now, too. An excited buzz rose all around him.

"—heard she wanted to kill us all—"

"—see her get what she deserves—"

"—people like that should be punished as severely as—"

Chess felt sick to his stomach. Were they talking about Mom? His mother, who wouldn't even kill a spider in the house? He wanted to put his hands over Emma's and Finn's ears, so at least they didn't have to hear. But he could only keep trudging forward and up the stairs, partly carried along by the crowd, partly pulling the others along.

The stairs ended in a long, flat surface, and then the crowd bottlenecked through a pair of narrow doorways. The doors and doorframes were marble, too, and ornately carved. As they squeezed through, Chess's face pressed painfully against the stone head of a creature that might have been a demon or just a man caught in the worst agony of his life. But on the other side of the doorway, suddenly there was space. Chess saw a giant pit-like auditorium filling before him.

Okay, we've come this far. Now just find Mom. . . .

After coming in from outside, he would have expected to need time for his eyes to adjust to the dim interior of the Public Hall, or whatever this huge, ornate building actually was. But he had the opposite problem: The glare at the front of the vast, open room was almost too intense to look at. Blinking and squinting helped him realize: The searing light came from a giant screen at the front of the room. It was probably the equivalent of two or three stories high, and maybe the width of a city block.

A dark shadow blocked the middle of the screen—was it a chair? With someone in it?

Suddenly the glow of the screen changed. Now there was a spotlight on the chair, and the overpoweringly bright blankness of the screen was replaced with a magnified image of the stage before it. The camera angle zoomed in and panned from the floor up, showing the bolts holding the chair in place, then blue-jeans-covered legs shackled to the rungs of the chair, then two wrists held together by handcuffs.

It was all wrong: the bolts, the shackles, the handcuffs, even the solitary placement of the chair. Those were all things for criminals, for prisoners, for people who couldn't be trusted.

It was all wrong, because Mom was the one sitting in that chair. Chess knew long before the camera reached her face. Maybe he'd even known when the chair was just a dark shadow, a dark blot in the overwhelming glow.

In spite of everything, Chess felt almost proud that Mom could sit so calmly—imposingly, even—in that cage of a chair. She kept her shoulders back, her head high, her expression firm and clear. This was her "Nobody can hurt me" pose. Chess had seen her look exactly like that in the days and weeks and months after Dad died, every time she left the house.

But he knew better than anyone that it had only been an act eight years ago. And surely it was only an act now.

The resolution on the screen was so precise that he saw Mom's chin tremble, ever so slightly. She only lost control for an instant, but it was enough to make the crowd jeer and cry out, "Coward!" "Traitor!" "Destroy her!"

Nobody silenced them. Nobody said, "She's innocent until proven guilty, remember?"

Chess sniffed, the foul smell of the alternate world filling his nostrils once again. He could feel the anger of the crowd growing around him like something physical—a beast devouring everyone. He felt a surge of anger himself. What could Mom say or do to defend herself against that mob? What could anyone do to help her?

The full meaning of the glowing screen and the chair on the stage finally sank in.

"We're already too late!" he turned to hiss at Emma. "If we try to rescue Mom now, every single person in this room will see us!"

FORTY-THREE

FINN

The big kids have a plan, Finn told himself. *The big kids have a plan. They know what they're doing. We're getting Mom back.*

Those words kept him moving forward, even as the crowd pressed in around him, constantly threatening the grip he had on Emma's hand in front of him and Natalie's hand behind him. He almost broke the link when Emma stepped through the doorway with all the terrifying carvings, and someone smashed Finn's hand against the stone head of some evil beast—a wolf, maybe? But then Natalie shoved him from behind and aimed her elbow right into some man's belly to make a space for both of them.

They were inside the building now, and Finn had never felt so small before in his life. The pillars that lined the walls around them soared high over his head, with more carved marble creatures staring down at him from the heights. The statues threw horrible distorted shadows onto the ceiling, because all the light in the room came from the front.

And then the floor before him sloped downward, and he could see the source of the light:

It was Mom.

Well, that wasn't exactly right. It was the *image* of Mom. She herself hadn't grown to thirty feet tall, or whatever the actual size was of the glowing screen before him. But there was her radiant face, bigger than life, framed by her familiar brown curls. Finn was so used to that face he had every detail memorized: the dancing eyes, the hint of freckles across the nose, the wide mouth that always seemed ready to smile at Finn's antics. Even when she looked serious—as she did now—her face held the *possibility* of joy and laughter.

Finn hadn't entirely understood what the sign had meant about a "trial and sentencing," or why anyone would call his mother a criminal. There hadn't been time to ask. But surely anyone seeing Mom's face right now would understand that she hadn't done anything wrong.

The crowd around them began to yell, and Natalie crouched beside him.

"Don't listen to them," she whispered. Her voice trembled. He had to tune out everything else to hear her. "And don't look at how your mom's trapped, with the handcuffs and all. I'm sure . . . I mean, she'll have a defense attorney, of course, and . . ."

"She's wearing handcuffs?" Finn asked. He stood on tiptoes, trying to see. Even though Natalie had told him not to.

"It's not showing on the screen right now anyhow," Natalie murmured. "But in person . . ."

And then Finn saw that there wasn't just the *image* of Mom, up there at the front, but she was actually *sitting* there. He felt a little mad at being tricked.

"Can't we get closer, to see her better?" he asked Natalie. He cupped his hands between his mouth and her ear, to block anyone else from hearing. "Or will that ruin the plan?"

He saw Chess and Emma conferring in whispers ahead of him. Probably in a moment they'd turn around and tell Finn and Natalie what to do.

But before that could happen, a man's voice boomed out from overhead, louder than any of the crowd's screams.

"Order! Order! The trial will commence. *The People versus Kate Greystone.*"

The crowd immediately went silent. Finn reached forward to clutch Emma's hand again.

Up on the stage, a raised platform slid out, along with

two large wooden structures. Finn had seen a cartoon version of a trial once—maybe for Bugs Bunny?—and that was enough for him to realize that these were seats for a judge and a jury. And maybe witnesses, too—didn't trials have witnesses?

The chair Mom was in slid back and locked into place behind one wall of the wooden structure. Maybe she was the first witness? But now Finn could no longer see her in person, only on the giant screen.

Then four guards marched out on the stage. The one in the fanciest uniform stepped to the front, and his face appeared on the giant screen, instead of Mom's.

Finn felt like he'd lost her all over again.

"The protocol will be different than previously announced," the guard said, somehow sounding stiff and formal and angry all at once. "The defendant has decided to confess. That will happen first."

Confess? Finn thought. Wouldn't that mean Mom *admitted* she'd done something wrong?

Around him, the crowd gasped and buzzed. The man held up his hand for silence.

"Let us begin," he said.

And then Mom's face was on the giant screen again. She leaned forward to grasp a microphone someone had put on a stand beside her; she had to reach with both hands, since they were bound together at the wrists. The handcuffs clanked.

Finn tugged on Emma's arm, and then Chess's, too. His brother and sister had to know how to stop this. They had to stop it *now*.

But when Emma and Chess glanced back, their faces were anguished, their matching dark eyes full of matching despair.

Emma and Chess don't have a plan, Finn realized. *They don't know what to do any more than I do.*

Finn turned to Natalie, still crouched beside him. She had her head down, defeated.

None of the big kids know what to do, Finn thought. *We're all exactly the same.*

Up on the screen, Mom opened her mouth and began speaking into the microphone.

"I am guilty of everything I have been accused of," she said in a strong, firm voice that was completely hers, completely the way she always sounded. "I committed all of those murders." Her voice filled the entire room. She paused only to stare more directly at the camera. "I even killed my own husband."

Chess and Emma slumped in front of Finn, staggering as if they'd been hit. Natalie buried her face in her hands.

Maybe they weren't all the same. Finn didn't stagger or slump or drop his head. He straightened his spine and lifted his chin. Because suddenly he knew exactly what to do, exactly how to help Mom.

He opened his mouth, too.

"None of that is true!" he screamed. "Someone's making her say that! She's just doing it to . . . to . . ." Ideas clicked together in his brain. "To save those kids! Somehow!"

He stepped forward, ready to run down to the stage and grab the microphone from Mom's hand and keep screaming, keep explaining until the whole crowd rose up and agreed, "Oh, you're right. We're sorry. We're sorry about those kids being kidnapped, too."

But before he could take another step, someone grabbed him from behind.

FORTY-FOUR

EMMA

Oh, Finn, Emma thought, one horror flowing over another. He'd said what she was thinking, but he'd said it *out loud.* When they were already standing in this dangerous place, surrounded by people who looked mad enough to kill.

For a moment, she was too paralyzed to do anything. Then she saw the angry faces of the crowd turning toward Finn. Now it looked like they wanted to kill *him.* She spun around and hissed, "Stop talking! Stop talking and *run!*"

How could Finn *not* see how much danger they were in? Hadn't he heard the terrible things the crowd had screamed? *Traitor . . . Killer . . .* Couldn't he see how much these people despised Mom without even knowing her? How the people at the front had started banging their hands against the clear Plexiglas wall separating them from the stage, as if that was the only thing keeping them from running up and attacking her?

How could Finn be so brave—and so stupid?

But Finn was no longer right behind her. She whipped her head left to right, and there was Chess still frozen beside her, all the color drained from his face, and Natalie scrambling up from the floor, her hands pressed over her mouth in horror. But Finn, Finn, Finn . . .

Finn was nowhere in sight.

An arm thrust out from the crowd and drew Emma in; an old lady in an orange cap put her face to Emma's ear and whispered, "If you run, you look guilty. Move with the crowd. Blend in. It's the only way to hide."

Emma yanked her head back. She would have started screaming as loudly as Finn—screaming his name, probably—except that in that moment the old lady moved her dark blue coat to the side, giving Emma a quick glimpse of Finn's brown hair and startled face, hidden behind her.

Emma pressed her finger to her lips. She let her eyes beg Finn: *Stay quiet, stay quiet, oh, please, you can't make a sound. I think this woman is helping us. . . .*

An instant later, the glare of a spotlight cut through the

crowd, reaching the exact spot where Finn had stood only seconds earlier. The crowd as a whole darted away from the light, leaving an empty space on the floor. Emma and Finn and the old lady moved back, too. Panicked cries rose around them: "It wasn't me!" "It wasn't my kid!" "Whoever it was ran away!"

Emma saw Chess and Natalie on the other side of the empty space, at the edge of the circle of light. They seemed to have unfrozen enough to call out with the others around them, "It wasn't me!" Chess's voice cracked. Natalie seemed about to cry.

The booming voice from the man on the stage called out, "Five-minute recess while the guards deal with a disturbance in the crowd. They need to make another arrest."

Mom's face disappeared from the giant screen, replaced by the blank, blinding light again. And that made Emma's eyes flood with tears, too. Emma *needed* Mom so much right now. Even if Mom was up there saying the most un-Mom-like things ever.

She didn't kill Dad, Emma told herself. *She didn't kill anyone. I know it. . . .*

It was like knowing that two plus two equaled four, like knowing how to breathe.

But how could Mom even speak those words? How could she think saying that would save anyone? How could anyone believe her?

Emma didn't have time to think it all through, because a dozen guards came shoving their way through the crowd. The shoving was unnecessary; all the clumps of people in blue and orange fell over themselves to get out of the way. A young woman with dreadlocks sagged against the man beside her; Emma wondered if she'd fainted in fear.

Emma took a shaky breath, fighting against terror herself. How had the mood of the crowd changed so quickly? Was just the sight of the guards enough to horrify everyone?

The acrid odor around them seemed worse than ever.

Maybe, maybe . . . maybe I don't actually know how to breathe anymore? Maybe it doesn't work the same here? Or breathing in makes me smell the odor more, and that's making me more and more afraid?

She held her breath, and somehow that steadied her. She could concentrate on locking her muscles, keeping herself from trembling. But as soon as she inhaled again, she felt lost.

Or maybe this time it was because the guards were so close now. They were so muscular, so stern in their dark blue uniforms. They thronged into the circle of light, just inches from Emma and the old lady—and from Finn hiding behind the old lady's coat.

"Who was yelling?" the guards demanded again and again as they stared out into the crowd. "Who dared disturb the trial?"

The crowd's panicky cries of "It wasn't me!" were replaced by mumbles: "I didn't see. . . ." "I didn't hear. . . ." "I was watching the screen. . . ." "That was behind me. . . ."

Could it be true that nobody saw Finn except the old lady? Emma wondered. *Or . . . is the crowd trying to save him, too?*

Did the crowd care about Finn, or were they only trying to stay out of trouble themselves?

Or were they all just too scared to think straight?

When the guards weren't looking directly at her, Emma tried to scan the faces around her, too. They were young and old, fat and thin, dark skinned and pale, surrounded by thick curls or bald scalps. . . . But all of the faces were twisted in terror, and that made them all look alike.

The old lady dug a bony elbow into Emma's side.

"Look down," she commanded, in a whisper so soft that Emma might have just been reading her lips. "Don't let them see your face."

But how could Emma see the guards and the crowd without letting them see her?

How could she see if it was time to grab Finn and run?

Emma compromised, bending her neck only partway. She peeked out through her eyelashes and the random strands of hair that slid down over her face.

She saw a man's dark shoe on the other side of the circle nudge something round and metallic toward the clump of guards. Was it a magnet? A bullet? A miniature *bomb*?

Emma's teachers were always telling her she had a scientific mind, but science only helped when you had enough data to come up with a good hypothesis. All Emma could see was a piece of metal rolling out into the bright light. The guards blocked her view, so she couldn't even see who had kicked it.

Are there light-activated bombs? she wondered. *Heat-activated bombs? Remote-control bombs?*

She shouldn't think about bombs. Or any other dangers besides the guards.

The round metal thing clunked against one of the guard's shoes and fell over on its side. Through her lowered lashes, Emma saw the guard bend down and pick up the piece of metal. Still crouched low, he held it up to the light. Then he stood and carried it over to another guard, the one whose uniform held the most medals and the fanciest braided orange trim. Was he the guard leader?

Emma held her breath again. She forgot the old lady's advice and lifted her head to watch.

The guard leader held the metal in one hand and tilted his head to the side to speak into his collar.

"Looks like it was an electronic voice we heard," he said. "The perp who set this up could be anywhere in the crowd by now. We'll reroll the security footage, do the facial rec—we'll have this arrest by the end of the sentencing."

Emma felt the old lady behind her stiffen at the words "facial rec."

Rec, Emma thought numbly. *Recognition.*

She couldn't understand everything the guard had said, but she'd caught enough. The guards thought they were looking for someone who'd set out an electronic device; they thought Finn's voice had only been a recording.

But there was security video of the crowd. And when the guards looked at it, they'd see Finn. They'd know he was the one who shouted. They'd come back for him.

The spotlight dimmed, then disappeared. The guards began marching away, shoving a few more people for no reason, as if the guards were just overgrown playground bullies.

Emma leaned back against the old lady who'd rescued her and Finn.

"Thank you," Emma breathed. "You saved us. Can you . . ."

She had a whole list of ideas to ask for. *Can you help us save our mother? Can you get us out of here safely? Can you tell us what to do?*

But the old lady was pulling away.

"You didn't see me," she murmured. "I wasn't here."

The old lady nudged past Finn and melted back into the crowd. Emma had never really gotten a good look at the woman—her main impression was of pruny lips and the orange cap that shadowed the rest of the old lady's face. So that's what Emma looked for.

No one anywhere near Emma was wearing an orange cap now.

Did the old lady take it off so I wouldn't find her? Emma wondered. *Or is she just hiding from the guards?*

"Emma, please . . ."

It was Finn, grabbing her around the shoulders and holding on tight. If he'd been too fearless before, he seemed terrified now. His eyes were wide and swimming with unshed tears. His lower lip trembled.

"It's okay," Emma lied, patting his back. "We're fine. Just stay quiet. We'll get back together with Chess and Natalie and maybe, maybe . . ."

She scanned the crowd. How could she explain that she was searching for a man she'd seen nothing of, except for a dark shoe? A man who may not have even known what he was doing when he kicked a little electronic device toward the guards? How had that become her only hope?

Maybe Emma didn't know anything about shoe fashions, and it'd been a woman instead.

Most of the men across from them were wearing dark shoes.

So were the women.

The crowd pressed forward, jostling Emma. Everyone seemed to want to get away from the spot where the guards had found the device. Chess raced over and grabbed Finn, and his arms were long enough to wrap around Emma at the same time. Natalie put her hand on Finn's head and Emma's both.

The others silently turned to the front. Even though the screen stayed blank and there was no movement on the stage, it seemed like the trial could resume any minute. Still, Emma kept facing backward. She gave up on trying to identify shoes and raised her gaze, studying all the people crammed in behind her. She was hoping for a wink or a nod or maybe a simple hand signal—something to tell her who she could trust. The man who'd kicked the electronic device had done nothing but buy a little time for Finn, but maybe he'd done it on purpose. Maybe Shoe Man—Shoe Person?—was braver than the old lady. Maybe he'd be willing to help more. Wouldn't he give her some sign of that?

The people behind her shifted restlessly: squinting, frowning, biting their lips, crossing their arms. . . . Maybe someone in the crowd behind her *was* trying to signal her, and she just couldn't tell. Why hadn't she learned sign language? Or semaphore codes? Or whatever people used in this alternate world?

Why hadn't Mom taught Emma, Chess, and Finn

everything they needed to know about the alternate world from the very beginning?

People were starting to stare at Emma for being different, for not turning around and looking back toward the huge screen at the front of the auditorium like everyone else. One tall, scowling man with thick glasses even tilted his head and made a shooing motion with his hand, as if her steady gaze was making him angry, and he just wanted her to go away.

No. He wasn't shooing her away. He was showing her something in his hand, but keeping his hand cupped so no one else would see it, too.

The thing in his hand was a paper.

A paper unfolded to reveal a crookedly drawn red heart.

FORTY-FIVE

CHESS

Chess was already having trouble standing up. He wasn't sure if he was holding on to his brother and sister more for their sake or his own. So when Emma began tugging on his arm and pulling him back, he almost fell over.

"We can't—" he began.

It was too hard to say the rest. Not to mention dangerous. *We can't stand out. We can't save Mom. Or the Gustano kids. Or ourselves.*

The only thing they'd achieved, coming to the alternate world, was to doom more people.

It made his heart ache to think of the people he'd

personally endangered by not sending them back: Finn. Emma.

And Natalie, who wasn't even related, who didn't have the same reason they all did for wanting to save Mom.

Emma pulling on him was just another reminder of how badly he'd failed.

"We have to follow someone!" Emma whispered, yanking on his arm harder and harder. "Someone who can help!"

It was odd: Emma didn't look or act like *she* thought they were doomed. She was practically jumping up and down. A moment ago she'd been as slumped over as Chess and Finn and Natalie. But now her eyes shone and her cheeks were rosy; it was possible to believe that if she touched his arm again, he'd get an electric shock.

"Okay, okay, shh," Chess whispered, more to calm her down than because he believed there was any hope.

The four of them silently began skulking through the crowd, with Emma leading the way. The people around them were milling about and muttering, clearly impatient for the trial to start again, so Chess hoped the kids' movements wouldn't stand out too much. Emma seemed to be following a man a few paces ahead of them in a dark blue jacket—not that that was unusual, since so many in the crowd were wearing dark blue or orange. This man was tall like Chess remembered his father being; he had dark hair and dark skin, and in his dark-colored clothes he could step into the shadows and hide a lot better than the Greystones or Natalie could. Even his horn-rimmed glasses seemed like a disguise.

When they got to the edge of the crowd, Chess thought maybe Emma had lost the man completely. Then he saw the man's hand reach out from behind one of the pillars with one finger curled back, summoning the kids forward.

Chess grabbed Emma by the shoulders.

"What are you doing?" he asked. "This is like every 'Stranger Danger' lecture ever! What—"

"We can trust him," Emma said. "I'm sure of it!"

"Why?" Natalie challenged.

Emma's answer was to speed over to the man and whisper in his ear. He pulled something out of his pocket and held it out. Even in the dark space behind the pillar there was enough light for Chess to see the heart on the paper.

"Hey, I drew that!" Finn said. "Well, not that exact one, I guess, but the heart just like it on Mom's phone. . . ." He spoke softly—for Finn, anyway—but he still glanced over his shoulder as if terrified the guards would come again.

Chess squared his shoulders and tried to look taller and more confident than he really was. He stared straight into the man's eyes, past the man's thick glasses.

"Where'd you get that?" he demanded.

The man seemed to cower back into the shadows even more. His eyes darted about.

"Someone mailed it to me years ago. Your . . . mother. That is, if I'm right about who you are." The man spoke slowly, as if he wasn't all that confident either. His gaze came to rest on Natalie's face. "Though, I thought there were only three of you. . . ."

"Natalie's just helping," Finn volunteered, and Chess despaired again. Hadn't Finn learned his lesson? Would he ever *not* talk too much?

Natalie took the heart drawing from the man's hand.

"You expect us to believe that Mrs. . . . uh, that *some woman* sent you this heart picture her kid drew?" she asked skeptically. "When you don't even recognize the kid?"

The man held his hands up, a gesture of innocence.

"Hear me out!" he begged. "It's true! We needed a symbol we could show, in case we ever had to meet and . . . and it wasn't safe to identify ourselves otherwise. I didn't even know what Ka—er, what the woman I was talking to—really looked like until today. It wasn't safe. But this heart . . ." His finger brushed the paper. His voice turned husky. "It's a good symbol. Everything we've done was for you and other kids like you. For our hopes for the future. *Your* future."

Chess wanted to weep. He wanted to scream, *Don't you*

see there's no hope now? Couldn't you have shown up and saved her sooner?

"So you do know who we are," he said, biting off the words. "We don't have to tell you. But we don't know you. Be fair. Tell us *your* name."

The man's face spasmed between sorrow and fear. He jerked his head around, and muttered as if he was only talking to himself, "I swept this area for any listening device. I rerouted the security camera on this pillar. It really should be safe. . . ." He clenched his teeth, looked back at Chess, and said, "Your mother knows me as Joe."

Chess had never been a violent kid. When other boys wanted to fight on the playground, he always walked away. But rage swelled within him now. He slammed the palms of his hands as hard as he could against Joe's chest. He didn't worry for an instant about Joe hitting back. He didn't even worry about guards hearing him. All he wanted to do was accuse Joe:

"It's your fault she's here!"

FORTY-SIX

FINN

Finn watched his calm, sane, *perfect* brother go crazy.

The big man—Joe—wrapped his arms around Chess, more like he was hugging him than trying to fight back.

Strangely, Emma was doing the same thing, as if she were on Joe's side, not Chess's.

"Don't breathe," Emma commanded, putting her hand over Chess's mouth and nose. "Don't inhale at all."

"What?" Finn said. "Emma, that's backward. When people are upset, you're supposed to tell them to take *deep* breaths. You say, 'Breathe in. Breathe out. . . .'"

"Not here," Emma said. "There's something wrong with

this air. Something that makes people more upset. It's worse every time the smell's worse."

"Really?" Finn said.

Chess stopped struggling. Joe pulled away from Chess to stare at Emma.

"You may be right," he whispered. "That explains . . ." He clutched his hands against his head. "What other horrors did they come up with while I was away that I don't know about? What *else* am I missing?"

"It's just a theory," Emma said modestly.

Natalie put her hands on her hips.

"Let's back up," she said. She narrowed her eyes at Chess. "*You* know this Joe guy?"

"I heard my mom on the phone with him," Chess said. His shoulders slumped. He exhaled a little, took a shallow breath—a mere sip of air—and admitted, "Or *somebody* she called Joe. It was the night before she left, and she said, 'If you don't fix this, I will.' I think she was talking about rescuing the Gustano kids."

Out of the corner of his eye, Finn saw Mom's image on the screen behind them again. He wanted to gaze and gaze at her. But he didn't want to hear if she told any more lies.

"Order!" the bossy man's voice came again from the front of the room. "We are about to resume."

Finn turned his back to the screen and glared at Joe.

"So she wouldn't even be up there if it hadn't been for you?" Finn asked forlornly. "She'd still be safe at home with us?"

Joe began shaking his head no. But the way the corners of his lips turned down, it was more like he was saying yes.

"I—I have kids, too," he said. "Kids *I* was trying to protect. And I didn't think her plan would work, to come back here. I didn't know what to do."

"But you're here now," Natalie offered.

Joe bowed his head.

"And I still don't know what to do," he whispered. "There's no way to rescue the four of you, the Gustano kids, and your mom—and get all of us out of here alive. This has gone too far."

Behind Finn, the public address system crackled, and then he heard his mother's voice boom out throughout the entire auditorium: "I killed everyone who disagreed with me. . . ." Finn put his hands over his ears. But he could still hear.

"What good does *that* do?" Emma asked, pointing back toward the screen. She had tears in her eyes. "How are those lies supposed to help anyone?"

Joe lifted his head and let out a bitter laugh.

"Oh, *she's* not saying any of that. This world—they have technology that doesn't exist in the other world. The leaders can take the image of anyone and make it look like they're saying anything. And no matter how much you analyze the video, you can't tell what's real and what isn't."

"But she's sitting right there—" Finn pointed behind him, though he couldn't look himself. His eyes were too blurry with his own tears.

"People can only see the screen," Chess muttered. "Not her. And they think they see what she's really saying and doing."

"It's like a magic trick," Emma said. "An *evil* magic trick. All about distraction."

"Yes." Joe put his hands on Finn's shoulders. "They're making it look like she's saying everything live, right now, speaking into a microphone this very minute. But that's a fake tape they prepared ahead of time. The leaders can destroy anyone they want that way, by controlling what people see and hear, so they only get lies. That's what we were fighting against, your parents and I. And our allies. We were gathering proof of the *leaders'* crimes—proof that couldn't be denied for once. We thought, in the safety of the other world, we'd have time and space to put it all together. But . . . then the leaders found the other world, too."

"This place sucks," Natalie said, and now it sounded like *she* wanted to punch somebody.

Was Finn the only one who still didn't understand?

"But *I* told people the truth!" he said. "They heard *me*! Why didn't that work?"

Once again he felt the horror of the moment after the old lady grabbed him. She'd whispered, "Hide, before they kill you!" And he'd peeked out from behind her coat, and people were looking back with murderous expressions.

Finn had never seen anyone look like that before. Certainly not looking at *him* that way.

But if it helped Mom, I'd do it again, he thought.

Wouldn't he? Couldn't he be that brave?

Joe shook his head. It seemed like all he ever did was shake his head.

"Only a few people heard you before the guards came. It was just lucky I was standing nearby. One little boy's feeble voice against an entire totalitarian government—it's not going to work. You'd need the entire auditorium hearing you all at once. And even then . . ."

"That one old lady did help us," Emma offered. She cupped her chin in her hand, as if that helped her think. "*She* didn't show us a heart picture. So she wasn't someone working with you and Mom, right?"

"Not that I know of," Joe said, spreading his hands helplessly. "We've had to operate in such secrecy—it hasn't been safe for anyone to know more than one or two contacts."

"So there could be lots of people here who are secretly

on our side!" Finn said excitedly. He thumped Emma on the back, as if they'd figured out something together. "They just need to know it's safe to unite! All we need to do is give Mom a microphone—a real microphone. And she could say from the stage what's true and what isn't. And then—"

"Huh," Joe said, tapping a finger against his cheek. Was that like Emma cupping her chin? Was Joe taking Finn's idea seriously?

"You had that little electronic device that made the guards think Finn's voice was a recording," Emma added excitedly. Her eyes shone. Finn *loved* seeing his sister this way. He could tell her mind was racing. "Do you have a microphone hidden in that coat, too? Could we drop it down from over the stage? Or, I don't know, there's got to be some way to make this work!"

Finn looked from Emma to Chess to Natalie to Joe. Chess and Natalie looked like they were thinking hard, too.

But by the time Finn's gaze reached Joe's face again, Joe was already slumped back against the pillar. Giving up.

"I'm sorry," he said. "There's no endgame in that plan. No escape hatch. See that clear wall keeping the crowd back from the stage?" He pointed. "We couldn't get past that to rescue your mom if the idea didn't work instantly. And there are guards by every door. We'd endanger ourselves even more. The guards would just take the microphone away from your mom before she got two words out."

Chess slouched. Emma hung her head. Finn blinked hard, trying to make sure that no tears began rolling down his cheeks.

But Natalie bolted suddenly upright, staring past Finn's ear. She grabbed Finn's arm and Emma's shoulder, and spun them around. Then she yanked Chess forward, too.

"Guys, guys, guys!" she hissed. "Do you see what I see? Or am I only imagining it, because . . ." She laughed, a strange noise that came out sounding strangled. "Because it's what I want most?"

Natalie pointed at the screen. Finn had been trying so hard to block out everything the booming voice of his mother was saying behind him. He'd actually kind of succeeded. And he'd kept himself from staring adoringly at her face the whole time.

But Mom's face had disappeared from the screen, replaced by another woman's. This woman had long, flowing hair and a ruffled collar. She had a firm chin, a determined gaze, a proud tilt to her head. She looked like she could take care of anything.

"Don't you see?" It was hard to tell if Natalie was laughing or crying. "It's *my* mom! *She* came to save us!"

FORTY-SEVEN

EMMA

"No, it's not," Emma said. This felt like the cruelest thing she'd ever done, killing Natalie's hope. "That's *this* world's version of your mother."

Natalie squinted at Emma. The corners of her mouth trembled.

"No! It has to be . . ."

"Your mother was wearing a neon green exercise shirt when she dropped us off at our house this morning," Emma said. Logic had never felt so mean. "She wouldn't have gone home and changed before following us. That woman is wearing a *robe* under that ruffle. Why would your mom do that?"

"And she's sitting in front of a sign that says 'Judge Susanna Morales,'" Chess added quietly. "Your mom isn't a judge."

Natalie let out a wail and turned to the side, hiding her face.

"Natalie's mom is nice in our world," Finn said. "So wouldn't this world's Ms. Morales be nice, too? If she's a judge here, won't she say, 'Order in the court!' and let Mom go?"

Now Emma needed to use logic to be cruel to *Finn*. She needed to remind him that he couldn't count on anyone or anything being the same in this world as back home. This world's Mrs. Childers hadn't been friendly like their familiar neighbor back home; this world's version of their house wasn't happy and welcoming like theirs was. . . . Whatever original difference had split one world from another had also led to one ripple of other changes after another.

How could Finn understand this, when Emma was struggling herself?

Before Emma could say anything, Joe bolted out of the shadows. He shoved Chess, Emma, and Finn to the side, and grabbed Natalie by the shoulders. He whirled her around, so he could stare her directly in the face.

"You're *Susanna Morales's* daughter?" he asked. "Who's your father? Is it . . . is it . . . ?"

"R-Roger Mayhew," Natalie stammered. She jerked away from him. "Let go of me!"

Joe was leaning in like he wanted to hug her, but he took a respectful step back. His expression, which had been so hangdog a moment ago, now glowed with joy.

"So you three crossed into this world with Natalie Mayhew," he muttered. "Natalie *Mayhew*. Genetically indistinguishable from Susanna Morales and Roger Mayhew's daughter in this world. Either your mom's a genius, or you kids are, or . . . or we are the luckiest people ever!"

"What do you mean?" Emma asked.

Joe waved his arms, like he was dying to hug *someone*. He settled on Finn, scooping up the little boy in his arms so joyfully that Finn's legs swung side to side.

"This changes everything," Joe whispered, holding Finn tight. "Now Finn's idea will work!"

FORTY-EIGHT

CHESS

"I don't understand," Chess whispered. But nobody was listening.

Natalie stood beside him, her eyes narrowed thoughtfully, her head tilted so far to the right that her hair seemed several inches longer on one side than the other.

"I'm someone important here?" she whispered. "Or my family is? Is that why those boys the other day were so scared of my mom?"

She gazed off toward the huge image of her mother—no, this world's Susanna Morales, the *judge*—up on the screen, pounding a gavel and looking severe.

Meanwhile, Chess's mother—his *real* mother, the only one he had in either world—was in handcuffs and shackles. And she'd just finished confessing to murders Chess knew she didn't commit. Because she couldn't have. He *knew* that, even if certainty about everything else had abandoned him.

Chess looked down.

On the floor by Chess's feet, Finn and Emma bent protectively over Joe, hiding whatever he was assembling out of tiny bits of plastic and wire.

"Ooo, Emma, this is like when you built that mechanical insect for me," Finn squeal-whispered. "After all this is over, you two should go into business together. Mr. Gadget and Kid Gadget!"

How could Finn flip from fear to excitement so fast?

He trusts Joe, Chess thought. *He believes we really are going to be able to save Mom. And ourselves. And—the Gustanos?*

Chess crouched down. Now he was at eye level with Joe, Emma, and Finn.

"Tell us exactly what you're doing," he asked Joe. "So we know our part. And so . . ."

So if anything goes wrong, the rest of us can still save Mom.

Chess didn't want to say that in front of the younger kids. Or even Natalie. He didn't want anyone else thinking about possible problems.

Joe's eyes met Chess's over the top of the man's glasses.

Chess clenched his jaw and kept his gaze steady. Wouldn't that make him look older and more trustworthy himself? Joe raised an eyebrow at Chess, a shadowy motion in the near-darkness behind the pillar. But this was like the looks Mom sometimes gave Chess over the top of Emma's and Finn's heads, the looks that said, *I know you are almost an adult, and so you are old enough to know things that I can't tell Emma and Finn. You understand, don't you? You trust me, right?* But this was different, because Joe wasn't Mom. He'd been a stranger until a few moments ago. Regardless of any heart drawing, he was a stranger still.

Chess wanted so badly to trust Joe anyhow. It *felt* like Joe wasn't just looking at him adult-to-near-adult. It felt like his gaze and his raised eyebrow were more . . .

Man-to-man.

"Are you building a drone?" Emma demanded, before Joe had a chance to answer Chess. "Do you think you can *fly* a microphone up to Mom? Won't the whole auditorium see that? You need to tell us your plan so we can double-check everything, make sure it's foolproof."

"I do want this to be foolproof," Joe murmured as he twisted a tiny screw into whatever he was building on the floor. He shifted his gaze from Chess to Emma, and it felt like he was answering both of them. "And I wouldn't be surprised if you could build this without me, given enough time. But there *isn't* time to explain. Just be ready to run."

"Where to?" Finn asked.

"Safety," Joe said.

Yes, Chess thought. *Get Finn to safety. And Emma. And Natalie. And Mom.*

He had to trust Joe. He didn't see any other choice.

FORTY-NINE

FINN

"Now," Joe said.

Finn had to hold himself back from jumping up and down with excitement. The five of them had wormed their way up to the front of the auditorium. Now they were right by the see-through wall that separated the crowd from the stage. Toward the center of the auditorium, the people beside the clear wall were pressed in close, pinned together by the pressure of the crowd behind them. But Joe, the Greystones, and Natalie were off to the side, away from the bulk of the crowd. They were beside a door in the clear wall. The *only* door.

"You really think Natalie's going to be able to open that because of her *genes*?" Finn asked. He wanted someone to congratulate him for remembering the science word.

Instead, Joe tugged gently on his shoulders.

"Stand back," Joe said. "An alarm might go off if the wrong person touches it. They might have set up that level of security."

He meant that the Greystones were the wrong people. But so was Joe, so Finn couldn't get offended.

All the others seemed to be holding their breath. But Finn couldn't tell if that was because they thought the air was dangerous or because they were scared.

Natalie reached one shaking hand to the knob of the door. She wrapped her hand around the knob.

Nothing happened. No alarms sounded.

Natalie let out a huff of air.

"Slowly, slowly," Joe coached her.

Natalie turned the knob and pushed forward, as gently as breathing. The door opened a crack.

"Yes!" Emma whispered.

Chess's pale, terrified-looking face turned even paler.

"Good girl," Joe said to Natalie. He glanced quickly over his shoulder. "And . . . nobody's watching."

He slipped his hand down onto the side of his leg. To anybody farther away than Finn, it would have looked like a man merely shifting positions. Joe didn't even look down. He peered off toward the giant screen behind the stage, just like Natalie, Chess, and Emma were doing. Just like everyone else in the auditorium.

But Finn couldn't resist watching a tiny crawling thing slither out of Joe's hand and down his pant leg. It moved like a lizard or a snake.

Joe hadn't built a drone that could *fly* a microphone up to Mom, in plain sight of the whole auditorium. He'd built one that could creep along the floor and up the side of her chair, unseen.

Joe tucked his other hand into his coat pocket, where Finn had seen him hide a remote. The drone lizard scampered through the doorway and up the first step toward the stage.

"It's working!" Finn couldn't help whispering.

"Shh," Emma warned him.

But she grinned, too.

Chess put a hand on Finn's head and one on Emma's shoulder. It felt like that was Chess's way of grinning, too.

Natalie hesitated by the door.

"Should I shut it now?" she asked. "Or open it wider?"

"Just wait," Joe whispered.

He still seemed to be peering intently toward the giant screen at the front of the room. But Finn knew Joe was really watching the screen embedded in his own glasses. That was how he could see the progress of the lizard drone as it moved the rest of the way up the stairs and onto a part of the stage completely cloaked in darkness.

Up on the screen, the too-serious, too-grim version of Ms. Morales—the judge—was using a lot of big, unfamiliar words.

"Some would contend that this confession would obviate the need for a lengthy trial," she said in a cold, heartless voice that made Finn miss the real Ms. Morales. Even when she was yelling at Natalie, Finn had never heard the real Ms. Morales sound so cruel. "But we are a society that believes in justice and—"

Joe snorted, blocking out her next words.

"This isn't justice," he muttered.

But behind him, the crowd cheered, as if they believed every word Evil–Ms. Morales spoke.

No, not just that—it was like they *adored* every word Evil–Ms. Morales spoke. Like they worshipped her.

"It's at the base of the chair now," Joe whispered, and Finn shivered with anticipation.

If the crowd could worship the evil judge, just wait until they heard Mom.

Finn watched Joe's face: His eye twitched, he winced, then the corner of his mouth moved just a little higher.

' "It's in her hand now," Joe said. "Success!"

Finn resisted the urge to grab Joe's glasses so he could see Mom's face when she looked down at the lizard drone. It'd probably be like her face on Christmas morning, or on Mother's Day when Finn made her *two* cards. She'd glow.

Because the drone lizard didn't just carry a miniature microphone. It also held a tiny paper with a message: another of Finn's crooked hearts with the smallest of words written below, "Kids=safe."

"Won't that make her think the Gustano kids are all safe *now*?" Finn had asked anxiously as he watched Joe write the words. "Won't that kind of . . . trick her?"

"Kiddo, there's not room on this page for future tense or conditional verbs or nuance," Joe had said. "We can't write out that Natalie's our secret weapon or that we're going to grab the Gustano kids next. What if the guards intercept this? Or . . . Judge Morales?"

Now Finn glanced toward Natalie, who stood with her hands pressed against the clear wall. How awful it must be for her to have a good mom *and* an evil one.

Or, at least, an evil one who looked like her real mom.

"Shouldn't Mom start talking already?" Emma whispered anxiously.

"Give her a minute to figure out what we sent her," Joe muttered.

Finn's heart started beating too fast. He hated waiting.

Then a boom sounded overhead—the exact kind of feedback boom a cheap, quickly built microphone would make when it was switched on.

Evil–Ms. Morales's frowning face remained on the screen, but another voice spoke over hers: "This entire trial is a fake!"

Mom! Finn exulted. *Go, Mom!*

"Your leaders are lying to you!" Mom's voice was steady and strong and perfect. It was everything Finn wanted. "I never—"

There was another boom, cutting off Mom's words.

At the same time, the whole room went dark.

FIFTY

EMMA

"Did you know this would happen?" Emma hissed at Joe in the darkness. "Did you know they'd shut off the electricity to shut up Mom?"

"No!" Joe protested. "I thought—"

"Finn!" Chess called, reaching out.

His hand brushed Emma's arm just as Finn shoved past them both, toward the door to the stage.

"We've got to get to Mom before the guards do!" Finn called back over his shoulder.

Usually Emma's brain worked as fast as Finn could move,

but now she wanted an extra moment to think, an instant to figure out the consequences of every action.

Behind her, the crowd went from shocked silence to a loud buzz. Did they believe Mom? Whose side were they on now?

Emma couldn't tell. She couldn't make out any individual words, just a deafening roar of . . . more anger? More fear?

"Finn's right! We can use the darkness!" Natalie called. "It helps us!"

In the next instant, some kind of emergency backup lights switched on. They were so minimal they only cast shadows—they seemed to emphasize the darkness, rather than fighting it. But now Emma could make out the dim shape of her little brother beyond the door, halfway up the towering stairs to the stage.

He looked so small, so defenseless. And that made Emma forget everything else: logic, Joe's plan, the crowd. . . .

"Finn, wait for me!" Emma called after him.

She pushed her way through the door, letting go of any worry about security systems or alarms.

Wouldn't a security system need electricity, too? she told herself. *Or is there a backup generator for that, also?*

She didn't touch the doorknob, and no alarm sounded, so

it didn't matter. She took the stairs two at a time. She didn't look back, but she thought maybe Chess, Natalie, and Joe followed.

She caught up to Finn right at the edge of the stage and pulled his head down beside hers.

"At least look before we climb on up!" she whispered in his ear.

Together, they peeked over the rim of the stage.

The dark shape of someone in a long robe stood over Mom behind the wall of her witness stand.

It was Judge Morales.

"Never . . . hello?" Mom was saying doubtfully, probably speaking into the microphone.

"Give up," Judge Morales sneered. "Can't you tell all the mikes are off now? And there's a practically soundproof wall between you and the crowd—no one could hear you, even if they weren't all shouting."

Emma realized the crowd noise seemed dimmer now, more distant. Maybe she could only hear it at all because they'd left the door open.

"I—I—" Mom stammered.

A cluster of guards rushed up beside Judge Morales.

"You want us to guard the prisoner?" the man in the lead asked. "Search her? *Punish* her?"

"There'll be time for that later," the judge snapped. "*She's* not going anywhere. We can look for accomplices later, too. The priority has to be subduing the crowd. This is a Protocol Six-Oh-Two situation. All of you—go!"

She led the guards to the other side of the stage, past the large wooden structures of the judge's podium and the empty jury box.

Now Mom was alone.

And again Finn was a step ahead of Emma, scrambling up over the edge of the stage and scurrying toward Mom.

Emma wanted to scream as she took off after him: *Mom! Mom! We're here!* She wanted to yell, *We love you!* and *Aren't you proud of us for finding you?* and *Oh, Mom, I thought we'd never see you again. This is the happiest moment of my life!* But she pressed her lips together and held it all in because they were still running through darkness, and Judge Morales and the guards were just on the other side of the podium and jury box, and the whole angry crowd was just on the other side of the wall.

And Mom wasn't free yet.

Still, as Emma caught up with Finn, she threw caution to the wind and launched herself around the wall of the witness box and into Mom's lap. Finn did, too. The two of them tumbled together into Mom's arms.

"We're saving you!" Emma whispered, just as Finn sighed happily, "Oh, Mom."

And then Mom gasped and began laughing and crying all at once, and alternately holding her hands over her mouth and holding on to Emma and Finn.

"*My* Emma?" she whispered in disbelief. "*My* Finn?"

And Emma understood why Mom might be confused in the near-total darkness, when she'd thought her three kids were still safely back in the other world, and only the Gustano children had been brought into this one. Mom began running her hands over their faces, as though she could identify them solely by touch.

"Yours," Emma assured her. "All yours."

It wasn't fair that she couldn't see Mom's face in the shadowy darkness. She wanted that so badly—not just to see Mom, but to see Mom seeing *her*. At least Emma could snuggle close; she could hold on tight.

"Mom?" Chess whispered behind her, moving around to the side of Mom's chair. Dimly, Emma saw that Natalie and Joe had arrived with him, and Joe was already bending low, diving toward the shackles that trapped Mom in her chair.

"You're all here?" Mom said numbly, reaching for Chess, too. "But—"

"We figured out your codes," Finn bragged. "Well, some of them. *I'm* the one who found the butterflies on your websites!"

"What? I never thought you'd see that until later,"

Mom whispered. "*Years* later. If ever. It was really meant for other—"

"Probably better not to talk much right now," Joe muttered. He seemed to be lying on the floor beside the witness box, his arms outstretched. Emma was pretty sure he had a screwdriver out to pry off the shackles, but she couldn't actually see it in the darkness.

"Joe?" Mom whispered, looking around. She let out a strangled cry, and her voice turned strangely bitter. "Funny how I know your voice so well, though I've never seen your face . . . *you* brought my children here? Into danger? How dare—"

"I *found* them here, Kate," Joe corrected. "They were a step ahead of me. And they even taped over the doorway to the tunnel, to try to guard it."

Emma thought that should make her feel proud—or proud of Natalie, anyway—but it didn't. There was something wrong with how Mom and Joe were talking, almost as though they were still using code.

Mom buried her face in her hands.

"I'm sorry," she whispered. "I've made a mess of things. But you *came*, and now you're all here, and—"

"And we've got Natalie, too," Finn interrupted. "She—"

Emma put her hand over his mouth, because if it was a mistake to talk about codes right now, it would be a really

345

bad idea to talk about Natalie being their secret weapon. Finn pushed back at her.

No—he was falling toward her, because the platform beneath Mom's chair gave a little jerk.

"Something's happening," Natalie hissed from the other side of the witness box. "Everybody down!"

FIFTY-ONE

CHESS

"Kids, save yourselves!" Mom whispered. "Hide! Now! Away from *me*!"

Chess wanted to argue, *We're not leaving you behind! We're not going anywhere without you!* But the words stuck in his throat. Joe was still working on the shackles on Mom's legs that bound her to the chair, but he hadn't even managed to pry away the first one.

Still, Chess crouched down behind Mom's chair, so that even if the lights came back on, no one would be able to see him from the crowd.

"Natalie's standing lookout for us," he assured Mom.

"We've got time. And even if someone sees her . . ."

Surely Mom knew that Natalie could just impersonate the Natalie Mayhew of this world; surely she knew that those two would look like exact doubles.

Mom turned her head toward Chess, and even though Mom's face was completely in shadow, he could feel the anguish in that one motion.

"Natalie's not . . . Have I just endangered another woman's child, too?" Mom moaned. She raised her head toward the crowd, and Chess understood: *What if this world's Natalie was already standing somewhere out there? She would know that the other world's Natalie didn't belong. So would everyone around her.*

The odds were, this world's Natalie was somewhere in the crowd.

"Natalie! You hide, too!" Chess whispered out into the darkness.

What other problems had he missed, because there hadn't been time to think?

Finn and Emma hadn't left Mom, either. If anything, they were holding on tighter.

From the other side of the stage, Chess heard Judge Morales's voice—so uncannily like and unlike the kind Ms. Morales's voice, all at once—as she called out, "Yes, we have enough power for that, even if we're making it look like a total outage otherwise. The plan's a go as soon as everyone's in place."

348

The platform beneath Mom's chair jerked again and began sliding away from the witness box, out toward the front of the stage.

"They're going to show me to the crowd!" Mom whispered. "Kids! Go!"

She pushed away at Finn and Emma, and turned and shoved at Chess, too.

None of them let go.

"Mom, it's still dark," Finn protested. "We're okay."

"Joe, hurry!" Emma whispered. "Do you have another screwdriver? I could help!"

The platform they were on had totally separated from the wall of the witness box now, sliding closer and closer to the front of the stage. If the lights came back on, all of them would be in plain sight.

"Chess!" Mom called. "Help me! Take care of Finn and Emma!"

There was a sob in her voice. There was a sob in Chess's throat, too, and it was threatening to burst out. And that would endanger everyone, even if lights and guards and evil judges didn't.

Chess reached down and began pulling on Finn's and Emma's arms.

He began pulling them away from Mom.

FIFTY-TWO

FINN

"Chess, *stop*," Finn moaned, because he didn't understand what was happening, and the only thing holding him together right now was being able to hold on to Mom.

The hard metal of her handcuffs dug into Finn's wrist, but he just clutched her hand tighter.

"Finn, Joe's doing everything he can for me," Mom said, and she had the same super-calm Mom tone she'd used that time Finn had broken his arm. "I need you to be brave, too."

I can't, Finn wanted to wail. But Mom was whispering something to Emma, and *Emma* started tugging on Finn, too.

Finn burrowed his face harder against Mom's side.

"Citizens, calm down," Ms. Morales's voice—no, *Judge* Morales's voice—boomed out over the crowd.

"Mom, if her microphone works again, won't yours work, too?" Finn whispered excitedly.

Even in the near-total darkness, Finn could see Mom shaking her head.

"They're using some sort of auxiliary system," Mom whispered. "They—"

Judge Morales's voice kept booming around them in the darkness, drowning out whatever else Mom was going to say. It seemed to silence the crowd, too.

"We apparently have saboteurs who believe they can shut this trial down simply by cutting an electrical line," Judge Morales said. "After they tried to throw us off with a fake recorded voice."

That was how she was trying to explain what Mom had said? Finn wanted to yell back at Judge Morales, just the way he'd yell at a playground bully, *You're the one with the fake recording! You're the one who shut off the electricity!*

"Believe me, all the guilty parties will be found and punished accordingly," the judge continued, her voice overpowering everything. "But right now, we all need to show the saboteurs that the will of the people is not to be tampered with. We have working microphones again, and in a second, we'll have the spotlights back. Even without our projection screen, it's time to call other witnesses alongside Kate Greystone."

The crowd buzzed again, this time with excitement.

"Mom!" Finn whispered. "They're not going to use the screen! They'll have to show you and your answers for real! No matter what anyone else says, all you have to do is tell the truth!"

"I can do that better if I'm not worried about you, Finn," Mom whispered back.

Was that true?

Finn still didn't understand everything, but he didn't want to be the reason Mom had to lie.

"What game are they playing now?" Joe whispered from below. "I don't see how—"

He broke off, because a blinding light appeared at the back of the auditorium.

"Run!" Mom whispered, shoving even more urgently at Finn and Emma and Chess.

But the light wasn't trained on Mom. It wasn't even swinging toward her. It was aimed at a pack of guards at the back of the auditorium. A pack of guards—and three small, huddled shapes.

And one of the shapes was calling out pitifully, in a voice

that sounded a lot like Finn's own, "Mom? Mom? Are you there? Please, somebody—they promised! They said they were taking us to our mom!"

It was the Gustano kids.

FIFTY-THREE

EMMA

That's how they think they're going to control Mom, Emma realized. *They still think those are her kids. Whoever's in charge doesn't know why she dared to tell the truth a few minutes ago, but they're reminding her whose lives are at stake.*

A chill ran through her, because *all* their lives were at stake, and had been all along.

A moment ago, Mom had whispered into Emma's ear, "Logic *and* love are going to triumph in the end, and in the meantime, I need you to take care of your brother. *Both* of your brothers. Trust me." And Emma had believed her. But now Mom sagged back against the chair she was trapped in, and Emma could feel her mother's despair like it was something contagious.

"I thought your message meant those kids were safe!" Mom hissed at Joe. "Otherwise, I wouldn't have—"

"Shh!" Joe begged. "I'm sorry! I had a plan!"

Had, Emma thought. *Past tense.*

Was he giving up, too?

"Joe, don't you have any more electronic devices to fool them with?" Emma asked. "Maybe we could record *our* voices and throw them out into the crowd. Or . . ."

"That device I dropped was just a fake," Joe protested.

"You built a drone lizard!" Emma reminded him. "Isn't there something else—"

"Anything like that takes time!" Joe whispered back. "And there isn't any left!" He seemed to be holding out his coat pocket, helplessly. "I have wires and screws and a few of *my* kids' things I thought I could build something with—sparklers and smoke bombs left over from the Fourth of July, Lego pieces and rubber bands and string . . . You tell me what good any of that does us now!"

If the situation hadn't been so dire, Emma would have thought, *Sparklers and Lego pieces? Joe's so much like me!*

But now she could only think, *He's totally losing it.*

Natalie came racing back to the others, even as Chess, Emma, and Finn reluctantly backed away from Mom and Joe.

"They're bringing those kids up to the stage," Natalie reported. "I heard fake Mom—I mean, the judge—she said that they won't put the spotlight on Mrs. Greystone until the kids are right beside her. They want the dramatic effect. But we can't let anyone see all of you here. Do you want me to run over and try to talk to . . . to fake Mom, to buy some time?" Her voice shook. "I don't know what I'd say, but—"

"Oh, Natalie," Mom said, her voice awash in helplessness. "We can't ask that of you. There's too much of a risk . . . a mother would see the difference. All of you—Joe, too—save yourselves!"

Joe kept stubbornly lying on the floor, working the screwdriver against the shackles. Emma liked him more than ever.

"What kind of a woman—what kind of a *mother*—doesn't answer even when her own children call out to her?" the judge taunted over the loud, booming mike.

But the judge didn't give Mom a working mike, so no one could hear her even if she did call back to those kids, Emma thought. *The judge is just trying to make Mom look worse and worse!*

Quivering, Mom bent her head low.

"There's still hope for me," she whispered with a sad little laugh. "They'll keep me alive because there are still things I know that they want me to reveal. But those kids, they're only valuable to the leaders if . . . if . . ."

She meant the Gustano kids were only valuable to the leaders as long as the leaders thought the Gustanos were truly Mom's children.

And the Gustanos would lose that protection if the leaders saw Chess, Emma, and Finn Greystone.

What if the Gustanos themselves give away everything once they're with Mom? Emma wondered.

Mom did *look* like the Gustanos' mom. If they really were two different worlds' versions of the exact same woman— and as much as Emma hated the idea, it did seem true—then Mom and Kate Gustano were probably genetically identical. It made sense the same way that there would be two Natalie Mayhews, the same way that Ms. Morales and Judge Morales undoubtedly held the exact same genes.

But Ms. Morales and Judge Morales were *not* the same otherwise. And probably there'd be some differences between Mom and Kate Gustano, too. Probably Kate Gustano and her kids shared some special code words and special, silly memories that were different from the ones Mom and the Greystone kids shared, just because they'd lived in different places and had different lives.

And the Gustanos would notice if Mom didn't act like their mom. If Finn Gustano was anything like Finn Greystone, it wouldn't take him long to blurt out, "Hey! This isn't really our mom! She just looks like her!"

And if Finn Gustano—or Emma Gustano, or Rocky—said something like that, it would be like signing their own death warrant.

Emma watched the three struggling Gustanos in their circle of light, as the guards around them prodded and shoved them up toward the front of the auditorium, up toward the stage. The crowd parted for them too easily. The crowd wasn't just terrified of the guards—it looked like they were terrified of the Gustanos, too.

Because of Mom, Emma thought, her heart sinking. *Because they think any kids of a horrible criminal like Mom would be horrible, too.*

The crowd didn't have any sympathy for sobbing little Finn Gustano, with his trembling lip and the bubble of snot in his nose. They didn't have any sympathy for the fierce way Emma Gustano held on to her little brother's arm, holding him up, or the protective way Rocky Gustano kept his arm draped around both his siblings' shoulders, even as they were already connected by handcuffs and chains.

The analytical part of Emma's brain wanted her to just keep staring at the Gustanos, to study and classify their every feature and move: *Oh, that's so much like us Greystones,* or *Hmm. That's not like us at all. Is that something that came from their father's genes, or is it because they lived in Arizona and we lived in Ohio?*

But the Gustanos and the guards—and the portable spot-light the guards carried—were getting closer and closer. It was only a matter of minutes before they'd be climbing the stairs, only a matter of minutes before the spotlight would shine on them and Mom together.

And on the Greystones and Natalie and Joe, too, if they didn't move quickly.

"Kids!" Joe hissed. "Go back down those stairs! Let Natalie take you—"

He pulled Natalie down beside him, and seemed to be whispering something in her ear. But Natalie sprang back, shaking her head no.

"We can't!" she protested. "There are guards beside that door now—I saw them! And they'll know we don't belong up here, they'll know I'm not really this world's Natalie Morales. . . ."

Natalie was practically sobbing. Emma saw everything in the slump of the older girl's shoulders. She saw how Finn had gone back to clutching Mom's arm, how Chess huddled helplessly on the floor, how Mom held her face in her hands. And, worst of all, how even Joe seemed to have dropped his screwdriver.

All of the others were giving up.

Emma decided to hold her breath again.

At first, she told herself, *I'm just testing a hypothesis. That's all. If everything's hopeless, it doesn't matter what I do. And if this world is going to kill me, I at least want to know as much as I can about how and why.*

It'd been a while since the bad smell of the alternate world had bothered Emma, but that didn't mean it wasn't there.

Maybe we've been immersed in this world's stink for so long we don't even notice it anymore? Maybe that's true for everyone in the crowd, too? And maybe the effects . . . build up?

Emma held her breath for so long that her head swam and dots appeared before her eyes. It wouldn't do anyone any good if she just passed out.

But she still didn't let herself breathe.

Logic and love, Emma told herself, remembering her mother's words. *Love and logic.*

Love was the reason Emma, Finn, and Chess had come all this way to rescue their mother.

In another way, love was the reason Mom had wanted to rescue the Gustanos. She knew the love the Gustano parents had for their kids, because of how Mom loved Emma, Chess, and Finn.

Love was what mattered most.

But logic was *how* Emma could make love win.

When Emma had been holding her breath for so long that she swayed with dizziness and her eyelids sagged down over her eyes, she finally thought, *We just need to buy more time. Just enough time for Joe to finish freeing Mom. And we can do that with the bits and pieces and kids' toys Joe has in his pocket.*

Her eyes popped open and she took the very, very smallest breath of air she dared. But she was still clearheaded enough to hiss down to Joe:

"Did you say you had string and rubber bands and Lego? And smoke bombs? I *really* want those smoke bombs! *I've* got a plan!"

FIFTY-FOUR

CHESS

The guards and the Gustano kids reached the door in the clear wall between the stage and the crowd. Now they were through the door and climbing the stairs. Now they were at the edge of the stage.

And Chess could only watch in frozen horror as the beam from the portable spotlight in the guards' arms swung closer and closer.

Then Emma was nudging him and shoving something into his hands.

"Throw these out on the stage," she whispered. "Hurry!"

Tiny wires poked Chess's fingers, but as far as he could

tell, Emma had handed him nothing but junk.

"You think we're going to hold off the guards with wires and rubber bands and bits of string?" he asked incredulously. "And . . . *Legos*?"

"It's dark! We could make them trip!" Emma whispered back.

Chess wanted to cry, that she could still sound so hopeful. Over nothing.

"All we have to do is confuse them," Emma whispered. "And when they see the smoke . . ."

Emma reared back her arm and threw something into the air. Chess heard a muffled thud a few feet away. Evidently Joe's smoke bombs were the type that splatted and set off smoke instantly, because Chess's next breath brought in an ashy odor.

And . . . somehow it brought him courage, too.

He blindly tossed the handful of trash toward the guards surrounding the Gustanos.

"Let me have some of those smoke bombs!" he whispered to Emma.

Chess sensed, more than actually seeing, that Finn and Natalie were throwing smoke bombs, too. And Joe had gone back to struggling with Mom's shackles with renewed vigor.

The guards screamed, and Finn Gustano wailed louder than ever.

"You're under attack!" Emma screamed at the guards. "Lots more rebels are coming to fight you! Run while you still can!"

And it was crazy, because anybody could tell Emma's voice belonged to a little girl. And the smoke bombs were just kids' toys. They did little but pop and fizzle and stink.

But maybe in the darkness the guards heard them as terrifying weapons; maybe the thin columns of smoke seemed to be the first sizzlings of a larger explosion. The guards reeled backward, clutching their heads as if they couldn't figure out what to do. One of the guards dropped the portable spotlight, and all the man needed to do was pick it up again. But he let the light careen about, shooting its beams out wildly.

Behind the guards, the crowd began to shriek and wail and shove their way toward the exits. In the crazily veering flashes of light, Chess saw dozens of other guards step out from behind the pillars and push the crowd back.

But the guards on the stage—the ones closest to the smoke bombs—just stumbled about, barely even managing to hold on to the Gustano kids.

"Joe!" Chess cried. "What was in those smoke bombs? Are they—"

"Magic" was the word he wanted to use, but that was silly. It didn't make sense that the little puffs of smoke made the guards crash into each other and mutter "Why am I doing this?" And "What should I do next?"

"I think it's just that they have air from the other world!" Emma hissed. "From the *better* world! It's like an antidote! I didn't know it'd work like this but—let's use it!" She smashed a smoke bomb down right in front of Chess. "Breathe deep, everyone! Breathe in as much of the good air as you can!"

Chess sucked in the ashy air, and it smelled different now that he viewed it as belonging to the other world. This air made him think of bonfires on autumn nights, of logs crackling in a fireplace, of Mom lighting candles on his birthday cake every single year, every single birthday.

This air made him think of home.

Behind him, Mom let out a sound that might have been a laugh and a cry all at once.

"Kids, kids, I love you so much!" she cried. "But you have to save the Gustano kids for me! And yourselves! You have to go! Now!"

"You, too, Natalie!" Joe yelled. "Run! Remember what I told you . . . Kate and I will be right behind you!"

"We'll meet you!" Mom added. "Back at the house! On the *other* side!"

Chess stood, torn even now. He'd come to rescue his mother. That was all he wanted.

But she wanted him to save the Gustanos. And she knew a lot more about this world than he did.

The beam of the spotlight swung closer than it had before, throwing a glow onto Mom's face. Everybody else ducked down out of sight, but Mom was still trapped in her chair and couldn't. And so Chess saw in stark detail that Mom was staring straight at him, her desperate wince full of not just anguish but hope—and maybe even faith as well—as she pleaded, "Kids, *please!*"

It was the "*please*" that did it. She wasn't ordering them anymore. She was begging. And . . . trusting them. Trusting them to make the right choice.

Chess looked down at Finn and Emma, both of them so little and so brave. He looked over at the Gustanos, weeping and wailing and reeling about blindly and helplessly, just like the guards.

He grabbed Emma's arm and Finn's hand and took off running.

FIFTY-FIVE

FINN

Finn was having so much fun.

The more smoke bombs he threw, the more he felt like himself again. What had they all been so worried about? They could ward off these guards with *toys*.

So when Mom yelled, "Go!" and Chess grabbed Finn's hand and pulled him along, Finn raced directly toward the guards.

"Finn, Emma, and Rocky Gustano!" he shouted. "Come with us! *We'll* save you!"

The guard beside Other-Finn was staring down at his hands as though he couldn't quite understand why he was clutching a little boy's arm. So it was easy for Finn to shove the man away and yank Other-Finn forward.

"W-what? Why . . . ? Rocky, what's going on?" Other-Finn screamed. His eyes were wide and terrified as the crazily rolling beam of light struck his face; the handcuffs slid back and forth on his wrists as he reached back for his older brother.

"We're getting you out of here," Chess was telling Rocky. Rocky squinted at Chess, then yanked on Other-Finn's arm the same way Chess was tugging on Finn.

Behind them, the crowd screamed and Judge Morales's voice boomed uselessly, "Silence, everyone! Guards, follow the protocol!" So Finn couldn't hear what Emma or Natalie told Other-Emma to get her to run. Maybe they didn't need to tell her anything; maybe she was like Emma: smart enough to figure out everything on her own. But the three Greystone kids, the three Gustanos, and Natalie began moving as a pack through the darkness, jumping past guards who did little but stare helplessly into the smoke.

"This way!" Natalie called, running ahead. "Away from the judge! There should be a door at the side—"

"Good idea!" Emma hollered back.

Finn threw his last smoke bomb over his shoulder, just in case any guards tried to follow.

"And don't kidnap anyone ever again!" he yelled.

He wanted to see if Mom and Joe were running yet, too, but the rolling light pointed the other way now; the rising smoke stung his eyes. He started to trip, and Chess yanked him up.

"Keep going!" Emma yelled.

Or maybe it was Other-Emma; it was hard to know.

They crashed through a curtain at the side of the stage and kept going, into more darkness.

And then Finn's shoulder hit a door, the kind that opened with a bar across the middle. He shoved hard, and there was light on the other side.

Light, and a new set of double doors.

These doors were surrounded by two rows of guards. They were still in formation, looking strict and tall and mean in their crisp, dark uniforms.

"Somebody throw more smoke bombs!" Finn called back over his shoulder. "I'm out!"

Behind him, Emma let go of Other-Emma's arm and held up both of her hands.

They were empty.

Finn whipped his gaze over to Natalie and Chess, who had their palms out, too.

Their empty palms.

Everybody was out of smoke bombs. They had nothing left to fight these guards.

The first guard stepped forward, reaching out to grab Finn.

FIFTY-SIX

EMMA

"Natalie!" Emma yelled. "Help!"

It was impossible to say in front of the guards what Natalie needed to do. Not when the guards could hear everything.

And not when one guard already had his hands around Finn's arm; not when a second guard was already reaching for Emma.

Emma stopped and pulled back and put her hands on her hips. It was time to speak in code.

"Don't you know who her mother is?" Emma demanded, pointing back at Natalie.

Behind her, Chess and the three Gustano kids were

jumbled together. Chess's face was red and sweaty as he struggled to keep a grip on the chain that linked the Gustanos' handcuffs. The three Gustanos were screaming and scrambling away from these new guards in a panic. Other-Finn's mouth was open so wide Emma could see his tonsils; Other-Emma shoved Chess away while Rocky yanked back on his handcuffs.

Rocky crashed back into Natalie, almost knocking her over. She threw her arms up helplessly and struggled to stay on her feet.

She did not look powerful.

But then Chess said, "That's Natalie *Mayhew*," pronouncing her name the same awed way he'd spoken it back in the basement the afternoon after Mom left, when he'd told Emma that Natalie and her friends practically ran the elementary school.

And that was all it took. A second later, Natalie whipped her hair back over her shoulder and thrust her chin high in the air and shoved past the Gustanos and Chess. She marched straight to the guard who was reaching for Emma and looked him square in the eye.

"My mother said for me to take these children out this door," she said, her voice ringing with bossiness. "All of them. The prisoners in chains *and* my helpers."

Emma suddenly understood what Chess had meant

about Natalie running the school. Now Natalie sounded like she could run the *world*.

"Er, miss, we don't have authorization for that," the guard replied. He sounded apologetic, though. And maybe a little uncertain. "Our orders were to let no one in or—"

Natalie made her back very straight. She was probably six inches shorter than the guard, but Emma suddenly felt as though Natalie was taller than everyone.

"Maybe it's too dark for you to see very well," Natalie said.

Sarcasm, Emma thought, because the emergency backup lights here were brighter than the ones on the stage. *But she's making it seem like the guard can't see well enough to do his job. Like he's not even capable of doing his job.*

"Oh no, miss, we—we—" one of the other guards started to stammer.

"I *am* Natalie Mayhew, and in an emergency situation like this, that is all the authorization you need," Natalie finished.

The guards looked at each other. They weren't bumbling like the ones on the stage. They still stood stiff and proud and stern. Emma wanted to blurt out, *Natalie, can't you say something else? Can't you do something to prove who you are?*

But that would be like a code, too. Emma couldn't make it look like *she* was telling Natalie what to do.

Natalie only tapped her foot impatiently. Like she was just waiting, and she knew the guards would obey. Eventually. If they knew what was good for them. And then . . .

The guards stepped aside. The one who'd been reaching for Emma let his hands drop. So did the one who'd been holding on to Finn.

"Do you need a detail of guards to accompany—" the first guard began.

Natalie whirled on him.

"Don't you think I have my own security force waiting outside?" she snarled. "My own *superior* guards?"

"Yes, miss. Of course, miss," the guard rushed to reply.

How did she do that? Emma wondered. *How was she so . . . perfect?*

The funny thing was, Natalie had sounded a little like she was just arguing with her mom. Like all that yelling at her mother had only been practice.

Now Natalie was making the Gustano kids and Chess, Emma, and Finn march through the door. She stood beside them like *she* was their guard.

The first door led to a dark, empty hallway and another set of doors.

And then they were all outside the building, blinking at their escape from darkness. The air out here was only slightly less murky than it had been in the auditorium, and it made

Emma feel almost as strange. But at least there was enough light to see by. For a moment, she just wanted to take in everything: the puzzled, terrified expressions on the Gustano kids' faces; the strange, ugly buildings around them; the emptiness of the street before them. And, most of all, the determination on Natalie's face.

Has anybody ever told you that you look a lot like your mom? Emma wanted to ask her. *That you act a lot like her, too, trying to fix everybody else's problems?*

But Natalie was still giving orders.

"Now run!"

FIFTY-SEVEN

CHESS

Chess ran.

It was amazing that his legs and feet worked, because his brain didn't seem to be functioning.

Maybe we should . . . If . . .

For a few blocks, none of them did anything but run, pell-mell, straight down the middle of the deserted street. Then it occurred to Chess that eventually someone was going to start chasing them, and they should probably try harder to hide. Just as he started to pull back to tell the others that, Rocky yanked his brother and sister away from the group.

"This is . . . crazy," the oldest Gustano gasped, slowing to a trot. Other-Finn and Other-Emma huddled beside him, their chains and handcuffs clanking. "We just need to find a *phone*. Was that . . . was that some sort of cult? And we're away from it now, so . . ." He appealed mostly to Chess and Natalie. "I guess you're trying to help, but . . . can we borrow a phone? To call the police?"

"The phone we have doesn't work here," Emma said. "And we think the police are bad guys, too."

The three Gustano kids just gaped at her.

Of course, Chess thought. *We're confused, and we've been working on figuring out everything for the past week. The Gustano kids don't know anything.*

"Are we in some foreign country?" Other-Emma asked. Her "I've got to make sense of this" squint looked awfully familiar. "With a corrupt government?"

"That's probably the best way to think of it," Chess said, trying to make his voice gentle. "We're taking you to safety. We promise. Then we'll explain."

The thin wail of a police siren rose behind them.

"Keep running!" Natalie screamed. "Faster!"

They took off again, full speed—or, at least, full speed for Finn and Other-Finn. The two little boys seemed to be struggling valiantly to keep up, and Chess saw that Rocky and Other-Emma kept having to force themselves to slow down to their little brother's pace. Of course, they were handcuffed to their brother, but Chess stayed by Finn, too. Natalie and Emma ran slightly ahead, in the lead.

So if the police come, Emma's going to be safer than Finn or me, but . . .

As the police siren seemed to draw nearer—was it just one siren? Two? Three?—Chess got an image in his head of a whole row of police cars pulling up behind them, maybe picking off Finn. . . .

None of us can outrun police cars, Chess told himself. *We have to find a route the cars can't follow.*

They were still blocks and blocks away from the abandoned house. Nothing around him looked familiar, though at least they'd gotten past all the towering buildings with their horrid blue-and-orange banners. Chess was pretty sure that the only landmark he'd recognized before—the retaining pond—was just ahead on the right.

Oh, the retaining pond . . . And behind it . . .

"Listen!" Chess screamed. "When we get to the pond, we run off the road and take the bike path behind it!"

"*Is* there a bike path in this world?" Emma shouted back at him.

"I don't know!" The police sirens were getting closer and

closer. The walls of fences and unpassable hedges rose around him. "It has to be! Or else—"

He couldn't say it, but the words rang in his head.

Or else we don't have a chance.

FIFTY-EIGHT

FINN

This is just like running home from the school bus after school, Finn kept telling himself. *It's just a slightly longer route. Keep running.*

Except, running home from the school bus always meant running home to see *Mom,* who would be waiting with chocolate-chip cookies or apples and Goldfish crackers or . . . or just a hug.

Finn was always hungry, and he liked food a lot. But sometimes what he wanted most was the hug.

But Mom said she'd meet us at the house today, Finn told himself. *So, see? It isn't different! She'll hug us all when we get there!*

"This way!" Chess shouted, veering off the street. He

pulled on Finn's arm, then Other-Finn's arm, too, tugging them both along with him.

"No confined spaces!" Rocky growled at Chess. "You can't take us anywhere we—"

"Just a bike path!" Chess shouted back at him. "Where we'll be out of sight!"

Rocky glared at Chess, but he threw a quick glance over his shoulder and followed along.

"Please let it be there. Please let it be there," Finn heard Chess repeat again and again.

Finn surged ahead, catching up with Emma and Natalie.

"It is!" he yelled back to Chess. "Just a little overgrown!"

The bike path was a *lot* overgrown. Branches whipped out at them, slashing at their arms and legs and faces and catching at their hair. A clearing appeared ahead, but Natalie held them back.

"Wait, just wait, shh, don't let anyone hear us . . . ," she whispered. She peeked past a thorny bush. "Okay, it's clear. Come on! Hurry!"

All seven of them dashed across a street and then back onto the rest of the overgrown path.

Why isn't anybody out? Finn wondered. *Why isn't anyone calling to us, "Oh, is something wrong, kids? Can we do anything to help?"*

Was it possible that every single person in this town had

been in that awful Public Hall?

The roar of police sirens behind them reminded Finn that even if that had been true before, it wasn't true *now*. The police were coming. And the police here were bad guys, too.

The sirens seemed to multiply and echo. Now it sounded like the police cars weren't just behind the kids, but ahead as well.

Can't be, Finn told himself. *Just keep running. . . .*

Beside him, Other-Finn kept glancing up at Rocky and Other-Emma. Finn wanted to say something encouraging: *You're doing great!* or *We're almost there!* But he found he didn't have enough air in his lungs. It was hard to breathe when the air smelled this bad. And when the air itself seemed to whisper, *You're not going to make it. You should just give up now.*

Emma fell back to run alongside Chess and Finn and ask, "Isn't it going to be hard to see the house from the path?"

Chess faltered, almost tripping.

"Oh, right, nothing looks the same, and there are all those fences . . . ," he murmured. "What if we miss it?"

"Should we go out to the street at the last block? At Chestnut?" Emma asked. "Or whatever they call Chestnut Street here?"

Finn didn't know all the street names in his neighborhood—it was just "the street where Tyrell lives" or "where that one old lady lets us pick raspberries" or "where they have that house that *I'm* going to buy someday, because it has a swimming pool."

When this is all over, I'm never going to any of those places again, he thought. *Maybe I won't even go to school. I'm just staying home with Mom.*

They burst out into the open again, and Chess and Emma screamed together, "This way!"

The broken-down street before them seemed a million miles wide and a million miles long. It should have been a relief not to have branches tearing at his clothes and hair constantly, but now Finn felt too exposed. Unless he could scale an eight-foot-high fence on one side or another of the street, there was nowhere to hide if someone showed up. The police sirens seemed to have faded in the distance, but maybe that was because Finn's ears had gotten used to them. Or maybe his ears weren't working right at all. The street before them seemed, if anything, too silent. The handcuffs on the Gustano kids' wrists clanked as they ran, and that suddenly seemed too loud.

And then someone stepped out from a gap in the fences. A woman.

Ms. Morales. The *real* Ms. Morales. He could tell, because she was wearing the same neon green exercise shirt she'd had on when she'd dropped them off at their house earlier that morning.

Finn decided neon green was his new favorite color. Definitely better than dark blue or orange.

"Natalie? Finn? Emma? Chess?" Ms. Morales called, her face a mask of concern. "I finally found you! But—"

It didn't matter that the concern on her face was almost immediately replaced by anger. Or maybe fear. It almost didn't matter for that moment that she wasn't *his* mom. She was *a* mom, and she'd always been nice to him, and right now he just needed a grown-up who would hug him and tell him everything was going to be okay.

He put on a burst of speed and took off running toward her.

In the next instant, he heard Ms. Morales scream, "Watch out!"

FIFTY-NINE

EMMA

Everything happened at once.

Emma had just turned her head to ask Chess, "That *is* our Ms. Morales, isn't it?" and Chess had replied, panting, "Neon green shirt, so, yes, I *think* so. It has to be."

At the same time, Rocky, Other-Emma, and Other-Finn had whipped around in the broken-up gravel of the street, as if they were about to run in the other direction.

And then, as Finn raced faster than ever toward Ms. Morales, she suddenly screamed, "Watch out!" and police officers appeared at the tops of every fence and started dropping toward the street below.

Finn skidded to a halt. All the other kids froze.

We're so stupid, Emma thought. *Those boys told us that first day there were SWAT teams everywhere on this street who captured Mom. We're going to be captured the exact same way. . . .*

Then Ms. Morales screamed, "Stay away from those kids!" and all the police officers froze.

"Ma'am?" One of the men gulped. He was a tall man with imposing muscles, but in that instant he sounded cowed and confused. "Did you say . . ."

"Mom! We've got to get out of here!" Natalie yelled. "I'll explain later!"

"Mom?" One of the police officers nearest Emma muttered under his breath. He seemed to be trying to peer past the tangled, twig-strewn hair hiding Natalie's face. *"Is* that the daughter? Or an impostor? And the orders we received, are they . . ."

Natalie flipped her sweatshirt hood up over her hair again, but it didn't matter. Now all the police seemed to be staring at her. While they were distracted, Emma took a testing step forward, closer to Ms. Morales and the gap in the fences behind her. The police didn't do anything.

That gap . . . Is that where the abandoned house is? Emma wondered. *Are we that close?*

Ms. Morales stepped farther out into the street, closer to all the police.

"I demand to know what's going on here," she said. Her eyes seemed to take in not just the police and Natalie and the three Greystones, but the Gustano kids cowering together, their handcuffs clinking in the sudden silence. "Why are those children—"

Natalie hurled herself at her mother, crying, "I did what you told me. Isn't that all that matters?"

Natalie plowed into her mother's side. Emma hoped it looked more like a hug than a tackle to the police officers. But Ms. Morales was knocked sideways, and she would have fallen if Natalie hadn't clung to her so tightly.

"Come on!" Emma called to her brothers and the Gustanos. The Gustano kids hesitated, seeming equally terrified of Ms. Morales and the police surrounding them. Then Chess grabbed Finn in one arm and Other-Finn in the other and took off running. Rocky and Other-Emma bounced along behind him, half running, half dragged.

"Mom, you better not have unpropped that door," Natalie muttered, pulling her mother along, too.

Emma raced around the corner of the fence, and, yes! The abandoned house stood before her. She sprinted for the front door. The can of corn was still there, holding it open. Emma crossed the porch in one step, burst through the door, and swung it open wide, making room for the other kids and Ms. Morales behind her.

"No! No! No!" Other-Emma screeched. "We'll be trapped! Again!"

"There's a tunnel!" Emma yelled back over her shoulder. "We'll escape!"

"A tunnel?" Some of the police who'd hesitated before began running after the kids.

Do they know about the other world? Emma wondered.

Then a worse thought occurred to her: *What if these awful people follow us into the other world?*

As soon as Natalie and Ms. Morales scrambled from the porch into the house, Emma reached out and yanked the door shut, slamming it as hard as she could.

Locked, she thought disjointedly. *It locks automatically. Now no one else can come in.*

She turned and sprinted toward the basement stairs alongside Natalie and Ms. Morales.

A second later she heard a crash and the sound of splintering wood.

The police officers were hacking their way into the house.

SIXTY

CHESS

Chess shoved Finn toward the basement stairs and screamed, "Don't stop until you get to the other side!"

Chess wanted to turn around and grab Emma, too, so he could make sure she was safe. Maybe Natalie and Ms. Morales as well. But he still held Other-Finn in his arms, and the little boy was struggling to get away. Rocky and Other-Emma were trying to pull Other-Finn away, too.

"I'm taking you to safety!" Chess screamed at them. "I promise!"

"We're not going into another dark basement!" Other-Emma sobbed. "We're not!"

Then a horrid thud sounded behind them. Daylight streamed in through a crack in the wall that hadn't been there a moment before. Chess looked back and saw the blade of an ax coming through the drywall.

A matching echo came from the kitchen, and then, from the other corner of the living room. Were the police smashing their way into the house from all sides?

"This is the only way!" Chess screamed, dragging all three Gustanos toward the stairs.

They screamed but didn't resist. Emma and Natalie came up from behind and shoved the Gustanos as well.

It was a wonder everyone didn't just fall down the stairs. Chess pulled and tugged and pushed as he ran, and he lost track of whose elbow he yanked forward, or whose handcuff smashed against his face. The lights came on when Chess was about halfway down the stairs, and he realized that Finn must have hit the light switch. In the sudden glow, Chess saw that Finn had also swung the door of the little side room open.

"Come on! Come on!" Finn called from beside the door.

"Keep running!" Chess hollered back. "Don't wait for us!"

Then they were at the bottom of the stairs. Chess heard footsteps from above. The police were in the house now.

"Go! Go! Go!" Chess screamed.

His voice blended with Finn yelling, "Come on!" and Emma and Natalie shouting, "Hurry!" and the Gustanos shrieking in such panic and fear that Chess couldn't make out any exact words.

He couldn't hear Ms. Morales.

He turned around and she was running, too—mostly, it seemed, because Natalie was pulling her. But she had such a dazed expression on her face, she didn't even look like herself.

"Make sure the next door is open!" Emma shouted ahead to Finn, and Finn disappeared into the little room. Chess and the whole jumble of everyone else followed along, aiming for the door back into the tunnel.

"It's dark in there!" Other-Finn wailed, and Chess was surprised to realize that he was still mostly carrying the little boy, still dragging him along.

"There's light on the other side!" Emma called back.

Chess kept running. Before, stepping back into the tunnel from the alternate world had felt so odd, almost as if he'd ceased to exist. But this time as he crossed the threshold, Chess felt his mind clearing.

Because I understand what's happening? Chess wondered. *Because I'm shaking off the alternate world, and that's* worse *than the tunnel?*

He could still hear the police in the abandoned house behind him.

"Shut the door!" he screamed over his shoulder to Natalie. "Lock it if you can! Or jam something against it!"

But the police had axes. What would stop them from hacking away at the door to the tunnel, too?

Blindly, Chess kept running forward, deeper and deeper into the tunnel. Two lights suddenly glowed around him—the flashlights from Natalie's and Ms. Morales's phones. Those lights provided just enough glow that Chess didn't trip or run straight into a wall. The whole group ran in silence now, as if everyone had lost words, or lost the breath to speak words. Chess's mind kept spitting half thoughts at him: *If they follow us . . . to our house . . . we should . . .*

What if there wasn't an end to that thought? What if there wasn't anything they could do?

Somehow, suddenly, there was more light around him, and Chess could see shelves lining the walls. Familiar shelves: the ones they'd been so surprised to see that Mom had stocked with cans of food and shoeboxes full of cash.

Mom . . . , Chess thought. *Where's Mom now? Did she escape, too?*

Chess heard footsteps behind him, but they were too heavy to be Mom's. And there were too many of them.

These footsteps had to be the police.

They were in the tunnel, too.

"Hurry!" Natalie gasped, breaking into the brighter,

more open space behind Chess. "That man—Joe—he said there's a secret way to shut off the tunnel if anyone follows us. He said we get to the area with the shelves, and then—"

"Don't let them catch us!" one of the Gustanos shrieked in terror. Chess was a little surprised to see that it was Rocky.

"Don't worry. We won't," Emma said, patting his back. "Natalie, how—"

"Oh, this is ridiculous," Ms. Morales said. She had an expression on her face like she'd just awakened. "What was I thinking? Running like that just makes us *all* seem guilty. No matter what happened out there, this isn't the way to handle it. I just need to talk to—"

"Mom, no!" Natalie said, grabbing her mother's arm. "You don't understand!"

"Natalie! The secret!" Emma called.

"It's the same lever as before," Natalie called, even as she tugged back on her mom's arm. "You pull it straight out from the wall like you're trying to break it, not just turning it side to side. But—"

"Chess, help!" Finn called.

He was already trying to climb up the shelves toward the lever. But it was too high over his head.

Chess heard the footsteps behind them getting closer and closer. How much time did they have? What if the secret lever didn't even work, and they still had to run and run and run? He saw the Gustanos on the floor, weeping. Would he have to carry all *three* of them up the basement stairs next? He saw Emma scramble toward the lever, too. He saw Ms. Morales shake off Natalie's hand and turn around, as if she still intended to solve everything by talking to the police. She took a step back into the darkness.

In one huge stride, Chess crossed the floor and grabbed the lever. He jerked it straight out from the wall, and it broke off in his hand.

A split second later, everything exploded.

SIXTY-ONE

FINN

Finn blinked and blinked and blinked. Dust settled around him, blocking his view.

"Chess!" he screamed. "Emma!"

"Finn?" Two voices answered: his brother's and his sister's.

No, it was three voices—there was an echoing "Is that you, Finn?"

Other-Emma.

And then a fourth, slightly deeper: "Are you all right? Is everyone okay?"

That was Rocky.

Finn lifted his head, still blinking. He was jumbled up on the floor with Chess and Emma: Her elbow was in his ear; Chess's knee was in Finn's rib cage. Beside them, the Gustano kids were equally tangled together.

But no one looked hurt. No one was bleeding. No one had any broken bones sticking out.

"Natalie?" Finn called.

"Over . . . here."

Her voice sounded weaker, but maybe that was just because she was farther away. The air seemed clearer now: The dust had settled, and the stench was gone. Behind Natalie, shelves leaned and sagged. A pile of cans and jars lay beneath the shelves, all of them dented and squashed and broken, scattered across the floor. While Finn watched, another can slowly dropped to the floor, a delayed reaction. He blinked again, trying to make sense of what he saw. In a few places, the wood of the shelves had splintered and cracked, and dirt and bits of drywall sifted down through the holes, as if the earth behind the shelves was straining to fill the entire basement.

There hadn't been shelves behind Natalie before. There hadn't been dirt either. There'd been a huge, hollow tunnel.

And Ms. Morales.

"Mom?" Natalie called. She sat up straight. "Where's Mom? She was right here!"

"She . . . she stepped back. . . ." Chess seemed to choke on his own words. He looked at the metal lever in his hand, and scrambled to his feet. He hit the broken lever against the wall. "There's no place for it to fit anymore! No sign that it was ever attached! It's like—"

"Like there was nothing here but a hidden room," Emma said, her voice stunned. "Like it wasn't a tunnel to anywhere."

Natalie whipped out her phone.

"I have service again!" she cried. She hit her finger against the phone's screen, then screamed into it, "Mom! Answer!"

A ringing came from beneath a pile of smashed jars at the bottom of the shelves.

"Her phone's here, but she isn't?" Natalie cried incredulously. She let her own phone drop to the floor. She stood and began digging her fingers into the dirt trickling through the broken shelves. "Mom!"

"The phone must have mostly been in this room," Emma said. "Ms. Morales mostly . . . wasn't."

Finn went over and wrapped his arms around Natalie's waist.

"Your mom," he said. "My mom. And Joe. They'll find . . ."

Each other, he wanted to say. *Another way out. Us.*

Emma and Chess limped over to the broken shelves,

too. They patted Natalie's shoulders and pressed their hands against the shattered wood and the wall of dirt. Both Emma and Chess moved with the same air of disbelief as Natalie.

"We went to rescue our mom," Chess said dazedly. "And . . . we lost your mom instead."

Natalie collapsed against the broken wall and splintered shelves, her face buried in her arms. Now it was more like Chess, Emma, and Finn were holding her up.

"We're sorry," Emma whispered.

Finn had never heard his sister sound like that before, so utterly defeated. So utterly lost.

He turned his face to the side, because he couldn't bear to look at her, couldn't bear to see her and Chess and Natalie reaching out again and again to touch the dirt that had replaced the tunnel. He couldn't bear to watch them trying to understand what couldn't be understood, or accept what couldn't be accepted. He couldn't even bear to watch the cans still rolling off the last shelf and dropping to the floor one . . . by . . . one.

But Finn caught a faster movement out of the corner of his eye: Rocky, Other-Emma, and Other-Finn on the floor behind him, all of them scrambling for the phone Natalie had dropped.

"Look," Finn whispered, and Natalie, Chess, and Emma turned around.

Before them, Rocky stabbed his finger against the screen, hitting numbers. Then all three of the Gustano kids clustered around the phone, screaming into it, "Mom! Mom! We got away from the kidnappers!"

"We're free now!"

"Come get us! Oh, please, come get us!"

Finn couldn't hear the voice on the other end of the line, and that was probably a good thing. It would have made him cry. He looked back, and Natalie had tears streaming down her face as she watched the Gustano kids. Emma and Chess did, too.

"We saved *them*," Emma said.

"We did what Mom wanted," Chess whispered. "And she said . . . she said she's protected by what she knows, and those kids weren't protected at all. . . ."

Finn realized that he'd been trying to say things wrong before.

"And next time we'll save *her*," he corrected himself. "And Ms. Morales. And Joe. We'll find another way in. Another tunnel. Next time."

He expected the big kids to get that look in their eyes that meant they were going to lie to him. He expected them to pat his head and put on fake cheer to assure him, "Of course! Everything's going to be fine!"

But Chess only straightened his spine. Emma lifted her

chin in the air. Natalie clutched his hand. It was like Finn had helped *them*.

And then Other-Finn tugged on Finn's arm. He smiled his gap-toothed smile, and behind the snot and tears and dirt smeared across his face, his eyes glowed. They were the exact same shape and color as Finn's. And for now, they held the exact same hope and confidence.

"You can do it," Other-Finn said. "If you could rescue us, you can do *anything*."

EPILOGUE

CHESS, EMMA, FINN, AND NATALIE

The kids emerged from the Greystone house into a neighborhood swarming with police and firefighters. Yellow tape was everywhere, stretching from tree to tree carrying the words, "POLICE LINE DO NOT CROSS." The Gustanos stiffened at the sight of the police, but Finn, whom they seemed to trust the most now, whispered to them, "No, no, *these* police are good guys. Everything's okay."

And somehow the Gustano kids had the sense not to ask questions in front of the adults, who were all shouting questions of their own.

"Did you smell any natural gas odor in there?"

"Did you see any flames?"

"Has everyone from your house been evacuated?"

Emma was the only one who managed to get a question in edgewise: "You think we just went through a *natural gas* explosion?"

One of the firefighters took pity on her and answered, "Well, that or an earthquake. Plain old sinkhole's another possibility—right now nobody's getting the story straight."

And then one of the cops noticed the handcuffs on the Gustano kids, and Natalie and the Greystones had to focus on getting *their* story straight.

"We've been away because our mother's out of town on business, and we came back to check on our cat, and *these* kids were trapped down there," Chess said.

"They said they'd been kidnapped in Arizona, and the kidnappers kept moving them around—they just arrived here today," Natalie added.

"Please, can you take care of them?" Finn ended, smiling his most innocent smile. "Get them back to their parents as soon as you can?"

And then the Gustano kids were whisked away, and the Greystone kids and Natalie only had to deal with firefighters for a while.

"I'm sure *your* parents are going to want to know that the

four of you are safe," one of the kindliest-looking firefighters said.

"Well, my mom dropped us off, and then she was just sitting in that SUV over there waiting for us, and . . ." Natalie did not have to use any acting skills at all to make her eyes widen at the sight of the empty SUV. She took off running toward it, crying, "Mom! Mom! Where are you, Mom?"

The firefighters ran after her, and for a moment, Chess, Emma, and Finn were left alone. They could hear the firefighters speaking gently to Natalie: "Young lady, can we call someone for you?" "Oh, your father . . . can you give us his number?"

Chess put his arms around his little brother's and sister's shoulders.

"They'll be asking us that question soon, too," he warned them. "And when they can't find Mom, we have to be ready to . . ."

"Go live with strangers," Emma finished for him.

Chess was surprised that she'd reached that conclusion so quickly, without first suggesting their old babysitter, Mrs. Rabinsky (who, he had to admit, always seemed tired out after just one night with them) or some neighbor like Mrs. Childers.

Finn was surprised that Emma had said that in front of

him, instead of making up some comforting lie.

Both of them could tell that Emma was only trying to sound brave when she squared her shoulders and added, "We'll be fine. We'll have each other." She gulped. "Just . . . just like Mom told us . . ."

But then Natalie was back, putting her arms around all of them, and telling the firefighters who trailed after her, "And these kids will come home with me, too. My dad will take care of all of us."

While the firefighters conferred about this, Chess whispered, "Natalie, there are *three* of us. All he'll know is that our mom has totally disappeared. He'll never . . ."

And Natalie jutted her jaw into the air and countered, "He'll agree to this because I tell him to. That's how it works with my dad. He lets me do anything. It drives my mom crazy." For a moment, her chin trembled. "Mom is the only one who . . . who . . ." She swallowed hard and dropped her voice to a whisper. " . . . *cares*."

Finn nestled in close, wrapping his arms around her waist.

"We'll find her," he reminded Natalie. "Her and our mom and Joe. We will."

Emma started to add, *We figured out the first part of Mom's coded message. Maybe all we need to do to find our way back is to solve the rest of the code.* She wanted to assure Natalie, *I'm really good at codes and secret messages. You know that, right?*

But maybe that wasn't what Natalie needed to hear. Emma thought hard as she hugged Finn and Natalie tight, then reached back to draw Chess in, too. The four of them stood together for a long moment. United.

"And in the meantime," Emma finally said, "until we get our mothers back, we'll *all* have each other."

ACKNOWLEDGMENTS

About thirty years ago, a newspaper columnist named Rheta Grimsley Johnson wrote about a sad, odd, *true* coincidence so compelling that the story has haunted me ever since. It took me almost three decades to realize it, but that column planted the first seeds of this book. So Rheta Grimsley Johnson is the first person I need to thank.

I'd also like to thank my agent, Tracey Adams, and her husband and co-agent, Josh Adams, for their belief in this book and this series at a time when I wasn't sure what I had.

Likewise, I owe my editor, Katherine Tegen, a great deal for her faith in this book and this series and me. Thank you as well to everyone else at HarperCollins who worked on the book, especially Allison Brown, Ann Dye, Mabel Hsu, Christina MacDonald, Aurora Parlagreco, Bethany C. Reis, Mark Rifkin, and Amy Ryan. And thank you to Anne Lambelet for the amazing cover art.

I'd also like to thank my niece Meg Terrell and my sister, Janet Terrell, who's a teacher, for their help with thinking about life in elementary (or intermediate) school. A shout-out as well to my daughter, Meredith, who helped with my research trip to the National Cryptologic Museum.

And I'm always grateful to my friends in my two Columbus-area writers groups, who provided love and support and listening when I needed it most: Thanks to Jody Casella, Julia DeVillers, Linda Gerber, Lisa Klein, Erin McCahan, Jenny Patton, Edith Pattou, Nancy Roe Pimm, Amjed Qamar, Natalie D. Richards, and Linda Stanek. My friend and fellow author Lisa McMann lives in the wrong place (though she says *I'm* the one who lives in the wrong place), but she provided moral support at a critical time, too, while I was working on this book.

And thanks as always to my family, especially my husband, Doug. A dinner with Doug and our friends, journalism professors Beverly and Mark Horvit, helped me figure out an important part of this book, so this is both a thanks and a "Sorry for completely zoning out for a while."

Finally, thanks to my friends Janis and Dan Shannon for showing me certain unique features of their new house, while our friends Sarah and Mark Fox and Barb and Gary Munn stood there saying, "Margaret, you're going to put this in a book, aren't you?"

People say that to me all the time, about all sorts of things. But this time . . . they were right.